A SHADOWING OF ANGELS

A SHADOWING OF ANGELS

W.T DELANEY

Matador
9 Priory Business Park,
Wistow Road, Kibworth Beauchamp,
Leicestershire. LE8 0RX
Tel: 0116 279 2299
Email: books@troubador.co.uk
Web: www.troubador.co.uk/matador
Twitter: @matadorbooks

ISBN 978 1785892 486

British Library Cataloguing in Publication Data.
A catalogue record for this book is available from the British Library.

Printed and bound in the UK by TJ International, Padstow, Cornwall
Typeset in 11pt Aldine401 BT by Troubador Publishing Ltd, Leicester, UK

Matador is an imprint of Troubador Publishing Ltd

CHAPTER ONE

THE TALIB AND THE ANGEL

Camp Bastion, Helmand, 2010

The Operations room was alive with activity since the teams had deployed into the pick-up area. The low-ceilinged office was only the size of a large sitting room and seemed packed; it smelled of a subtle, but not unpleasant odour of sawdust, plastic, and freshly brewed coffee. The office was strange mixture of ultra-high and low-tech make-do and mend. The office furniture was reclaimed, made, stolen from, or donated by the Americans, and invariably repaired with standard black British Army masking tape.

Desks had all been made very quickly from standard half inch MDF, a material all too familiar to all those who have served in Afghanistan.

In contrast, the focal point of the office was the computer and communications equipment, including a 50-inch HD TV and two smaller monitors that relayed real time satellite footage of the action on the ground. There was an extra edge of tension in the Ops room today, a tangible sense of concern; the planned debriefing of agent 3010 was going wrong.

The face of Danny McMaster reflected his concerns. His eyes blinked rapidly as he focused on the TV monitor while gently biting his lower lip. He was experiencing that empty falling feeling in the pit of his stomach. *Something's not right,* he thought.

A legendary character in DHU (the Defence Human Intelligence Unit) he was truly old school Intelligence Corps. He had scaled its ascending hierarchy from Lance Corporal to Colonel and he had plied his trade over a period of twenty-five years from Northern Ireland to Afghanistan. Each crevice of his well-worn face represented the effort needed to plan out one operational worry or another; he was the guy who carried the responsibility for his boys and girls.

Danny's eyes had seen their fair share of the casual mayhem of terrorist violence in their time. How that unholy trinity of a planned act of terrorism, the victim or victims, and the organisations need for publicity, ensured that politically justified violence was always bubbling under the surface of modern society, ready to raise its ugly head. Danny thought it was like some bizarre game of whack-a-mole, as soon as you hammered one, another popped up in its place. The only bright side, as Danny saw it, was that he would never be out of a job!

He hated terrorism of all kinds, whether it was left-wing, right-wing, secular or religious. He had been there to pick up the pieces when just being in the wrong place at the wrong time had destroyed the innocent. He had seen the results from Belfast to Baghdad, and from Bosnia to Kabul. He had visions of the slaughter hard-wired into his memory, visions that were sometimes hard to shift. He was often jolted from sleep by stark horrific images of the past. Severed heads bobbing in the Tigris River, the handy work of sectarian murder gangs in Baghdad or a young mother cradling the lifeless, torn and bloodied body of her baby after a suicide bombing in Kabul. So sometimes Danny did not sleep so well, but sometimes he did, because he also knew that over the last twenty-five years he and his agent handlers had prevented more things like that happening.

He had also developed a feel for trouble, a sort of sixth sense, a hybrid mixture of common 'dog fuck' in British Army parlance, a mixture of experience based street sense combined with the stringent application of practical risk management. Danny solely judged the abnormal by the absence of the normal and that had kept him and his troops alive over the last quarter century. In short, in Danny's world, if things weren't right, they were wrong, and after two recent tours in Afghanistan he knew that things in this particular shit-hole could go horribly wrong, very, very quickly.

Danny always worried about his teams on the ground. As the commander he was, and also felt, totally responsible for them. The relayed images from the screens intensified this almost parental responsibility. Danny knew that even on a routine operation, in an environment as hostile as Helmand, sometimes shit just happens. Afghanistan was just totally different from anywhere he had served before. The extreme poverty, the tribalism and the endemic corruption at all levels of society made it unique. All this was superimposed on the misery and utter despair of thirty years of war. Danny often thought that Afghanistan appeared to be a fucking mess and despite the media hype promising a Western-style democracy and regeneration, a nation seemingly without hope.

In contrast in such an utterly hostile environment, the previous risks of special duties in Ulster did not measure up to the risks his troops ran here every day. A Ra-man (an PIRA member) after all, would never blow himself up just to kill you, not intentionally anyway, and even in a worst-case scenario if you were snatched on an operation and ended up hanging upside-down on a meat-hook in South Armagh, getting the cattle-prod and rubber hose treatment, at least you still had a chance to keep your head attached to your body when it was ditched on the border later.

The early years of Britain's reoccupation of Helmand were a steep learning curve for all. Danny had seen his guys' operational techniques and tradecraft slowly adapt and evolve in an almost Darwinian way. The early mistakes had been made and the unit had adapted to stay ahead of the game. It was obvious that ever-changing situations needed ever changing solutions and so far they had adapted well. Danny also knew that one mistake, one assumption, one piece of over-confidence, could have life-changing consequences for his troops.

Pressure from above had instigated the operation; source 3010 was a top Taliban commander and had provided the proverbial 'golden nuggets' of information. He had saved lives in the past, but now the source had been out of contact for a full three days and had failed to react to his re-contact procedures (REVCON). Something wasn't right, so it was wrong, and now in early 2010 with a major push into Helmand gathering pace, Danny's reservations had been noted by his upper chain of command and ignored. Therefore the agent, 3010, pronounced as Thirty-Ten, needed to be met and debriefed, safely, securely and without compromise, *In-fucking-shallah*, Danny muttered in thought.

Despite his nagging doubts, the operation had been planned and orders given. Things then were further complicated when a late call from the source explained that he only had a finite time-window to meet. This rang definite alarm bells for Danny. You did not need the brains of an Int. Corps Colonel to know that if your timings are bracketed by circumstance, and the agent knows the general area of the pick-up, then the complicated, safe and secure military operation, meticulously planned at a time and location of the teams' choosing, veers unnervingly into the realms of a fixed-point meet. *It might as well be 'see you under the fucking clock at twelve'*, thought Danny.

Things got drastically worse as the source had failed to show. Danny's gut began wrenching. He had insisted on every possible precaution, a full multiple of a twelve man QRF (Quick Reaction Force) from Zulu Company Four-Five Commando, which was mounted in two Sea King Naval helicopters from the Royal Marines Brigade Air Squadron burning and turning on the ground. He had also sat in on the excellent set of orders delivered by Captain Sam Holloway, his star player.

Everything was covered in orders: Ground, Situation, Mission, Execution, Friendly Forces, Enemy Forces, Communications and Logistics. Any small inattention to detail could be disastrous: not checking the vehicles for fuel, water and oil, a door that would not open properly, a forgotten tow-rope, the wrong frequency for the radios, all could have dire consequences on an operation. The Royal Marines LO (Liaison Officer) had sat in on the orders and now had an envelope containing photographs of all the vehicles and personnel involved and the details of the OOB, the 'out of bounds box' in which the operation would take place. This was an area sanitised of other military for that particular operation to prevent the dreaded 'blue on blue', the military fratricide that had sometimes cursed military operations in Afghanistan in the past.

Lastly the Int. Corps collator read out the 'be on the lookout' for or BOLO list, a list of suspicious vehicles. It was the usual mixture, a white Toyota Corolla, the most common car in make and colour in Helmand that a source report said was being prepared for a suicide operation in Nad E Ali. The operators committed the registration to memory as it was repeated three times. The next items were two white police Land Cruisers stolen from the district centre in Lashkar Ghar, again the operators memorised the details. Finally, the most worrying: a lorry, known by the troops as a 'jingly truck', the type decorated with ornate, garish Pakistani-type decorations, make unknown, being prepared as a 500-kilo truck bomb. The team exchanged glances. *That's one to avoid,* they thought.

Then there was the visual side of the preparation, how things actually appeared. A DHU team preparing for an operation in Afghanistan was akin to actors dressing for a costume drama. Every aspect of the operation had to look right to an unsuspecting local Afghan farmer. The Ops vehicles themselves were indistinguishable from any of the other cars negotiating the dusty tracks and potted roads of Southern Helmand. The team's cars were Toyota Corollas from the mid-nineties. They were popular in Helmand because their high wheel arches gave that little extra bit of ground clearance to cope with Helmand's severely potted roads.

The Ops cars were seldom washed but were well maintained. Externally they looked no different from the usual misused pieces of shit used by the locals. The Ops vehicles were, however, specifically designed for the task with some protective upgrades, including the application of some lightweight ballistic armour. The REME engineers had also thoroughly checked and perfected the mechanics of this all-pervading piece of 'Japan in Afghanistan' and the engines had been ripped out, replaced and upgraded. Most importantly and last fitted was the radio system that allowed for long-range communication.

Lastly, he had deployed a very experienced team, who had prepared themselves well. All had two tours of Helmand under their respective belts. Each member carried not only his or her personal harness mounted radio, but also a personal locator beacon in case of a snatch. All were highly armed and wearing lightweight body armour, covered with the standard covert chest rig containing 120 rounds of assault rifle ammunition under their local garb.

The team was experienced and had learned how to blend in with the local population, what they could wear and what they couldn't, and how to wear it.

A visitor to the compound before they deployed would have seen the six-person, three-vehicle team, appearing in their operational Afghan guise, appearing to the outsider like the bearded extras in some pirate movie. But this was not a film; they had to appear like the locals, this was survival; this was one aspect of pre-operational preparation where things had to be 'Afghan good' as a minimum, and not just 'Afghan good enough'.

Danny again nervously studied the monitor. It focused on a dirty white Toyota Corolla negotiating a dusty track beside a ragged concrete canal on the outskirts of Nad E Ali, deep in Taliban country in what was called the 'Green Zone'. Danny still found this a strange experience; this was technology that was in its infancy in Northern Ireland. Real time, instantaneous coverage of events as they were occurring, *that also gave commanders the real time consequences of their plans*, he thought.

The camera panned out and the car became smaller, framed by green vegetation on one side and the reflected silver sheen off the jagged gash of the canal on the other.

The split screen monitor showed the grid and direction of the ordinary-looking white Toyota, bumping slightly, as it negotiated the heavily rutted track with a plume of Helmand dust streaming from its rear tyres. Danny knew that the vehicle was Sam Holloway and Taff Thomas's Ops car. He also understood that they were the most at risk because, as the handler's car, they were at the periphery of the operation and deep in the 'Green Zone'.

Afghanistan's 'Green Zone' was a uniquely dangerous place, not to be confused with the 'Green Zone' of Iraq's Baghdad where things were relatively safe, and life was good for soldiers and internationals alike.

The 'Green Zone' in Helmand was where our soldiers died or lost their legs; it was an amazing piece of 1950s American civil engineering gifted to an Afghanistan at peace. It had changed Helmand's arid desert into a rich agricultural area. However, after thirty years of war and in Afghanistan's strange and uniquely topsy-turvy, fucked-up way, that international aid and US largesse would have an inverse and opposite effect.

Because it was in this fertile crescent of life gouged out of the surrounding desert by American bulldozers, where the poppy was sown, grown, and easily harvested, it was therefore the area from which the Taliban drew its financial strength. It was this

'Green Zone' that produced the unending vomit of processed heroin that gushed into the Western world and it was, at that time, the epicentre of the Taliban insurgency.

American ingenuity, know-how and millions of dollars of US taxpayers' money had inadvertently created the ideal terrorists' playground. The mixture of irrigation ditches and canals, interspersed with small tracks and roads, channelled and contained ISAF's military movement, therefore supplying the Taliban with a thousand ready-made ambush positions. It was at that time, in 2010, the most dangerous place in the world for a British soldier to be stationed, especially if you were a British Army covert operator.

Danny knew things were starting to go pear-shaped when Thirty-Ten had failed to show. This was accompanied by a rapid increase in enemy radio chatter, with ICOM intercepts indicating that the Taliban was very active and looking for something or someone. Sam and Taff's car, the pick-up car, was the furthest away and therefore the most vulnerable. Although the threat would be over in another fifteen minutes as the Toyota closed towards them, Danny decided not take any chances. He turned to the Royal Marine designated as Zulu Company Four-Five Commando's LO (Liaison Officer) and said, "Let's get your boys in the air, I think the shit is going to hit the fan big style."

Danny shifted his radio headset into a more comfortable position on to his head and spoke concisely into the radio mike. "Hello all stations, this is O. QRF will over-watch Two-Zero Charlie, all call signs to proceed to the nearest hard cover."

The deployed call signs responded in numerical order. "Hello O, this is Two Zero Alpha, roger that."

"Hello O, this is Two Zero Bravo, roger that."

And then a girl's voice, very feminine with a slight upper-class twang, sounded clear and calm across the radio net. "Hello O. This is Two Zero Charlie, roger all your last, we are from Red

36 to Green 16 and appear to have some company." It was Sam Holloway, the main handler for the op.

The whole Ops room then concentrated on the large monitor as the controller scanned out and back to pick up on a large dust trail caused by two white SUVs travelling at speed. The operator focused onto what appeared to be Afghan police vehicles.

The duty radio operator asked Danny, "Have we got ANA Cops in the out of bounds box, boss?"

Danny knew straight away what was happening, he remembered the BOLO list and said, "No, this looks like trouble, son." Danny immediately broadcast, "Hello 20C, this is O, you have hostile surveillance closing fast."

Sam's voice was calm and measured. "Roger that, we are going open mike, OUT." Sam checked with Taff, the heavily built, bearded figure that was driving the Toyota. "Hi, Taff, you got that?"

"Yeah, roger that, Sam, looks like our day has just got a whole lot more interesting."

Danny suddenly came through clearly. "Hi Sam, this is Danny, you have permission to go hot."

Sam immediately understood the implications of that statement. The ROE or the 'Rules of Engagement' had just been changed, she had now just been informed that they could use deadly force if they considered their lives to be in imminent danger from armed enemy forces, and that it could be done pre-emptively if needed. "Hi, Taff, you roger that?"

Taff's thick southern Welsh accent responded reassuringly. "Yeah, that's a roger, let's get prepped."

Sam, who was wearing a full-length burka, reached into a dusty, dirty carrycot covered with a tatty blanket nestled next to her on the back seat, and a baby immediately started crying.

The burka is not a functional piece of kit, thought Sam. It was hot and stifling in the summer and offered no warmth in the bitter Afghan winters; but it offered excellent camouflage and nobody looked at you when you were wearing one, especially if the garment, like Sam's, was faded and slightly dirty.

Sam knew that nobody wanted to make eye contact with what looked like a poor Afghan woman, even if that were possible through the face-piece, which it was not! It meant they were poor and they might be begging. There were literally hundreds of homeless women, many with children, begging on the streets of Kabul or Kandahar because after nearly thirty years of war the amount of widows outweighed the number of people who wanted to look after them.

Sam squinted through the gauze-type net of the face mask; she could see the dust cloud to their rear quickly change into the solid shapes of two white SUVs moving at speed and seemingly with menacing intent. She felt her pulse begin to race, that old familiar feeling, the empty feeling in the pit of her stomach, that scary feeling when you had to inwardly wrestle the self-preservation demons within. *Keep calm, keep calm,* she thought, and then she was through it, and was again focused on the job. *When it comes to it you will need to move quickly to take out both vehicles before the passengers can deploy.* She remembered that the first ten rounds of the thirty-round magazines now firmly attached to her HK 53 assault rifle had been arranged as alternate tracer and armour piercing rounds. *That might be handy,* thought Sam, as she continued to make her own individual battle plans.

★ ★ ★

Back in the Ops room all eyes were focused on the white Corolla as it moved at speed, the camera operator scanned ahead on the dusty track to the next crossroads and immediately understood the danger. "Boss, we have problems."

The camera picked up at least three armed insurgents by the crossroads appearing to be setting up a checkpoint; they were pulling large pieces of metal from what was once a Russian vehicle onto the road. In that instant just as the threat became doubly clear, the duty signaller said, "Just got an enemy ICOM radio intercept, boss, they know we are on the ground and they say they have our car."

"Roger that, bleeps," replied Danny. Danny thought, *that's as bad as it gets*, it was almost his and the unit's nightmare scenario: the last car on the ground, and a Taliban unit planning to snatch it.

Danny immediately directed the action. "Hello Sam, this is Danny, you have a Taliban checkpoint ahead and hostiles behind, I confirm you have permission to go hot."

A clear, calm, measured voice responded, "Roger your last, Danny — we're good to go."

The Toyota was fast approaching the Taliban checkpoint. Sam quickly checked her kit. Under the burka she was dressed in a dark blue long sleeved tee shirt and Levi jeans, her long blonde hair tied neatly back in a ponytail. Her Levis were held in at the waist with a gun belt on which a Sig 228 reassuringly nestled on her right hip, on the left side of her waist she had the usual three thirty-round magazines of 9 mil bullets for it, and just above the comfy KSB lightweight rock climbing boot on her right ankle there was an ankle holster with Sig 230 9 mil short pistol. She felt and checked both weapons; she knew that they both had one up the spout ready to go. She then patted the HK 53 concealed in the carrycot with the butt folded, that was prepped with one up the spout as well, and the baby was still crying.

At about 400 metres out, Taff slowed the car. He could just make out two armed insurgents crouched behind a makeshift barrier, a quick assessment assured him he could not drive through. *They'll have a cut-off on the road*, he thought, and the light Kevlar in the seats and door panels of the Toyota would not respond well to a couple of bursts of .762 short from the Russian made RPD, the Taliban's standard machine gun. The adrenalin had kicked in, Taff felt that familiar lightness in his chest as the blood started to course through his body, he concentrated completely and calmly rechecked the pistol grip of his Sig 228 nine millimetre pistol. Taff recognised the old familiar feeling. *It was fight or flight, so I guess it was a scrap these fuckers are after?* he thought. He was totally focused now, he had to make this look as natural as possible.

He looked at Sam in the rear view mirror. "Looks like this is it, Sam," he said quietly. He had made the assessment, so now he gave quick QBOs (Quick Battle Orders). "I'll take front, you do rear, and I'm going from the draw."

Sam was instantly reassured by Taff's calm voice in her earpiece, and responded with "Roger that, Taff, standby all stations, rolling in now."

"Right, let's look natural, I'm slowing to stop."

The Taliban waiting ahead could not have time to realise what was coming their way; they effectively had a very nasty ambush rolling towards them.

Sam peered through the gauze face-piece of her dirty-looking, light-blue full-length burka, and reached into the dusty, dirty, brightly-coloured carrycot nestled beside her on the back seat of the car where a baby was still crying. She looked to the rear, the two hostile Land Cruisers were closing fast, and that was her job!

The moment seemed to freeze in time — the thought occurred to her that this was the situation they had trained for, the regiment guy's voice from training sounded in her head. *Keep calm, harness the fear and SAS, Speed, Action, Surprise, and let the drills take over.* She reached into the carrycot with her right hand and felt the pistol grip of her folded H & K 53 assault rifle; she slipped the selector switch to three-round bursts and waited.

Time seemed to stand still in that last few seconds before contact, and Sam bizarrely thought of the Rudyard Kipling poem that an SBS Major had once introduced his anti-ambush lecture; it was called Ithuriel's Angel:

12

Sooner or late – in earnest or in jest –
(But the stakes are no jest) Ithuriel's Hour
Will spring on us, for the first time, the test
Of our sole unbacked competence and power
Up to the limit of our years and dower
Of judgment--or beyond. But here we have
Prepared long since our garland or our grave.

As the car rolled up to the crossroads the two Talibs gestured at them to stop. They looked young, agitated and unsure.

Taff murmured under his breath, and Sam heard him in her earpiece. "OK, Sam, standby, STANDBY."

CHAPTER TWO

CONTACT

Sam knew that this was what she had trained for, thousands of rounds of live training ammunition, SAS and DHU instructors and countless repetitions of likely hostile encounters, called 'situation awareness training', just clicked in. She had controlled and harnessed her fear. "CONTACT, wait out," she said in a cool, calm voice, making sure that they had priority on the unit radio net.

The car rolled to a controlled stop, and Taff opened the driver's door slowly and said in perfect Pashtu, "What is wrong, brothers, my son is ill." The Talibs heard a baby's plaintive wailing.

Sam then reached inside the baby's cot and grasped the pistol grip of the HK 53, rechecking that it was on bursts with her thumb still enveloped in the burka, a small tape recorder playing a baby crying was still wailing away.

Taff thought he could detect that final recognition of threat and fear in the young Talib's eyes, his eyelashes had been elaborately blackened like a girl's with homemade soot for mascara and this emphasised the abject look of horror as Taff drew his Sig and placed two shots, a double-tap, right between his eyes.

BANG-BANG!

Taff then engaged the secondary target, a fat little Talib who was already firing his AK47 wildly in panic; again Taff double-tapped him twice in the chest.

BANG-BANG!

He then took cover as a long burst of machine-gun fire ripped over his head. *That'll be the cut-off machine-gunner*, he thought.

Sam had prepped the door lock and on the first double-tap had simultaneously pushed both her feet out of the Toyota's rear passenger side reinforced door until they were firmly anchored on the dusty track. She then turned on her right foot, threw off her burka and lengthened the butt of the 53 to engage the two white SUVs that were closing fast at 200 metres to the rear.

She then adopted the kneeling position and took careful aim through the mounted single point sight. The red dot held steady and she squeezed the trigger smoothly twice as two three-round bursts seared into windscreen of the driver's side of the front vehicle, hitting the driver in the upper body. She moved aim slightly and then sent another deadly mix of armour piercing and tracer into the passenger side. The first vehicle careered off the track and turned over.

Sam was already engaging the second vehicle with another three, three-round bursts. The potent mixture of rounds had a similar effect tearing through the vehicle as it turned off the road and came to rest in a ditch. Sam now moved towards the threat, with the butt of the 53 firmly in her shoulder. All pretence was gone, the burka discarded, as her blonde ponytailed hair caught the afternoon sun. She moved quickly as she had been trained, in short bounds, to close on and kill the enemy.

A rear occupant of the second vehicle was now out and trying to bring his machine gun into action, Sam heard it rattle into life and felt pain. Then she aimed, framed the man's shape into the red point sight and slowly and deliberately applied smooth pressure to the trigger. The 53 barked sharply and fired a long burst that ripped completely through him, and then the empty 53's cocking handle stayed to the rear, indicating that she had an empty magazine.

Sam deftly dropped the empty magazine by depressing the

magazine release button as she made herself a small target by going to ground. "Ammo!" she shouted as she took cover in the lying position and then, rolling onto her back, removed another mag from her chest rig and slapped it in to the weapon, simultaneously releasing the opening and holding device to automatically re-cock the 53. No fear, no panic, just the mechanics of a fast mag change under fire, practiced a thousand times. She then almost simultaneously rolled into some low cover and came on aim in the lying position and fired another three-round burst towards the muzzle flashes of the enemy.

She then felt the assuring crack and thump of Taff's 53 on her left hand side; he had retrieved his Long from the car and was now in the fight. She heard Taff's call. "MOVING NOW!" She almost felt Taff's burly reassuring presence on her left-hand side.

"ENEMY LEFT!" Sam had spotted the glint of a weapon in the tree line at about fifty metres. "DOWN, TAFF!" she screamed.

Taff took cover as Sam fired over Taff's back at the suspected firing position with a short three-round burst, a piercing scream of pain confirming her success. Taff moved swiftly to give Sam covering fire.

"MOVE, SAM!" he screamed.

BANG-WHOOSH!

There was a sharp explosion and a flash and distinct whoosh from the tree line as a seemingly slow RPG round spiralled lazily over both operators' heads and imploded into the Ops car. There was another explosion and flash as the petrol tank exploded.

Taff shouted, "MOVING NOW!"

Sam provided covering fire, with two three-round bursts to the area of the flash from the RPG.

At that precise moment, the vast airborne bulk of a black, sleek-shaped Royal Naval Sea King helicopter swooped in low over the firefight, and the air gunner with the mounted GPMG (General Purpose Machine Gun) suppressed the tree line with short bursts of fire where they had seen Sam's outgoing tracer rounds impact.

Taff shouted, "RALLY, RALLY, RALLY!" He had found some hard cover besides an old Russian BMP (Boevaya Mashina Pehoty-Infantry Combat Vehicle) left over from some earlier Afghan ambush.

"MOVING NOW!" screamed Sam as soon as she heard the sound of Taff's 53 to her left. "I'M IN!" Sam screamed as she joined Taff. She dived onto her stomach in a lying position in the opposite direction from Taff, with their feet nearly touching. Both operators were laying in a small hollow in the ground some twenty metres from the old BMP; they instinctively knew that the obvious cover of the old Russian tank would draw fire. A long burst of .762 from an RPD then rattled against the side of the BMP as if to confirm their training, then the incoming fire suddenly stopped. The tempo of the firefight changed as they heard the sharp distinctive crack of several British SA 80 rifles — the QRF had arrived and the remaining Taliban were busy.

They could tell the difference between the combatants, long wild bursts from the Talibs answered by the distinctive controlled double taps from Zulu Company's Marines, ably accompanied by long bursts of suppressive fire from two air gunners that circled the immediate area mounted in the Sea Kings flying low that filled the dusty-coloured sky like large and very deadly birds of prey. The Taliban were losing the firefight.

Sam shouted to Taff above the din. "AMMO AND CAS, I HAVE TWO MAGS LEFT AND I AM HIT!"

Taff responded, "TWO MAGS LEFT AND I'M OK."

Taff immediately went into first-aid mode and pulled a FFD (First Field Dressing) from his chest rig and an OMNIPON (morphine syrette). Both Sam and Taff had taken their compromise hats from their webbing and placed them on; these were camouflaged, Army-style hats with a difference, as ARMY was emblazoned in day-glo yellow letters across the front of each.

Taff moved around to lie next to Sam to dress her left upper arm. "You good, Sam? You need this?" Taff said, offering the syrette of morphine.

Sam gently replied, "It's not that bad, Taff, just a scratch, I want to keep my wits about me."

"You OK, kid?" Taff enquired.

Sam looked towards Taff and caught his gaze; she saw reflected in his deep, dark brown eyes a kindly glint that registered both his concern and his comradeship.

"I've never been as scared in my life, Taff, but I'm alive, and so are you, so I've never been better."

The operators stayed firm overlooking the road as the Marines moved in two man teams, one covering, and one moving, to check the Taliban dead. Taff shouted "ARMY, ARMY, ARMY," and pulled the pin from a red smoke grenade, the recognition signal, and threw it to their right and downwind. The Marines shouted, "ZULU, ZULU, ZULU," both the responding code word on their orders and coincidentally the old Zulu Company battle cry from the Falklands. Within a minute, a Commando medic was checking Sam's injuries and preparing both operators for a helicopter extraction.

An older Marine introduced himself in a broad Scottish accent.

"Hi, I am WO2 Jock Moran, Z Company's Sergeant Major. Great job guys, there was nearly very little for us to do, we will have you back sipping coffee at the Green Bean in Bastion in fifteen minutes max."

"Thanks, it is very good to see you, Sergeant Major," answered Sam as the approaching thump, thump, thump of the Sea King's rotor blades made further communication impossible.

In the eerie calm after the hectic action the Marine Commandos set about clearing, searching and photographing the dusty crossroads by the canal that had, fifteen minutes earlier, been a life-or-death battlefield.

WO2 Jock (Steph) Moran was an old school bootneck, an ML (Mountain Leader) specialist with twenty-five years' experience of every shithole the Corps had been in, and he had been in a few. He was with a young Marine, awed by his first full contact with fresh memories of the carnal mess that was the second Land Cruiser, who said, as the first Sea King lifted up to cover the other as it searched for the LZ (Landing Zone) to extract the handlers.

"That was fucking outrageous, I've never seen shit like that, Sergeant Major."

"Welcome to the 'Ghan, son," he said ruefully.

Twenty minutes later as the QRF prepared to extract one of his Marines, he had handed him a plastic evidence bag containing all the documents collected from the dead. One item was a blood-splattered Afghan NDS (National Directorate of Security) identification card with the name in Afghan and English. It apparently belonged to a Major Marouf. Jock's face instinctively grimaced as he realised the implications — the faded photo behind the worn, scratched, clear plastic, looked very worrying like the older bearded guy in the passenger seat of the second vehicle, whose brains lay splattered behind him on the grey leather of the Land Cruiser. He muttered under his breath, "Oh, fuck, blue on fucking blue."

A wounded Talib peered towards the scene, his RPD was smashed, one of Sam's armour-piercing rounds had entered just above the magazine housing, and another had gone through his shoulder. He knew he was badly wounded, dying maybe, probably his only chance would be medical help from the kuffar (infidel), he could not call them, maybe they would find him, *Inshallah* (God willing), he thought. He had been in the fight and had seen how this little Western woman with bright blonde hair had fought; she was the most beautiful girl he had ever seen, but he had never seen a more competent killer, she went about her business like an angel of death.

Chapter Three

Shock and Loss

London, Cardogan Square, 2015

Sir Ian Cameron was a man with impeccable bearing and manners, and possessed the supreme self-confidence that Eton, Cambridge and a commission in the Scots Guards had imbued in him. A harsh isolated upbringing with traditionally distant upper-crust parents and the character-moulding experience of the British public school system, had failed to adequately prepare him for the emotional bereavement of life's more mundane challenges; the trauma of divorce, for instance, or the violent loss of a friend in battle. His life had not been easy.

An estrangement from his parents, triggered by teenage rebellion and his early life-style choices, including a tramp along the 70s hippy trail had led to his parents removing his financial stabilisers early. He had to battle his way through life and had not lived his life in an upper-class bubble. After living life teetering on the edge for a while, he had dropped off and rebounded onto a more conventional path and decided to join the Army.

He found, to his amazement, that he was rather good at it. He let the comradeship and shared experiences of Sandhurst that had churned out young British officers for hundreds of years forge him. Then, as a twenty-year-old subaltern, he had experienced extreme violence and the haphazard lottery of war on the mad charge up Mount Tumbledown on the 13th of June

1982. He lived with the memory of his own limitations when tested with the crack and resounding thump of Browning 50-cal cracking within inches of his combat helmet.

He not only felt that gut-crunching fear for his own preservation, overcome by training and pride, but also the more intense secondary fear, as any decent leader feels for the men under his command. It was a strange dichotomy, an intense protective fear for his platoon with that swinging sword of Damocles inching nearer to the realization that some might die. Tumbledown was as tough a martial challenge as fate could devise for him. An uphill battle, bayonets fixed, against an enemy who had dug themselves in well, who were not conscripts but regular Argentinian Marines. It was a long hard fight and they, the best regular soldiers the Argentinians had, had lost, but Sir Ian had also lost. Not only some close personal friends but also some of his men that had followed him on the final assault, and there was not one day when he did not feel the loss.

His early forays into the business world were now legendary. He had the analytical edge over his competitors, he realised that technology had become the key future driver before others, and invested accordingly. He had built his business well and extremely quickly. He understood people, he understood leadership, and he understood life, and therefore charged hard at it. He was then a hard man to fool. He was successful, extremely ruthless in business, and although gifted with a head start as far as background and education was concerned, he was also a very driven self-made man, and also in 2015, one of the most wealthy men in Britain.

He worked from home, one of the few luxuries he allowed himself. Work dominated his life and he preferred to work to a set routine. Up at 0630, into running kit and a thoughtful jog from Cardogan Square to Hyde Park. He was also security aware, and was always accompanied by two members of his security detail trailing discreetly to the rear. At Hyde Park he would meet his personal trainer Steve and train for half an hour with a sequence of cardio and strength conditioning, and then repeat the run for home, this time with Steve setting the pace with the BGs slightly more stressed, trying to keep up. Then it was a shower, time to dress in an immaculate Savile Row suit, freshly laundered shirt, and invariably a Guards tie, properly shod with a pair of his twenty-year-old gleaming Church brogues, and he was then always in the library office by 0900.

The best part of the morning was the first coffee of the day presented by his super-efficient elderly secretary along with a copy of the Times. "Thanks, Mrs. Eldridge," he said with genuine warmth.

"My pleasure, Sir Ian, but nothing very uplifting in it this morning,"

"There very seldom is, Mrs. E," Sir Ian replied.

Again, the news was focused on Islamist terrorism, with the sad news that an American photojournalist had been seized near the town of Mosul accompanying a Kurdish Pershmerga patrol. The other story focused on the colourful London Mayor Boris Johnson, who had succinctly, and correctly in his opinion, summed up the newly joined British born recruits to ISIS as porn-addicted self-abusers, or as classically trained Boris had called them, 'onanists'.

Sir Ian then switched on the television, as always set to Sky News, and his heart stopped. In that instant time seemed to freeze. He could not focus on anything said by the newsreader; his mind became oblivious to the accompanying story. He found himself in a horrific emotional void; he was looking directly at his son, a son he had not seen since his very traumatic and troubled divorce from his first wife twenty years ago.

He studied his son's face, it was like he could see Caroline's features fused with his own and frozen in time, etched with fear. His face was swollen on his right side; a deep weal indented across his forehead where he had obviously been beaten. His son was featured in a group photograph with two other previously seized hostages; all were wearing Guantanamo-style orange jumpsuits.

A Danish aid worker from Save the Children and an Italian doctor who had been working for Medicins Sans Frontiers looked sheepishly into the camera, eyes seemingly trying to adjust to the light. In the instant that Sir Ian had recognised in his own son, in a surreally horrific setting, he felt a sort of fusion with him, a strong feeling of love coursed through his inner being and he felt a total connection.

He also recognised a sort of family trait, a glimmer of defiance in his son's gaze, as he looked through the camera, head up, fearful, but seemingly un-cowed by his captors. In that moment through the shock and horror, he swore a solemn internal oath that he would save him. He would use every penny, every connection, pull every string and lever, push any button and use any method legal or illegal to snatch him back from the heart of darkness. Sir Ian made some calls.

Sir Ian knew whom to ring; he had friends in the security services, a brief explanation and a short period of time later he had arranged another person to attend his next training session in the park.

To the unsuspecting there would have been nothing unusual about the watchers providing a protective screen for the meeting in the park, it was what they had done professionally every day of their lives and they looked like everyday people. Sir Ian's fitness entourage left at the same time and eventually a senior intelligence officer joined him for PT.

Tim Broughton was a fit guy in his mid-thirties. He had joined MI6 from Oxford. He was a comprehensive school kid from the new wave though; the new wave liked to think that they combined 'book smart' with 'street smart'. Tim was both, and had already investigated both the circumstances and possible solutions to Sir Ian's problems.

"What can be done?" asked Sir Ian, in between bursts of

exercise. "It is difficult, Sir Ian, HMG can do very little directly, but we can help indirectly."

"What help can you give?" Sir Ian said tersely.

"We advise you to put this into the hands of a recommended civilian agency. This is a highly recommended company that we have had dealings with in the past. The name I can give you is Danny McMaster, he's an ex-British Army Colonel and the company is called Hedges and Fisher. On the back of their card you have my confidential and encrypted phone numbers, please do not hesitate to call, but please do not use any other means of communication. We will help, but cannot directly, we can assist quietly, under the radar so as to speak, but our assistance will be substantial if a solution can be forged. We would thoroughly recommend that you do not advertise your interests in the release of this man, be assured that our colleagues in the CIA are also very active in his cause and will offer support."

Sir Ian recognised the reality of the situation, an offer of help was all he was going to achieve. "Very many thanks, young man," he offered.

"Not at all, sir," answered Tim. "My CEO sends his best regards, by the way."

"Tell him it is deeply appreciated, Tim," Sir Ian responded.

Back in the library at Cardogan Square, Sir Ian examined the card. It had an embossed emblem of a trident and net on one side and what looked like a Greek-style Corinthian helmet on the other, and it was emblazoned with the title 'Hedges and Fishers Security Services'. It might at first sight, and especially to the uninitiated, seem an unlikely name for a security company, but Sir Ian understood the hidden meaning, the two names refer to the two British Army Intelligence Corps organisations that the founders of the company belonged to. Both organisations were born and evolved from the initial chaos of the Frank Kitson-inspired intelligence apparatus formed to combat the Provisional IRA during the early years of the so-called 'Long War' against them.

Hedges refers to Mark 14:23, "*Go out into the highways and hedges and compel them to come in,*" the biblical quote associated with 14th Intelligence Company, more commonly known as the DET, which has now become the Special Reconnaissance Regiment or SRR. The DET were masters of the extremely exacting discipline of surveillance and masters of the complicated tradecraft that they required to succeed.

'Fisher' refers to the other part of what has been referred to, along with the SAS as the Unholy Trinity, the Force Research Unit later to become the Joint Support Group whose motto, 'Fishers of Men', had similar biblical connotations referring to their pivotal role as agent handlers for agents inside the Provisional IRA, and all the other major terrorist organisations across the religious divide during the Troubles. The third element of the company was the intelligence analysts versed in the full spectrum of multi-skills needed for information collection, from which reliable intelligence could be gleaned, plans based on, and jobs completed. The cutting edges of the company were a collection of extremely accomplished independent security operators with a proven track record of obtaining results in extremely hostile environments.

The company was doing well. It had a variety of clients on a multi-national basis with commercial tentacles reaching out globally; encompassing services ranging from bespoke security surveys to personal protection details for visiting pop stars and dignitaries. The spectrum of clients' only uniting factor was their ability to pay for good results. The company also filled another niche part of the market, which other firms avoided, because it recruited people with a unique ability to think outside the box.

Added to this potent mix was the all-important network of supportive contacts that pointed the way to success. These ranged from friends in the contemporary British and American armed forces, the CIA, FBI, MI5 and MI6 to senior politicians.

Danny McMaster had retired from the British Army's

Intelligence Corps after a fury of recrimination of the 3010 incident. The Afghan knives were out as soon as the guys had extracted and the Special Investigation Branch (SIB) of the British Army was soon called in to investigate the whole incident. Senior Afghan politicians demanded, quite literally at times, the heads of those involved. It had, as far as they were concerned, been a calculated murder mission against innocent villagers and had involved the brutal murder by ambush of a senior NDS officer who had friends in Government.

Sam and Taff were investigated under caution and accused of at least a calculated over-reaction, and at worst involvement in a preconceived murder plot. The unit was grounded as senior British politicians danced to President Karzai's tune. Danny resigned in disgust, the Whitehall warriors had, as far as he was concerned, said to the quite supportive commanding General they had "failed to support and actually betrayed his guys, and undermined his unit". He suggested that they try a quick drive around the 'Green Zone' to see if they found it to their liking. It annoyed him that the cold, calm, courage of his lads and lasses had been so abused.

He told the ensuing enquiry that Sam and Taff had reacted in entirely the right way and that he had personally changed the 'ROE'. The buck stopped with him, and added that the enquiry team had absolutely, as Danny told them, "diddly squat knowledge of Helmand."

They asked why had he allowed the operation when he knew that a white Toyota Corolla, very similar to Sam and Taff's Ops car, was on the BOLO list. Danny took a deep breath and explained what every soldier in Helmand who had actually been on the ground knew.

"Gentlemen," he had said very calmly, looking very directly into the faces of the members of the enquiry, "there are literally thousands of white Toyota Corollas in Afghanistan, they are imported from the Gulf States and bought in bulk. On every

BOLO list there is a white Toyota Corolla and that's why we use it as an Ops car." He looked at the confusion in their faces and realised that they did not live in the same world as him.

It took two months and several boards of enquiry before the unit was comprehensively cleared of any operational improprieties. It slowly emerged that Major Marouf was actually a double agent himself in the employ of Pakistan's ISI, and that the voice intercepts collected from both radio chatter and Marouf's own mobile phone indicated that he had been actively coordinating the attempted kidnap of British intelligence operatives. The body of 3010, the source involved, was found two weeks after the attempted snatch; he had been brutally tortured and decapitated. All involved were exonerated and Danny's previous paperwork writing Sam and Taff up for an award was grudgingly accepted. However, for Danny, the incident was the final push he needed to finally announce his retirement and walk.

Hedges and Fisher Security Services was the result of discussions with an old friend called Kenny Hanraran who was also retiring as a Lt Col from the DET, or as it is now known the SRR (Special Reconnaissance Regiment). By the time they had landed at Heathrow on the flight back to England, and numerous gin and tonics later, Hedges and Fisher was a viable concept, two months later it was a reality.

Kenny brought with him twenty-five years' experience of operating surveillance against dangerous targets in extremely hostile environments. He had joined the DET, also known as 14 Intelligence Company, in the mid 80s as a talented Royal Marines Corporal from 40 Commando, and left as a half Colonel in the Intelligence Corps. He had first met Danny on 'Camp One', at an undisclosed location during the gruelling selection procedure that all DET personnel, apart from those already qualified as Special Forces (SAS & SBS), had to endure.

Their joint suffering bound the two together, as in all extremely arduous selections. The final eight successful candidates from the initial selection of fifty volunteers had not only thoroughly prepared in all aspects of the skills needed for life in the DET, but had also produced some side-splitting moments of comedy, as both men fondly recalled on the long journey home.

Entirely apart from their complementary and interlocking skills, the two men, between them, knew just about everybody there was to know in the intelligence world. They had a joint knowledge of who to talk to and how to get things done. Therefore when they received a call from Tim Broughton, it did not surprise them. Danny and Kenny knew very early on that this was a job that the security services would cut them some slack on; they also knew that it was also a job that would need every joint resource and contact that they could muster.

The research process on the possible destination of the task was immediately instigated to assist with the initial planning stage; it helped immensely to have a depth of knowledge of the operational area before the pitch to the client. The company's experienced team of collators and IT specialists concentrated their initial focus on what is termed open source material. Mapping was drawn of the suspected areas of operations and the target pack and profile slowly emerged as the numerous intelligence gaps were researched and closed.

The huge amount of data produced from the extensive debriefing of previously released ISIS prisoners from France and Italy was meticulously researched to trace any reoccurring patterns or personalities. It was quickly established that the ISIS hostage holding cell was previously situated in Syria and staffed by Jihadists from the Salafist cells operating out of London. By the time Danny Mac and Kenny had arranged their first meeting with the client, they had a background target pack, and they had an outline plan of how it could be done and they thought that with enough resources and unofficial governmental support the hostage could be retrieved.

Chapter Four

The Circle of Knowledge

Secrets are by their very nature, hard to keep; the analogy used by agent handlers is the idea of a finite circle of knowledge. Preventing the leakage of information by limiting the number of people who know it, controlling its release on a 'need to know basis.' Therefore, successful terrorist organisations use a closed cell system to protect vital information. One of the handlers main questions on a source debrief will always be, "Who else knows this?"

If a source is part of a four man cell then any operational specifics that he discloses could have serious security implications for him. A good source handler, who wants to keep an asset running, must always assess the operational importance of that information with the safety and security of the agent. If, however, as in some cases, especially as in social systems in the Third World, if half an Afghan village knows the information, the information can be acted on without fear of compromise.

Danny Mac was acutely aware that the key to a successful extraction in this case revolved solely on keeping their circle of knowledge tight. He had arranged to meet Sir Ian and Tim Broughton therefore at an address in London that they all knew. It was comfortable, secure, and because of its long and distinguished history, was extremely security aware. The Special Forces Club was set up as a post war old boys club for members of the SOE, (Special Operations Executive) and wartime Special Forces; it was a gentleman's club with an edge!

Danny Mac arrived early with Kenny H to set up the library meeting room and to set up the visual aids and to double check the area with a quick electronic security scan for any listening devices; although he knew that the club was scanned on a regular basis. The initial target pack had been prepared and contained everything they knew at that stage; with mapping, possible locations and likely personalities and was available to the client. It also contained, as importantly, what they did not know. Or, put another way, what they had to discover to make a hostage rescue a viable option.

Tim Broughton arrived soon after to join them. "Hi, Danny, Kenny, I have some watchers outside, some of your old troops, I think."

"Excellent stuff, Tim, we have swept the room and it's all good," Danny replied. Tim looked at Danny and caught his glance; he had worked with Danny Mac in Afghanistan and had the greatest regard for him. He knew that with Danny it wasn't about money, it was about integrity.

"Danny, is it a goer so far, is it doable?"

Danny cupped his chin in his right hand and adopted his Danny Mac thoughtful look, and answered, "Yes, Tim, it is doable, but we will need your help, we can do the mechanics of an extraction, but for it to actually work this project needs to know precisely where he is, we need a definite location, and we have a finite amount of time to find out."

Tim nodded in agreement. "Yeah, fully understood, we are working on it and we might have a good lock-on quickly, I will explain once you have finished your pitch and we are on our own."

Sir Ian arrived by taxi minus his usual entourage and was greeted by Kenny H. "Good morning, sir," Kenny said as they shook hands swiftly. Kenny opened the heavy teak door leading into the Library room; it creaked open and slammed satisfyingly shut, Kenny turned the ancient key and the door locked with a clunk.

Danny stood in front of a white screen onto which was projected the company's logo. He shook Sir Ian's hand and handed him a target folder.

"Good afternoon, Sir Ian," Danny started. He was a very good speaker with a very clipped and precise upper-class English twang; the ex-British Army Colonel he was now was a world away from the poor northern grammar school boy who had first joined the Army in the late sixties.

He addressed Sir Ian directly. "Tim has informed us of your requirements and we have prepared a brief presentation that will last about forty-five minutes, we will then, between us, attempt to answer any questions you might have. It will be divided into two separate parts. I will present what our research has uncovered thus far, or the known variables, and then my business partner Kenny will present what we need to know to proceed successfully, in other words, what is the 'intelligence gap', or what we need to find out."

Sir Ian nodded and Danny then started the first part of the presentation that consisted of the known variables. At each juncture a new PowerPoint slide flashed up to emphasise or explain a point. The projected images used a predictable military sequence, including Ground, Situation, Mission, Enemy Forces and Friendly Forces. An overview and explanation of the possible ground using sequential slides in time frame to explain the expansion of ISIS and the current socio-political situation in relation to them in both Syria and Iraq. He then pronounced and repeated what the company at the moment considered a mission statement. "The aim, gentlemen, is to safely extract David Slater and his fellow detainees from ISIS captivity safely, securely, and return them home."

The enemy paragraph contained information on the very brief history of ISIS, its current disposition, and its known intentions. Then a slide flashed up of six fresh-faced, but bearded, young men appearing to be of Middle Eastern extraction. Danny

31

described the slide: "Here are the men suspected of joining ISIS from the London area in the past three years, we believe that these young men, four of which are from East London and two from the Luton area, are part of the English-speaking cell that are tasked by the leadership of the Islamic State to act as prison guards to the European-based hostages."

"They all entered Syria in or around 2012, and either proceeded there on the tourist route through Turkey or under the auspices of running aid conveys organised by London-based Salafist groups. We know that the first two men are now dead; Mohammed Islam who is on the extreme left, upper row, was killed in a US airstrike in June 2013, the guy next to him, Faisal Rahman, was killed by Pershmerga in September 2013."

Danny used a laser pointer to indicate which person he was currently discussing. "The four men remaining have all been positively identified by former hostages as having been actively involved in the ISIS hostage holding cell as recently as January 2015. I would like to bring your special attention to the heavily bearded guy on the extreme bottom left. He is the one with the dark blemish on his forehead, which is caused by constant contact with a prayer mat. His name is Abdul Rahman, the previously mentioned dead Faisal's brother. He also has a quite famous, or infamous, depending on your point of view, brother called Mullah Hamid Rahman whose name might be familiar to you. Mullah Rahman is a Salafist preacher who is closely aligned to Al Majhouroun in London. He also believed to be the main fundraiser and recruiter for ISIS in England."

"So, gentlemen, the first part of the presentation is complete, you now know what we know. My opposite number Kenny will now explore what we need to find out to perform a safe and successful extraction."

Kenny stood up and replaced Danny by the PowerPoint screen and with his low Scottish burr very concisely said, "Gentlemen, so you now know what we know, but unfortunately," Kenny paused, "what we do not know is everything else. Gentlemen, at this juncture without a considerable research phase and considerable luck, the task is unworkable."

"We have three main intelligence requirements we need to nail. One, we need to access their communications systems, two, we need to know the timeframe we have to work within and three, and most importantly, we need to fix and find the exact location of the US hostage David Slater."

"Initial research indicates that IS move their hostages from their point of capture to their main power base in Raqqa within two to three weeks. At this time we believe that we can far easier affect a rescue from the far more fluid area of the Kurdish front. This effectively means that we have a three-week window to find, fix, and extract the hostages. Gentlemen, we need to do this within the next twenty-one days because with ISIS hostages, time is not on our side."

Kenny then described how the company intended to proceed and flashed up on the screen the selected primary team for the London-based operation. A montage of four separate individuals was displayed. The extreme left hand top picture under which was written 'Team Leader' showed a good-looking blonde girl in her late twenties or early thirties. The picture looked out of place on a security montage, the strikingly blue eyes, fine cheekbones and long blonde hair falling demurely across her face could have featured in a fashion magazine.

"This is the team we have selected for the research phase. On the extreme left is one of the most accomplished and skilled intelligence operatives we work with, a Miss Samantha Holloway MC (Military Cross), Sam is a former intelligence Corps Captain, and has served with both DHU and the SRR. Alongside her is Taff Thomas MC, who served alongside Sam in both units. Taff is an ex-Royal Marine who is not only a top intelligence operator but also a talented linguist and speaks Pashto and probably more pertinently in this case, fluent Arabic."

"The guy on the extreme left, bottom row, is an ex-SAS Sergeant Major called George 'Pat' Patterson alongside his close colleague and ex-SBS WO2 Ricky Scott. All of the team are trained in advanced surveillance techniques and not only have years of operational experience behind them, but more importantly they have all worked on many London based tasks and have a detailed knowledge of the ground."

"This project, if the concept is accepted by the client," Kenny directed his comments solely to Sir Ian's extremely alert eyes and detected a steely determination that boded well for the answer, "will run through three distinct phases. Firstly the research phase, based here in London, that will attempt to discover access to ISIS communications systems and to access their London-based support cell to gain a fix. If such research is successful, the project will move to stage two, the forward deployment and mounting stage. This will be achieved with an augmented and reinforced team with a strictly military intention based in Erbil, Kurdistan. The final phase will be the extraction, at this moment in time the only option is a strictly military Special Forces style extraction. At any time, the company could advise the client that due to insufficient information that the task is unworkable. You, Sir Ian, will only pay for one phase at a time, securing the services of Hedges and Fisher for fifty per cent up-front fee per phase."

Kenny paused, looked at Sir Ian and said, "If the company cannot achieve its initial objectives then half of this fee will be returned. Each phase will be arranged the same way, to ensure that you will only pay for results. A full contract is available for your lawyers perusal on completion of this presentation and here is a personal copy for you."

Kenny tried to gauge Sir Ian's reaction. It was hard to read his thoughts; he was probably an accomplished poker player. The clients face remained impassive as he removed his glasses from an inside pocket of his immaculately tailored jacket and put them on. There was an icy quiet as Sir Ian quickly leafed through the document.

Sir Ian broke the silence. "This all looks in order, I will get my legal people to look it over but I think I can say that you can start your 'Phase 1' immediately. I will of course need a full breakdown of the initial and projected costing." Sir Ian paused and looked towards both men, in his world, everything was based on personal recommendation, and he knew he had the best men for the job. "What is it going to cost me, ball-park figure?"

Danny responded, "A lot, this job will need the very best people and the latter stages will have a strong military element. Initially you will be charged for the surveillance and associated work in London at London surveillance rates. However as the project proceeds the cost will increase. The company will need funds for both political influence in Kurdistan, import licenses for weapons and equipment, and also a comprehensive insurance package for its nominated operators. However, this company promises that you will only pay for the work undertaken, and that you will be strictly informed of all developments."

Sir Ian quickly gathered the contract and said, "Sounds reasonable, go ahead, get him back." Sir Ian sealed the agreement with a firm handshake and quickly left the club.

CHAPTER FIVE

THE LONDISTAN CONNECTION

As soon as Sir Ian had left the club, the three remaining men sat down on the deep leather Chesterfields in the library and continued the briefing. Only this time it was Tim who supplied the surprises. He took a short nervous breath and then gave his, or rather MI5 and MI6's input. "Gentleman, I will not labour the quoting of the Official Secrets Act, I am pretty sure you two could quote it verbatim, however, I must mention that it applies in this case. What I am about to tell you only has a very finite circle of knowledge and compromise would have disastrous consequences for our future operations against the ISIS support organisation based in the UK."

Tim paused and glanced at both men to emphasise the point and continued. "There are two main, almost game-changing dynamics affecting the Islamist world since you two last worked for Box. Firstly we have had the rapid expansion of the Islamic State through military conquest, followed more recently by them suffering some significant military reverses at Kobani on the Syrian border, and also on the front line against the Pershmerga in the Kurdistan salient. Secondly and more pertinently for us, especially in relation to this venture, is the extremely corrosive effect on our ability to monitor ISIS intentions caused by the Snowden disclosures. As you know, since the leaking of our most technically advanced monitoring procedures, it has become increasingly hard to access ISIS communications, in actual fact we are now operating with methods more consistent with how you guys worked in the 80s and 90s. Gentlemen, we are trying to monitor these people using old school methods, because in reality, they are the only ones that now work. ISIS is extremely IT savvy and now understands how to circumvent our technical interventions. We have had to revert to both old-time surveillance methods and agent recruitment, now let me again reiterate my earlier point, reference our limited circle of knowledge."

Tim then paused and made separate eye contact with each man to underline the seriousness of what he was about to say. "At present we have two top sources within ISIS operations in London, both are familiar with ISIS operations in Iraq and Syria and both are actively seeking the present location of the Iraq based hostages." Tim then allowed himself a wry smile. "This may be something that will also uniquely match the skill sets of your people. It is linked to source information and it concerns the purchase of ten MacBook Air computers from Rasheed Electronics in Ealing, London, by an organisation called Syria Action Aid Direct. SAAD is the cover for the import of both material and personnel into the ISIS heartlands under the guise of Islamic Aid for Syrian refugees. We know that five of these computers are now in Iraq, they left on an aid convoy last week and we think that they are now in the vicinity of the hostage holding cell. My source believes that the next five are due to be delivered to the same ISIS unit. Those five computers have been delivered to Mullah Hamid Rahman and are now held by him. We believe that they are now in storage at his house near the Al Furquan mosque in East London and are now ready to be dispatched. Unfortunately, because of political restrictions and governmental sensitivity reference these computers, the proximity of the mosque, and because they belong to an Islamic aid charity, we cannot quickly gain permission to covertly access the laptops. A warrant to gain covert access has been refused by the High Court but here I have something that might interest you. Here is Mullah Rahman's personal file, with his known pattern of life and addresses; I hope you have better luck. This of course, gentlemen, is totally unauthorised and my organisation would not hesitate to deny that I ever gave that to you. I am going to leave it here for about ten minutes because I am sometimes somewhat, shall we say, absent minded?"

Tim quickly left the room, closing the heavy teak door behind him.

Danny and Kenny exchanged glances and knew that the pendulum of chance had just swung in their direction; maybe there was a chance to actually fix and find this guy.

In around ten minutes Danny and Kenny heard a slight tap on the door and Tim re-entered the room replaced the file into his briefcase, and with a conspiratorial grin said, "OK guys, that is what we have so far, completely off the record, without my big boss finding out, how can I help you?"

Danny looked, walked to the library door, opened the heavy door and briefly glanced outside into the hall, he then secured the door and turned to talk to Tim, "This is top notch, Tim, our profound thanks, I know you have given us a start point but we will need you to ease open doors for us all through this project. We need everything you can get for us on how these shitheads communicate, we need decent profiles of the players involved, and we will also need some help from our former colonial cousins."

Tim laughed, "Yes, that sounds like vintage Danny Mac, be assured, guys, our CIA friends have displayed extreme interest in getting these people back, you will have on the ground support from certain assets already deployed into the general area of Erbil in Kurdistan if you can progress the project to Phase Three."

Kenny then produced three cut-glass whisky glasses and a bottle of Laphroaig single malt whisky. He then placed them on the coffee table and neatly poured two fingers of amber liquid into each. "This is how us Jocks start a project, gentlemen." The three men stood and raised their glasses.

"To success and the damnation of the devil," pronounced Danny Mac.

All three swiftly downed their drinks, they all knew that the rescue was on, it was achievable, it was doable, and it had the chance of striking a very painful blow to an organisation that had caused carnage wherever it popped up. If Danny and Ken and the team could hurt ISIS, they would do so at any opportunity; this project had an extreme military solution! The game was afoot, the gloves were off, and the dogs of war were about to let slip.

Chapter Six

Flashback London 2015

Sam and Taff were sitting together again in yet another very ordinary-looking saloon car, but this time it was a ten year old Ford Mondeo, and they were not in Helmand Province, but in the East End of London and looking towards the entrance of a drab, very ordinary-looking terraced house. Some things had not changed; Taff still wore a thick black beard and a prayer hat, Sam was again engulfed in a full face black niqab and an all-covering black silk abaya, not much improvement on a burka but a little bit more comfortable.

They had been in the Whitechapel area for the last three days, at varying times, in varying vehicles, in various guises, trying to confirm a workable pattern of life to enable a covert entry of Mullah Rahman's rather dingy looking house near the Whitechapel Road. In very basic terms, they had to know when he was out so they could break into his house. Surveillance is an exacting task; it needs high levels of concentration and the ability to think on your feet, but it was sometimes also very time consuming and even boring, and also gave you, probably, much too much time to think about the past.

Five years had passed and the incident that had shaped all their respective lives still had daily repercussions. Sam had had to resign from the Army. Even after the MC, the 'Angel of Death' epithet had clung around her like a particularly loathsome smell especially after the media had exploited the story. It had therefore been a hard few years involving both heartache and an intense period of personal readjustment. Sam's marriage had car crashed due to both the press attention and by her husband's staff job as a Major at DSF (Directorate Special Forces). Before the Afghan thing they had half-admired, half-loved each other, but they always had been like the proverbial ships that passed in the night. Due to her husband's total lack of support during the daily attrition of press intrusion, both ships had well and truly steamed in the opposite direction, and, like that ship, Sam had broken that emotionally important bottle of bubbly across the relationships bows and wished him well.

She left the relationship feeling like a huge weight had been lifted from her shoulders. As her Dad always used to say, "Never worry about the past, aim for the future," and her recently deceased and unashamedly Commando with a capital 'C' Dad did not really like him that much anyway.

Sam had kept her sanity together by keeping busy with her unusually gruesome CrossFit training regime and her love of Thai boxing, which she combined on a daily basis. She also had spent the last couple of years getting a Masters from St Andrew's University in Scotland in Terrorism Studies. She loved the unique combination of challenges; competing in Muay Thai bouts and CrossFit competitions, while also getting a mega cerebral work out with the latest essay or lecture. Sam still had sleepless nights and the odd attack of the horrors, but she just cracked on, refusing the offers of counselling. It wasn't Sam's style.

Taff had coped better; five years had produced the good in equal measure with the bad, the MC had helped with his promotion to Warrant officer and his time spent with SRR, with two of those years working on attachment with 'Box' (MI5) in London as their liaison officer with the SAS. After a messy divorce, brought on partly by the stresses and strains of the job, but mainly by a total breakdown of both his own moral compass

41

in the bright lights of London, and his own incompetence in his personal black-ops, involving a stray text message.

Now, he was no longer married and also no longer in the Army, and, to his great pleasure, working for his old mates Danny Mac and Kenny. He had also jumped at the chance to work with Sam again; she was probably the best officer he had ever worked with. She was super-smart, brave, funny, and reliable, and he realised, not in a soppy way, that he sort of loved her. Not that it would have occurred to him to tell her!

Five years had also seen something that he would never have suspected when he operated with Sam in Afghanistan. The enemy was the same, the reasons they professed to fight for remained the same, but the war had morphed and was now here in their own back yard on the streets of London. This part of London, Whitechapel and Brick Lane, was multi-cultural, diverse or just mono-cultural, depending on your political perspective. The shops and market area reflected the dominant Muslim community and their need to link to their Bangladeshi routes. The clothes shops displayed various types of ethnic clothing, some brightly coloured, some not. There were money transfer shops, mobile phone shops and of course halal butchers and sweet shops.

This was an East End of London that had always started as a foothold for the dispossessed. Victims of historical pogroms and warzone refugees since it welcomed the French Huguenot Protestants in the rein of the previous Queen Elizabeth to a vibrant Jewish community before the Second World War. It is, was, and always has been, a down at heel area of the Capitol, with, in London tourist board spin-speak, 'an endearingly sooty exterior'.

Its present inhabitants, however, apart from the odd hip student from the artsy Hoxton, were adherents from one of the most severe versions of Wahhabi Islam, so the need for subterfuge was as important here as it was in Helmand. Taff looked around, it actually seemed thousands of miles away from the London of two miles down the road and they were effectively operating in a mini, closed, and hostile environment, all within the sound of Bow Bells.

Apart from the very obvious looking British buildings and flats thrown up by hip architects in the sixties, and the British registration plates on the cars, it looked more like Londonistan than London. The more militant of the local male youths had even previously mounted so-called 'Muslim Patrols' to stop such affronts to their religion such as young people enjoying themselves, the dreaded alcohol, and of course, gays, girls in short skirts, or young couples from the local University holding hands.

Sam and Taff were now 'eyes down' in Ernest Street just off the Whitechapel Road and observing a run-down terraced house with a battered-looking black door. The windows of the house were shrouded in net curtains with the front room window draped in a thick heavy purple more usually seen in a Catholic church. The house was near a converted pub that now served as a mosque; the peddlers of eternal redemption had superseded the trade for alcohol in this part of London.

Young Bangla guys passed in and out of the bright green door, seemingly struggling through an assorted pile of old trainers and sandals and the odd shoe outside the mosque door. Sometimes they glanced towards the Ops vehicle. They had been there a while, were they OK, so far the covert dress had seemed to work?

Sam spoke from under the niqab, "We will need to relocate soon, Taff. We have been here for a wee bit too long, and we are getting some looks."

"Yeah, roger that, give it five and I will call in Scotty to give us cover. It is fairly busy though Sam, and it does not look like we have been sussed, and it'll soon be dark."

"It never does till you are, sweetheart, we tend to attract the worst type of attentions when we're sharing a car," Sam said with a giggle.

"Yeah, fuck that last time in Helmand for a game of soldiers, hopefully though these fuckers haven't got a spare RPG in their front room," Taff whispered with a suppressed chuckle. Taff then broke off the conversation with, "Hang on, standby."

Both operators had spotted a bright light shine through the heavy curtains, on the right-hand downstairs window. The curtains moved and a heavily bearded face appears at the window. The front room light then was quickly switched off, but not before Sam and Taff had made a positive ID of the rather podgy bearded face of Mullah Rahman.

The door of the rather jaded-looking terraced house then opened, and a strangely dressed, almost biblical-looking figure moved out onto the street and looked very slowly in either direction up the street. This was done in the manner of the grossly overweight; he seemed to shuffle to his right and then change direction and totter to his left. The young people outside the mosque nodded reverentially towards the Mullah, they had just heard him preach many times and he was a powerful figure locally.

"If that is his attempt at counter-surveillance, Sam, it looks like the lads have an easy follow," said Taff.

"Roger that," said Sam.

The heavily bearded man peered through thick black-framed glasses; the long white beard extended down to his protruding stomach. He was dressed in a white dish-dash with a white prayer hat on the back of a shining baldhead. His white cotton dish-dash bottoms flapped around his shins, showing his fattish ankles jammed into a nifty combination of bright red socks and brown leather sandals. Mullah Rahman was not such a comical figure though; the team had read the files and knew he was a prominent member and the spiritual advisor of al-Muhajiroun, the London based Jihadist organisation, and he was also suspected by Box (MI5) of being involved in the radicalisation of the young that attended his mosque. He was ISIS's London representative.

44

Mullah Rahman then walked to a dark green Volvo Estate car, opened it remotely, and returned to his open door. He briefly entered the house and returned with a large, seemingly heavy cardboard box. The team realised from the previous three days that the box contained various tapes, books and ISIS promotional material. He paused for breath, briefly resting the box against the car as he fought to find his car keys in his long flowing pyjama bottoms and eventually opened the tailboard of the estate. He grunted, heaved, and finally placed the box inside and locked the car remotely and shuffled back to lock his front door.

The team responded. "Hi all stations, this is Taff, X-ray One is on the move in a dark green Volvo Estate, registration, Lima Alpha Victor, three, five, seven."

"Roger that," all operators heard through their ear-pieces.

"This is Pat, stood by."

"Roger that, this is Scotty, stood by."

Pat was parked 100 metres at the end of the street, 'eyes down' on the green Volvo, driving a black, battered, ten-year-old Ford Fiesta. Scotty was 'eyes down' at the other end of the road, driving an equally nondescript but new VW Polo. Whichever way the Volvo went one, of them would tag it, and then the other operator would become the backup car.

The puffing Mullah carefully closed his front door with a seemingly endless turning of locks, fumbling at intervals for the correct keys.

"How many fucking locks has he got on that door, kid?"

"He has five, two Chubbs, a conventional Yale, and two Yale deadbolts, all from the CTR 'Close Target Recce' early doors this morning." Sam giggled. "Just as well I am going in the back, where he only has a dodgy old Yale."

"Yeah," said Taff "and look, he's left his front window open!" They both laughed at the absurdity of it.

Taff watched the subject open the driver's side door and squeezed behind the steering wheel of the old Volvo.

"Hello, all stations, X-ray One, is moving east."

"Roger that" said Pat.

"Roger that, I have," said Scotty, as he waited to start his follow.

Scotty waited until the Volvo had passed and slipped in behind him after another car from traffic had conveniently positioned itself behind the target. It was always better to have a slight standoff, especially if it was going to be a long follow or the target was particularly security aware.

Scotty transmitted "That's me, towards Blue One." Blue One was the junction of Commercial Road and the Whitechapel Road.

Pat's car followed to cover any sudden changes of direction and Sam and Taff's car tagged on at the rear. The heads-up display on the GPS marked all the Ops cars, which made things much simpler. The target car was now on the main road in fairly heavy traffic and seemed to be making its way in a rather haphazard manner with a combination of some pretty appalling driving and copious use of the Volvo's horn at every opportunity. The Volvo passed the East End Mosque on the Whitechapel Road.

"That's X-Ray One at Green Three." Scotty reported his location.

"Hi Sam, this is Scotty, I think he'll get a pull by the Old Bill, kid, his driving is terrible and he's forgotten to put his lights on."

A fourth voice sounded on the net. "Hi all stations, that's me on the plot."

Jimmy Cohen was thinking, *what's a nice Jewish lad like me doing in this part of town just before the call to prayer?* It was ironic really because Jimmy was actually born in Bethnal Green, just down the road to Jewish parents who had fled the holocaust.

The timings are right on time, he thought, just as Sam had given on the Op orders at the safe house, *it looks good.* He loved working with his Hedges and Fisher mates.

Jimmy was small and wiry, with blondish, slightly receding

hair, sporting thick-framed light-blue glasses, which gave him more than a passing resemblance to Brains from the old Thunderbirds International Rescue TV series that he loved as a kid. He was now though driving his own version of Thunderbird 1, a newish RAC recovery van, along with a load of specialist kit and a large personal collection of registration plates to suit every occasion.

Jimmy Cohen was good at what he did; in fact he was considered the best. That is why he was always busy. He had started his career as a Paratrooper in the British Army before joining the IDF (Israeli Defence Force) mainly because it was the only scrap at the time and it made his Mum happy. Then came the Israeli SF, and then Shin Bet where he had been the only spy with a 2 Para tattoo, and now after nearly twenty-five years of practical experience, he had both the technical expertise and the operational know-how to bug or monitor anything, anywhere, at any time.

He was an expert on encryption, computer analysis, and cryptology, and was one of the few people at that time, globally, to have the technical know-how and equipment to intercept and record 4G mobile telephone conversations. He had worked for many different agencies, governmental or otherwise, but particularly liked working for Danny and Kenny.

Tonight's task was much simpler, all he had to do was to unpack five MacBook Air computers, making sure that they had not been covertly marked against interference, and then to install, probably, he thought, the most advanced piece of bugging technology he had ever seen devised. The kit was simple, undetectable, and long lasting, because it appeared as, and also performed the same function as the chunk of Apple circuitry it replaced.

The beauty of this kit was that it was virtually undetectable even to an Apple computer engineer who might routinely service the computer. The device replaced the circuitry it was substituted for and was therefore charged by the computer itself. It would not only give the planners at Hedges and Fisher the constant GPS location of the laptop, but it could also hijack and remote the camera at their command and simultaneously record voice conversations. It also had the ability to 'hoover up', or drain all wireless communications within a hundred-metre radius and transmit that data to a remote base station within fifty kilometres of its location, and to Jimmy's ultimate amusement, a good old Israeli firm made it.

Jimmy knew all about Arabs and mobile phones, as he had once placed a small explosive charge in one that had blown its owner's head off. The same firm had done the technical stuff on that, simple improvisation at its best.

Jimmy's workshop was situated in the back of the Transit van in which he was driving down the Whitechapel Road. Although the large, box-shaped Transit van's livery advertised it as an RAC recovery vehicle, which it was before he had bought it, the rear was now refitted with a high tech workbench, a HD digital camera linked to a 40-inch TV monitor, high powered lighting, a large magnifying lens that hovered seemingly weightless over the bench, and all the tools and technical paraphernalia needed to open the five laptops, replace the circuitry, and to reseal all of them within the original boxes and wrapping within a time scale of fifteen minutes per computer.

Jimmy knew that with this job speed was everything; he would park the van as close to the covert entry target as possible, and make sure that the super-bugged laptops were back at the target before they could be missed. He only hoped that with all this super-expensive technology, along with his considerable fee that he would gratefully receive from Hedges and Fisher, they would get the result they were after. Jimmy had already asked to go with the team if they deployed; it was an exciting task, a mixture of technical and practical that he knew he could help with.

Scotty's Highland Scots sounded over the net; the Volvo was indicating left. "Hi Guys, Alpha One X-ray One is intending left into which seems like an industrial Estate."

"Roger that Alpha One, this is Two, I have."

Scotty's vehicle glided past the slip road signposted Archway Industrial Estate, and Pat seamlessly took up the position of the lead follow vehicle.

Sam and Taff watched the heads-up display on their GPS and saw Pat's car turn into the estate as Scottie's rolled on ahead to find a convenient place for a U-turn.

"Hi all stations, X-ray One has parked close to a row of viaduct type lock ups, and he appears to be unloading the Volvo, that's me going foxtrot," (walking).

Pat quietly opened the door of the Polo, the interior light had been disabled with a simple switch on the dashboard. He slipped soundlessly out of the car and checked the immediate area, old habits from a Helmand die-hard. He still found himself automatically doing his five, ten and twenty-metre checks as if checking for possible IEDs.

Pat was wearing his standard surveillance gear: jeans and dark clothing with a two-coloured reversible jacket. In his jacket pocket he had a woollen hat that doubled as a balaclava if needed. He held a small night-scope to his right eye and peered around a very old, somewhat crumbly, red brick wall. He stood back from the wall, being careful not to break the outline.

He could clearly see X-ray One through the site, and then the site whited-out as the interior light that beamed as the Volvo's tailgate as it opened. Again Mullah Rahman sorted through a large set of keys, muttering each time he made the wrong selection. Finally he made his way to a lock-up garage under a railway arch. It was a fairly large building with two blue-painted, inward opening doors, one with a seemingly carelessly painted number 'eighteen' scrawled in white paint. Mullah Rahman crouched and applied the selected key to a large padlock, and quickly released it with a clunk that caused the large chain that secured the doors to rattle loudly. He then stopped and looked around to check whether the sound had carried. He opened the door and switched on an interior light.

After a couple of minutes, the Mullah left the lock-up door open and returned to the Volvo, where the tailgate still gaped. Again he appeared to struggle with the weight of the box as he returned to the garage and moved inside with his burden; he was inside for a short time and appeared again empty-handed. He then moved outside the garage and looked both to his left and right, seemingly checking for watchers, and then noisily reattached the padlock and chain.

Mullah Rahman then returned to his Volvo and struggled inside. The lights were turned on, the engine sounded and with a crunching of gears the Volvo appeared to lurch its way towards the entrance to the arches. His pattern of life now indicated that he would go to the East End Mosque to preach.

Scotty heard Pat's voice in his earpiece. "That's X-ray One lifted off and clear, you have control."

The remainder of the team now knew that Pat would now follow to make sure that the Mullah did not return to his house.

CHAPTER SEVEN

THE BREAK IN

Scotty again made a call. "Hello, all stations, that's X-ray One at Blue Two, the plot is all yours." The team at the house now knew they could proceed with the covert entry.

The Mullah's car turned into the East London Mosque car park and Scotty observed him exit the vehicle and make his way to the main door; he removed his shoes and went inside. Scotty knew he could not maintain his 'eyes down' position for long. Apart from the unofficial Muslim Patrol, the mosque sometimes also had a group of designated police community officers, recruited locally, that were particularly diligent during this particular time of increased cross-community friction.

Scotty decided to go technical. *It's good that beards are considered pretty hip at the moment,* he thought. He quickly placed a white prayer hat on the back of his head, left the vehicle hidden clear of the numerous CCTV cameras that festooned the mosque and made his way towards the Volvo.

He knelt by the driver's side wheel and pretended to tie his shoelace, and quickly placed a magnetic GPS device on the inside of the front sill. The bit of kit had a range of twenty kilometres; it would allow the team to monitor X-ray One's movements, which would now show on the teams GPS devices. Scotty returned to the Polo and exited the car park. He removed the prayer hat and replaced it in his inside pocket; it was always handy to have it on a job like this. He had bought it in Baghdad. *Never thought I would be using it in London for the same reason*, he thought, *instant camouflage*. He would now stay mobile in case the Volvo moved, and would change the Polo's plates as soon as he could.

"All stations, Scottie, that's me mobile, X-ray One is now on our system and stationary."

The remainder of the team quickly sprang into action. Pat broke the radio silence with, "That's me, lifting off to provide back up on the plot."

Jimmy and the team responded.

"Hi Taff, that is me towards you with my kit in ten."

Sam then called. "All stations, roger that, I'm foxtrot towards the target." Sam quickly checked her equipment, lifted the door lock and said to Taff, "Right, I'm off for a spot of burglary."

"Enjoy, kid," responded Taff.

Taff looked across the car at the fleeting image of Sam as she walked towards the alley that led to the target, the black abaya seemed to float towards the target. *Fuck, that girl can actually look sexy in any fucking thing*, he briefly thought, and then watched as the bleeping dots converged on the screen of the car's GPS. Pat's car was the first to arrive and pulled up on the side road at the junction of the alley to the rear of Mullah Rahman's house. In the next couple of minutes Jimmy pulled the RAC van right up behind Pat's vehicle with the lights flashing. Pat had released the bonnet catch and raised the hood into which he gazed confusedly, in that familiar bemused pose known to any that have driven vehicles that suddenly go rogue.

Scotty had parked at the opposite side of the street. Taff would supply close support to Sam in the immediate area of the operation.

Sam had exited the Ops car, still wearing her black abaya and full-face niqab, along with long black satin type gloves to complete the ensemble, and retrieved a large black shoulder bag from the boot. Underneath, she was wearing jeans, a black reversible reefer jacket and her favourite black New Balance barefoot trainers. The Chanel shoulder bag contained all the equipment she needed for a spot of covert MOE (Method of Entry). It was one of Sam's many talents, honed on numerous tasks whilst working with the SRR. She could let herself in most places with her personal set of lock-picks. She also carried in the smart shoulder bag a fourth generation set of night vision goggles. As soon as she entered the back alley at the rear of the target house, she quickly removed the abaya and niqab and stowed them in the bag.

She then tucked her long blonde hair inside a black woollen hat that could double as a full-face balaclava. Her belt kit, hidden under a thin cashmere top, contained her radio and everything she would need in case of a hard compromise. She walked with her hands in her pockets to hide the clear latex gloves she wore on her hands. She checked for any obvious surveillance, waited for a moment until the Ops car pulled away and depressed her prezzle switch and muttered into her chest mike.

"Hi Taff, that's me on the plot."

"Yeah, roger that" replied Taff.

Sam arrived at the back door and placed her bag on the floor on the rear step. She removed the night vision kit from the bag and put it on, she then spent some time adjusting to the green eerie light before examining the lock. It was a straightforward Yale lock, it would take her seconds, but first she would check the whole door to see if it had been covertly sealed. Sometimes people were not as stupid as they looked. Security tape was easily available in any locksmith's. The brittle serial numbered tape, once broken, had to be replaced. Sam had twenty different rolls of it, as sold by all major manufacturers, in her bag. She examined the door, some peeling paint, but no tape; it looked OK.

Sam then removed a small leather tool roll from the Chanel bag; she untied it and unwrapped the roll to reveal a long line of bright steel lock-picks of various sizes. She removed two, and by combining them she very quickly turned the lock and opened it with a click. She then eased the back door open and squeezed inside. The inside of the kitchen was now illuminated by the NVGs. Mrs. Mullah had obviously been away, on a family visit to Bangladesh according to Box's source. The small back kitchen was cluttered with various dishes and pans along with empty cans and plates of uneaten food.

Sam stood and readjusted the NVGs; it always took a little while to acquaint the brain with this strange green tinged, night-time world. You needed to let your natural perspective or awareness to click in before you actually searched a house. A stumble or stupid accident could break something not easily replaceable and could compromise the whole operation and eventually cost someone his life. *Very little changes*, thought Sam.

The consignment from Apple, according to the MI5 agent, should be in the downstairs office but Sam still needed to wait until all her senses became attuned to the darkness and the ambience of the house. You could also smell the presence of animals, like a family dog, although there was very little chance of that in a devout Muslim's house. *They're not great dog lovers*, thought Sam, but she still waited and listened. She knew what she was looking for and had seen a mock-up of the Apple shipping container; it was branded on the outside with the famous half-bitten apple logo and should also have the shop's details on the exterior paperwork in a plastic sleeve, attached to the top of the box.

She moved from the kitchen, easing the door open into the carpeted hallway. Again she checked that she had left no ground-sign. A carpet was good; a dusty hallway with tile or wood flooring would not have been, as the outline of her trainers would have been visible afterwards. She knew that the office was the second door on the right in the hall from the research phase. She again tentatively eased the door open and peered inside, and bingo, there it was, perched, not very neatly, on an old mahogany desk.

Sam quickly took some IR photos with her iPhone for

comparison when it was replaced later and then pulled a piece of chalk from her jacket pocket and quickly marked the exact location of the box on the desk with four light chalk marks so it could also be replaced precisely. Sam scanned the room for cameras, *nothing obvious*, she thought, and then took another piece of equipment shaped like a small chunky box from her left hand pocket. She scanned the room with the bit of kit to again confirm the absence of covert cameras or bugs, and replaced it in her pocket. *All good,* she thought, the package was on its way to Tommy.

Sam then transmitted, "Hi guys, that's me towards you." Sam very deftly lifted the bulky box and within two minutes she was handing it to Taff at the back door. Two minutes later it was safely nestled on Jimmy's surgically clean steel workbench and was first bathed in infrared light to check for obvious IR security markings against interference.

Meanwhile Scotty had donned his second disguise of the day and now wore the day-glo orange jacket of an RAC patrolman, always kept in the back of Tommy's van, and had joined Pat muttering to each other under the bonnet of the old Fiesta. He and Pat would supply close security for this part of the operation.

Jimmy worked quickly; he only had two hours maximum to get this done. After the IR scans he took the first of a series of photos of the systematic unpacking of the laptops that were instantly displayed and recorded on the large monitor in the van. He would record every stage of the unpacking and packing procedure to ensure that the packaging went back together exactly as it came apart. The shelves near the workbench contained every possible combination of Apple packaging material in case of accidents.

Jimmy soon had the insides of one of the laptops exposed and was replacing the circuitry with the replica part and lovingly soldering it into position, aided by a large illuminated magnifying glass.

He had set himself a time of fifteen minutes per laptop; by

the time he had reassembled the final one it had only taken him ten. The laptops were then repackaged using the photo scans for reference at every stage. Sam collected the box from Taff at the Mullah's backdoor and within ninety minutes from when she had first opened the back door it was back on his desktop. Finally, Sam wiped the slight chalk marks that had indicated the outline of the box and then transmitted, "Hi guys, that's enough fun tonight, we're out of here," and she quickly and silently closed the back door.

Taff led the way out, looked left and right down the alleyway and gave Sam a raised thumb indicating the all clear; he then went left towards the Ops car.

Sam quickly looked right to check the now very dark alley running along the rear of the house. She then removed the NVGs and black woollen hat, and stowed them quickly into the Chanel shoulder bag. She then checked her belt kit to make sure nothing had come loose and studied the area to find a convenient place to switch back to 'obedient woman' mode. She took the black silk abaya out of the bag and was about to put it on when she heard the sound of footsteps coming into the alley. She quickly stowed the garment back into the bag.

Sam waited. *The back alleys of Whitechapel have probably not changed much since Jack the Ripper*, thought Sam. It was an odd feeling being alone in one, not fear; it was more like a feeling of being watched, not by an individual, but almost like being quietly observed by hundreds of years of history. The old Victorian red brick walls seemed to blend seamlessly into each other generating their own unpleasant memories. Sam felt a little spooked.

She reached down with her still gloved hand to her right hip, and was reassured by the outline of the 18-inch ASP extendable police baton, nestled in its holster under her cashmere top. She also checked for the small red-coloured CS and pepper spray she had in her pocket and looped its small linked chain around her index finger. *These are handy things to have in this part of London, especially at night*, thought Sam, *bet those Victorian chicks wished they had this kit.* Sam stopped and listened.

She could hear footsteps at the end of the alley, along with the odd female laugh. It sounded like the girl was in high-heeled shoes accompanied by a man's heavy footfall. Sam stepped back into the shadows; it was best that she did not bump into anyone on the extraction, and especially so close to the target. The giggles came closer, along with the clip-clop of high-heeled shoes and semi-drunken giggles. The man's footfall became louder, *probably a hefty old lump,* thought Sam.

The previously oppressive atmosphere of the back entry was immediately lightened though by the sound of a girl's laughter and the responding deep chuckle of her companion. The young couple seemed to be making their way, quite obviously and quite drunkenly, back to their apartment. Sam suppressed a giggle as she observed the man hold up his smartphone in front of him like a cross between a lucky talisman and a schoolboy compass.

The girl's voice had a deep Irish brogue. "You've got be fecking kidding, Mick, this is definitely not a fecking shortcut!" Sam detected a Dublin lilt in the accent, because, as Sam thought, the Southern Irish accent is one of the few that actually makes that particularly Irish version of the sexual swearword sound quite nice.

She heard the guy reply, struggling to focus on his smartphone in a deep Irish brogue. "This is a scientific experiment young lady, we are on the right route, and Paddy O-fucking Google, the most accurate navigator in the Irish nation, says so!"

"Yeah right, that's why we are so hopelessly fecking lost, yer a fecking eejit," the young girl said with a giggle.

The spell of Victorian London was suddenly broken and Sam felt better. She waited until the couple passed, again checked her equipment and quickly adjusted the bag onto her right shoulder. The sound of the young Irish couple faded as the couple walked past Sam and their paths diverged. Sam finally, faintly heard the man declare, "Follow Paddy O'Google, gorgeous, and you will never go far wrong."

This was followed by some raucous laughter from the girl as the sounds of laughter were swallowed up by the thick Victorian walls as the young couple sought home, doubtless guided by Paddy O'Google.

Sam's fears had lightened. *It does not matter how hard you think you are,* she thought, *we all sometimes experience those mini-moments of self-doubt and uncertainty.* She quickly flicked her long blond hair with her right hand, and carried out that weird procedure of sort of scrunching up either side, so it sort of fell better to either side of her face, and immediately decided that she was running late and needed to get to the pick-up and especially to the safeness of Taff, as soon as possible.

Sam visualised what the team should be doing now. Soon she would get the call from the guys that they are leaving for the pre-arranged debrief back at the safe house in Putney. Pat and Scotty would stay mobile to supply support as Taff supplied a rolling pick-up for Sam on the Whitechapel Road. She reached the end of the alley and turned towards the pickup.

Taff's voice then sounded in her earpiece.

"Hi Sam, this is Taff, I'm at Blue Two, stuck in traffic, kid, add five minutes to the timings."

Sometimes, shit happens, thought Sam. "Roger that, sweetheart." She knew that a well-planned operation also needed a degree of flexibility. She vaguely remembered some quote from a World War Two German general. *No plan survives contact with the enemy, it does not survive contact with the traffic in London either.* She quickly worked out a walking loop to extend her approach to the pick-up area. "Roger that, Taff, add ten and the same route."

Taff was definitely stuck in traffic and could not proceed without compromise. Training instils in you that you should always be able to turn out of traffic; a good operator will always make sure that he has room to drive out. Taff was three cars back, but a major altercation was about to kick off in front. An Asian taxi driver had managed to drive into the rear of a black London cab and both drivers were shouting at each other and trading pretty choice swear words. Not a good mix in a volatile environment thought Taff, with all the racial tensions that are generated in East London; non-racial ones like the vendetta between black cabbies of all races, and unlicensed Asian taxi firms is probably the worst. "Hi Sam, make that add fifteen, kid, I have a major scrap brewing in front after an RTA," Taff transmitted resignedly.

"Yeah, roger that," said Sam. "But don't stand a girl up." Sam continued to walk along the Whitechapel Road. To any passing motorist or bystander who looked at Sam they would have assumed she was a very West End, Sloane Street type of girl slumming it in the East End. Sam's long blonde hair and immaculately cut short reefer jacket and Chanel shoulder bag jarred with the surroundings. Sam knew it was too late for the covert abaya option and she also knew that she did not exactly blend in.

If things are going to go wrong on an operation, it will usually be something minor that tips something that could be major. As Sam walked close to a group of Asian youths, she knew that things were about to go a wee bit pear-shaped.

"Cover your hair, you slut!" shouted one of the young guys.

He was about eighteen, dressed in a black dish-dash and waistcoat, with a traditional white prayer cap on the top of his head. He was about six foot, and a little bit on the podgy side. A straggly beard protruded from his chin and his voice seemed to quaver with nerves.

"Yeah, cover your hair and show some respect for our area," said another older man in his late twenties next to him. This guy was about six feet tall, fattish, and had a long scraggly ginger beard, and although dressed in the same local Islam-cool look, he spoke in a really broad cockney accent. "We are the Muslim Patrol and we are keeping prostitutes and slags out."

Sam was absolutely stunned, her old bootneck dad, who taught her to scrap when she was a child, would always say, "It's not the dog in the fight, it's the fight in the dog." Why did these guys assume they could bully her? They had just crossed the Rubicon of carelessness, and Sam decided that they would pay.

A local Asian shopkeeper now forced his way in front of Sam, as to protect her. "Why don't you idiots leave the young girl alone, you are ruining our businesses here!"

The older man grabbed the shopkeeper around the neck and then Sam struck. She moved her bag to her left shoulder and swiftly moved within striking distance of the older man. Her target was the fleshy area on his left thigh over his femur. Sam spun, almost on her tiptoe of her left New Balance trainer and fluidly brought her desensitised right shinbone crashing into the target through the lever generated by her knee and hip, it hit with sickening force. The epithet "hard as nails' is awarded to many, but in Sam's case, it was almost literal. In her Muay Thai training she regularly hardened her shinbones on a full man-sized bag filled with sand, this had devastating results in its application and the man screamed in agony and collapsed.

Sam then moved very quickly and as the younger man reached down to assist his senior, she delivered a classic right hook to his chin, just above his pubescent beard that seemed to change his body position from bent over vertically to totally horizontal, all within a millisecond. To the casual observer both the men would have seemed to hit the ground at about the same time. The young man was knocked out; the older man squirmed in agony crying. "My legs broken, call an ambulance!"

Sam calming readjusted her hair and addressed the shocked Asian shopkeeper in her best Sandhurst English. "Thanks very much, sir for your kind concerns and gentlemanly behaviour. When these guys get back from hospital, tell them what my father told me." Sam paused and thought lovingly of her mad old bootneck dad who had brought her up alone since she was five. "If you want to bark, first learn how to fecking bite." Sam quite liked the Irish version! Dad was usually more explicit. *I suppose that's me banned for life from Raj Mahal sweet-shop,* she thought.

Sam quietly walked off, but took the precaution of drawing her ASP from its holster and holding it concealed in her pocket. A small crowd had gathered around the two guys, now both lying on the ground outside the sweet-shop. She moved quickly to try and put some distance between her and the incident. The street was fairly crowded and she quickly made her way onto the main Whitechapel Road. She looked ahead and spotted Taff in the Ops car, still stuck in traffic, and said into her comms, "Hello Taff, it's me babes, move over."

Taff looked into the left hand mirror and observed Sam's lithe figure silhouetted against the brightly-lit shops and inwardly smiled. There she was, just another pretty girl in the crowd, but probably the person he felt closest to on this earth. Taff leaned over and unlocked the passenger door and Sam slipped in, throwing the bag onto the rear seat and secured the door.

"It's probably a good idea to get us out of here, sweetie, I have just dropped a couple of guys down the road."

"Yeah, I can see that" said Taff as an ambulance, lights flashing and siren sounding tried to negotiate the traffic towards them. He knew Sam, and had seen her train. *The ambulance would be needed,* he thought.

Almost as quickly as the traffic had backed up, it cleared, and within twenty minutes Taff and Sam would be back in the safe house. Sam was fairly deep with her emotions; Taff knew her well, not only because of the joint trauma of the contact in Helmand, but also because of the hours banged up in the same car together keeping each other sane and awake during long and sometimes boring surveillance serials. It was unofficial therapy for them both and they both knew that their totally connected comradeship was the ultimate guarantee of confidentiality. He knew she was upset, but he also knew that she would never admit it to anyone but him.

"What's bothering you, Sam, that has shook you up, hasn't it?" Sam looked in the passenger mirror, which served not only to do the girly thing and check her hair and makeup, and reapply some lippy, but also to check if she recognised any of the vehicles behind after the recent surveillance or incident. She had noticed a white transit van with B&G Halal Produce emblazoned on the side that the two guys she had slapped were standing by. She had memorised the last part of the number plate, and would give it to the collators when she got back. The van was nowhere to be seen and she relaxed a little.

"No Taff, it's not that, it is really about me, it is about what I have become." Sam paused and again checked the mirror. "I should have let that go, just took the verbal shite these people come out with and made myself scarce. They did not really offer me a threat, just more like a challenge, do you know what I mean?"

Sam looked thoughtful; there was a sadness reflected in her deep blue eyes. "I am really annoyed at myself, I am becoming someone I don't really like."

Taff touched her shoulder fleetingly with his left hand. "Yeah, I think I know, Sam, I think it was easier for me to put up with things when we were actually in the 'Ghan, I find it harder here."

"Hey, but you are the educated one with the Masters, why is that?" Sam looked across at Taff; he was such a good man, with a heart as big as the valleys he hailed from. She had known him now for more than six years and found it increasingly hard to tell where the comradeship and respect ended, and the love started? Why was it that he was the only person she really felt comfortable with, the only person she really could relax with?

She was quickly jolted back into Rupert (Officer) mode by the question, "I suppose it is all about context Taff, from where you are actually viewing the problem, the academics of an organisation called the Runnymede Trust invented the word that they all use, Islamophobia, meaning an irrational fear of Islam. The thing is, from our joint experience, there is nothing irrational about it."

Sam paused and looked towards Taff. He was important to her, he was safe, he was strong, and he seemed to radiate that confidence and strength; he made her feel safe. She had not really felt that way about anyone since her dear old dad had died. Sam looked at his big, rough, spade-like hands carefully cradling the steering wheel, his bulky heavy shoulders and his heavily bearded profile, and she knew for the first time that she felt more than just respect, she knew that she loved him.

Sam shook herself from her thoughts, and back to the job. She rechecked the rear mirror, still all clear, still normal. Sam paused and looked across the car. "It is just that I am really annoyed with myself, Taff, I could have compromised the whole thing tonight, just because I was not professional enough to walk on by, I really wanted to hurt them."

Taff looked towards her and touched her arm. "You are just the same as the rest of us, kid, don't beat yourself up about it. You are not in Kabul or Helmand now, and it was nowhere near the Ops area. I would have done the same myself, but as you know, they would not pick on a big old lump like me. They like to intimidate and bully the weak, they only seen a slightly-built girl with blonde hair, not the Sam I know. They are the ones who should show remorse, but I guarantee they won't. The only plus side is I bet they are fucking sorry now." Taff laughed. "I hope it turns up on YouTube, I doubt it though, as it would not do much for their cause, and knowing you it would've been over too fucking quick to video. Good effort Sam, that is what you call girl power!"

Sam remained thoughtful. She had fucked up and she would tell Danny as soon as they got back.

Chapter Eight

Safe House

The company safe house was a semi-detached, Edwardian building on a leafy lane on the outskirts of Putney in South West London. It had been purchased by Danny Mac and Kenny and was a cross between a convenient operational base for work teams in London and an excellent investment. It was comfortable, well-appointed and fairly private, as private as you could get in London anyway. It was a place to mount an operation from and in which to conduct a debrief after, and it also served as a crash pad for guys like Pat, whose own house was on the outskirts of Hereford, and Scotty, who lived in Dubai normally.

Sam met Danny at the front door and quickly explained that she had been involved in an incident. Danny had known Sam a long time and knew that she was upset. "Danny, we need to talk, just the two of us, I have severely fucked up."

Danny led Sam to the quiet office area at the back of the house. "What is the problem, Sam? I am sure it cannot be that bad, kid."

Sam took a deep breath and tried to control the urge to sob. *What the fuck is wrong with me?* she thought. "I have just dropped a couple of idiots on the Whitechapel Road, Danny, and I really did not need to!"

Sam then explained the whole incident to a thoughtful-looking Danny who then said, "OK Sam-Sam, lets debrief it, and go from there." Danny was the only person apart from her Dad who affectionately doubled up her name as an endearment.

Danny then asked a series of Op related questions.

"How far from the target house?"

"How long did the incident last?"

"How many people witnessed it?"

"Were there any CCTV cameras?"

"Were the police called?"

"What was the crowd reaction?"

Danny then summarised. "Sam-Sam, you have nothing to reproach yourself for. On operations, whether it be in Kabul or London, your training has prepared you to make an instant appreciation of the dangers and to respond accordingly. It was well away from the Ops area, and since these local vigilante patrols have been mounted from that section of the community the press is full of it. More seriously, what if they had opened your bag and seen the Ops kit and NVGs, that would have been disastrous. I think you done exactly the right thing to extract yourself," Danny smiled, "and it has taught those deranged young men a valuable lesson."

Danny reached towards Sam and placed a fatherly hand on her shoulder. "Sam-Sam, Iraq and Afghan has changed us all, and sometimes it is hard to put it behind you, especially when you face the same ideology and stupidity in your own country."

Danny thought briefly of some of the shit he had seen from Bosnia to Afghanistan, a visual snapshot again of those severed heads bobbing in the bloodied waters of the Tigris flashed momentarily into his subconscious and out again. Danny had been in Iraq during the civil war between Sunni and Shia murder gangs and the image often haunted him. He then snapped back to the present. "Anyway Sam, you have told me but there is now work to do. Let's go debrief the Op."

Danny then led Sam into the large comfortable, art deco styled lounge where the rest of the team had gathered to discuss the operation. A debrief is always an excellent way to improve future operations and was standard practice with Hedges and Fisher.

"Hi guys, a good job so far it seems. Sam, as team leader, you kick off." Sam then outlined the conduct of the Op so far and at each juncture called on a particular member of the team to elaborate on his piece of the operation. Everybody had something small to add; small points can sometimes be the difference between success and failure. Everybody agreed that the cars should now be totally changed if the surveillance phase needed to continue. The key question for the evening, as Sam summarised, was addressed to their technical expert.

"What do you think on the tech-side, Jimmy, is this thing going to work?" The team knew that the whole success or failure of the deployment not only relied on his technical adaptions but also on the final destination of the laptops.

Jimmy removed his glasses, wiped them thoughtfully, and replaced them. He looked around and said in a broad cockney accent, "I'm fucked if I know, Sam, it now all depends on Mullah Rahman and on what he does with the jarked (bugged) kit. What I do know, is that we have the best kit in place for the job, and if that kit gets to where we think it is going, we will have intelligence gold, if he decides to send it anywhere else, or not send it at all, then we are fucked! We now have a chance to put into their coms system the ultimate 'Trojan horse', and I am talking Ancient Greek fables here, not IT viruses. If this kit gets to where it is supposed to go, it will totally tear their communications system apart. Western intelligence agencies realise ISIS's vanity is their Achilles heel. They really think they have the upper hand as far as the media thing is concerned and consequently they concentrate a lot of their efforts into it, but that very need to get their actions publicised that could bring them crashing down. In short, they think they are sophisticated, but they're not. Let me explain; they have managed to recruit some Westerners with the technical savvy to put together their IT systems, but these guys are only second rate technical college standard, and it has not been done very well? They are almost totally dependent on social media systems like Facebook, Snapchat and Twitter they do not really understand. For example, the majority of the traffic from ISIS in Iraq and Syria is conducted on Snapchat and Yello, which is a walkie-talkie type telephone-y system that suits their purposes because they consider it encrypted, but trust me, if our kit hits the ground it definitely won't be."

Jimmy paused for effect and very carefully looked around the room. "In short, guys, everything depends not only on what we have done to the laptops in that box but also whether they get to Iraq at all. I suppose it all depends on Mullah Rahman."

CHAPTER NINE

HUMINT

Imran Sarwar picked up the box from Mullah Rahman's desk and carefully examined it to make sure it had not been interfered with. These Apple computers were the best Syrian Action Aid Direct (SAAD) could afford until the next tranche of funding came in from Qatar's London Embassy. He looked at all the outer packaging and then checked the invoice attached to the outside of the box. He then opened the outer box and individually unwrapped each laptop to check the serial numbers against the invoice. He was personally responsible that these computers got to 'the brothers' in Iraq.

He was slightly annoyed, because Mullah Rahman had asked him for one of the laptops and he had to choose which one, and he would much prefer to be choosing one for himself. It was typical of the fat Mullah, he thought; he was so puffed up with his own importance that he always needed something from the deal. Deep down, Imran did not like Mullahs very much, it must be the alter-ego British part of him butting in. In actual fact he did not even like old people very much, and old Mullahs in particular. He had seen how they controlled things here and in Syria and Iraq; basically, they did very little, and expected a lot.

He had also seen how some of the brainless shit that they came out with actually worked out on the ground. He remembered having to mete out some punishment to one of the boys that had been caught smoking in Raqqa. The brothers had heated up a steel kebab skewer until it was red hot and made him smoke it; he still smelt the burning flesh and heard the screams. It affected him now, back in the safety of London; he internally winced as he remembered that he had laughed at the time, he knew then that his concern would be seen as British weakness.

He felt the cigarette packet in the pocket of his long waistcoat and he smiled as he thought how he would enjoy a smoke. At least here, in good old liberal, democratic Britain, all there was to worry about was cancer and the health warning on the packet.

Imran knew the ISIS system, inside and out, along with fuck-ups, the tribalism, nepotism, and the horrifying and terrible realities of war, because he had been out there and done it. He had actually fought with the Al Nusra Front before the even more extreme Islamic State had swallowed them up and moved him to Iraq. He had been at the great victory at Mosul, he had also seen the aftermath and taken part in the butchery at Camp Spyker; he still had many sleepless nights thinking of the horror of what he had been forced to do. Over last two years he had watched all his mates die on both fronts. He knew that the reality of the new Caliphate was very different to the picture that these new computers would eventually help generate.

He inwardly cringed when he thought of how he had crossed the Turkish/Syrian border a couple of years ago with a couple of his mates from Luton, dressed only in the clothes they stood up in, armed with two different books they chipped in together to buy at WH Smith at Heathrow before the Turkish Airways flight. They were 'Basic Arabic' and 'Islam for Dummies'. *I guess in the end we were the dummies,* thought Imran, *and like dummies we were used, fucked up, and spat out. We provided the military muscle, the cannon fodder, but the bosses and Mullahs kept the cars, the women, and the money.*

Imran was especially bitter about the whole thing because he had to make a terrible, life-changing decision and therefore had inherited a mind-bending secret, one that he had to live with for the rest of his life. He moved towards the backdoor of the house and carelessly opened it. He needed that cigarette. He removed the packet and opened it, fumbling with the packaging, as his hands suddenly felt shaky. *It is a bit late for nerves* he thought; as he withdrew a long, white-tipped Consulate from the packet and placed it in his mouth. He lit the cigarette and took a long hard pull. He needed to think. *How did I get myself into this game*, he thought, and he thought of the past.

He was the only one of his friends to get back alive and he initially thought he could put the experience down to a terrible misadventure. He even thought that maybe he could learn to live with himself and forget the abject horror of the experience. He even hoped he could, at some point in the future, like some of the older Afghan War guys, even enjoy the mini-celebrity of being a returning Jihadi, even maybe write a book!

Imran therefore thought he had developed the perfect plan to put this episode of his life behind him. He thought that in a virtual Facebook war; it would be easy to facilitate a virtual Facebook-based death. A couple of brief announcements on his normally busy Facebook page and he had declared himself dead fighting bravely in Aleppo, martyred by the Syrian Army. *"In a battle last night, our beloved brother Abu Daigham al-Britani died bravely, May Allah accept him."*

He then decided to go home and using some money put by from some recently acquired war wealth, he then planned, organised, and bribed his extraction through Turkey and was picked up by his trusted cousin Tariq, now a Luton taxi driver, in Eastern Europe. *It was a great plan*, he thought to himself, *just two guys coming back from a road trip through Europe.* After all, he had a proper issued, one hundred percent real British passport, supplied through a proper London Embassy in the name of a guy called Omar Khawali. It had cost him five grand and was totally genuine with his face on it and as part of the deal, it had even been scanned on an outward journey to France two weeks before.

He had memorised the details, his date and place of birth were the same, he was officially, or at least 'Facebook dead', and he considered his plan foolproof. However, everything changed at Dover!

Imran had meticulously planned their arrival. He had been involved in doing some low-level smuggling when he worked as a bouncer in Luton, mostly cigarettes and the odd load of weed. He was confident that things would go well; he had shaved his beard and had dressed in his favourite jeans and G Star T-shirt. The two men however had argued loudly before they drove onto the ferry when Imran had decided to take down the small, dangling 'Holy Koran' charm from the rear-view mirror.

"That's bad luck, bruv, that's denying the prophet," said his cousin Tariq. Tariq had always been a bit more devout than him, although he was a talker not a doer.

"Don't give me that shit, mate, you were always more interested in making a profit rather than serving the prophet, that's why you stayed and we went."

The argument had unsettled Tariq, he had been unusually nervous driving onto the ferry. It was really unlike him, they had done this crossing many times together in the smuggling days and he knew the routine. You just had to look normal and smile at the cop and security guys while they checked the passports. Imran's thoughts were disturbed by a terrible crunching of gears. The worst possible thing happened at this stage, just as the old Opel Zafira joined the departing traffic and slowly moved down the ramp of the ferry. Tariq had stalled the car.

"You fucking moron" whispered Imran.

"Sorry," said Tariq, "but I have more to lose than you do"

"Get this fucking thing rolling, you tosser," Imran muttered under his breath, and after a seemingly endless amount of time and after they had truly drawn attention to themselves, the car started and rolled down onto the quay and joined the queue of other cars being checked by security.

The Zafira halted at the covered checkpoint and all seemed well. Imran calmly handed the passports to Tariq, who again nervously fumbled them into the immigration guy's hand. *Fuck, fuck, fuck*, thought Imran, *this is not going well; we are going to get pulled here.* Then, there was that horrible sinking feeling as the guy said, "Do you mind getting out of the car, gentlemen, we would just like to ask you some questions."

It all happened very quickly then, both men were separated and shown to different offices in the small security complex. When Imran entered the room escorted by the customs official he knew things had gone wrong, the customs guy quickly turned on his heels, leaving him in the darkened room that contained three men.

The office was an extended prefabricated single-storey building and through the darkened interior, Imran made out a large conference table with chairs neatly around it, as if arranged for a meeting. The two men standing on either side of him were stocky, hard-looking guys, scary-looking fuckers, dressed in dark casual standard street gear. They both moved quickly to his rear and blocked the door on either side and before Imran could plead his innocence, the one on the right nudged him forward saying, "We are the Special Branch, do exactly as you are fucking told."

Imran made out a third man in the darkness that was sitting at the end of the large oblong dark mahogany table. Imran could see in the gloom that one of his elbows was casually resting on what looked like a thick file. He couldn't see his face properly but the man's frame was silhouetted against a lit PowerPoint projection. The PowerPoint clicked on and Imran gasped as he recognised a picture of himself in his black ninja kit, crouching over a heavy machine gun with his right index finger pointing upwards towards Jannah, or Heaven. Imran's own face was grinning at him, seemingly taunting him; his past had just exploded back into his present.

The man spoke slowly and clearly. "Hi, my name is Tim and you are 'Abu Diaghan al Britani', the recently deceased member of ISIS, I presume, or should I call you by your Luton nickname?" He paused and said with a warm emphasis, "Welcome home, Barbie."

Imran's heart sank. He had been betrayed, what the fuck was he going to do?

Chapter Ten

The Pitch

Imran was panicking, he was sort of drowning inside. How much did they know, did Tariq shop him? He needed to think but he did not get time for that. The two heavy guys sort of grabbed and pressed him into a chair facing towards the 'Tim' guy, and he was gently but forcefully held in place. Tim spoke. "OK, Imran, we have a presentation for you. Watch it carefully and then I will give you your options."

Imran tried to look downwards, but a powerful hand pushed his head up to the screen.

"That is not a fucking request, it is an order" Tim said forcefully.

Imran then watched the story of his life unfold on a slick, well-edited PowerPoint presentation, accompanied with short video clips woven into Tim's narrative. They even had a picture of him at primary school.

The presentation ranged from. "This is the house you were born in Southhall," to, "this is the door of the nightclub you worked at in Luton in 2010," ranging to the really explosive stuff, "Here is a picture you released on Facebook in September 2011."

The picture clearly showed an unmasked Imran holding up human heads with the caption, "Heads, kuffars (non-believers), disgusting."

These people knew everything about him, and more worryingly, Tim knew exactly what he had done.

At the end of the presentation the lights came on and Tim stood up. He slammed the file that had been on his desk in front of Imran and slowly and said, "Your life story, mate, along with detailed witness statements from three different individuals from your group, describing what happened at Camp Spyker after the fall of Tikrit, all attesting to your willing involvement in the beheading of Iraqi prisoners. We have enough here to put you away for thirty years. It is your choice and have two minutes to make it, you can put this thing behind you and get amnesty and a place back in England, and earn a good living doing it, or we can have you in Belmarsh Prison looking at thirty years minimum tomorrow."

In that instant Imran knew he had no choice. What the fuck had ISIS ever done for him? "Yeah, I've got it, I will work with you. What about my cousin?"

Tim smiled. "Don't worry, Barbie, we have that covered."

In that instant everything fell into place, the stalling of the vehicle, the nervousness, the arguments about the religious charm. Was that a bug? Was Tariq with them?

Things happened very quickly from then on. He was instructed to get into the back of a small Peugeot van where he was blindfolded by one of the escorts and moved to a house which was about a fifteen-minute drive from Dover. When the van stopped, he heard the electric motor of a garage door opening before the van was driven inside. He was taken from the back of the van inside what he presumed was a garage, which appeared to be at the side of a large house. He was then guided still blindfolded until hands guided and pushed him into a chair. The blindfold was suddenly removed and he found himself seated fearfully bolt upright in the sitting room of what seemed like a normal family house.

As his eyes adjusted to the light, he recognised the one who called himself Tim. There were also two other guys he had not seen before. One big, heavy, fit-looking guy, who was clean-shaven with blond hair and blue eyes, *obviously the minder thought Imran*, and another man of Asian appearance, light-brown skinned with bright black piercing eyes, with a neatly trimmed short beard and dressed in a black Pakistani-style salwar kameez suit. The Asian guy lounged back onto a leather armchair and beamed a smile towards him displaying bright white teeth. Imran's confidence was shaken, he was scared and his barriers were down. He was experiencing what prisoners of war call the 'shock of capture', and he then talked non-stop for three days.

He told them everything, how the organization worked, who financed it and its links, but he was mostly amazed by how much they already knew. Sometimes he was just confirming it.

They also treated him well, they said he could leave whenever he liked and they would give him time to reassess his options, but the choice was still the same: work for us, or do the time.

He was shown countless ISIS personalities from Britain and Ireland; Tim called them 'players'. He identified and named many they did not know and he identified the aliases they were using and told them where in Syria and Iraq they were.

Tim and Ahmad were particularly interested in the hostage holding guys and where the current crop of hostages was held outside Raqqa. Imran particularly disliked this group, they lived it large while others fought, and they were usually babysitting and brutalizing prisoners because they were too militarily inept to do, as he said, "fuck-all else."

They talked about how ISIS was organised, and they knew who financed it, and where the profits were returned, they knew about the Qatar and Saudi funders, and they also knew whom the London middlemen were. By the end of the first day he was beginning to feel his confidence return as his fear subsided; he was beginning to feel like he was part of a team.

On day two they introduced him to security procedures, his REVCON (re-contact procedures) and his emergency extraction routines if compromised. They promised to relocate him if his work led to life-endangering compromise. They also introduced him to the guys he would be working with. Tim was the big boss, he was the guy that had narrated his life-story, but his everyday contact would be a guy very like himself, the one dressed in the black salwar kameez, he was called Ahmad. Ahmad introduced himself. He beamed confidence, he was a Muslim, he was British, he was working class, and like Imran, he spoke Punjabi with a slight London accent. Ahmad had previously served in the Army in Afghanistan and was now a MI5 agent handler. He would be Imran's case officer.

On day three he was briefed on how to gather and pass the information they needed, simple ways how to memorise the numbers, places and faces, and how to encrypt that information, store and pass it. They also spent a lot of time teaching him how to organise his own personal security, training that really impressed Imran. These guys really were professional and were actually concerned for his safety, a quantum shift from his previous organisation. He was rehearsed in telephone procedure and his local walking routes for both routine and emergency pick-ups for debrief. He was given phrases to memorise in a phone conversation that he would use if he were being forced to get in touch, Ahmad called this his 'duress code'.

The whole afternoon of day three was spent rehearsing his cover story from the time they were arrested to their release. The names of the policemen who interviewed them, the solicitor who represented them, computer imagery of the inside of the police holding facility they were held at. What they had to eat. What they had been asked, how he had replied. He and his cousin had been detained for questioning over suspected drug smuggling and he now had been released without charge. Imran half-believed the cover story himself by the end of the day.

The final meeting of the day was with Tim and Ahmad. Imran was again rehearsed in relation to his cover story and contact procedures. After dark that day, he was thanked for his cooperation and then blindfolded and gently guided back into the van. He once again heard the electric motor of the garage door operate, and fifteen minutes later he was back for processing and release at the Dover holding facility.

He thought of Tim's last remark: "Remember, you're with the good guys now."

Imran knew there was no turning back; his life had changed irreparably and forever. He was now running with a different crew. It was strange though, it worried him but it also excited him; he did not feel bitter, it seemed more like a type of divine retribution, a sort of payback for all the bad stuff he had done in the past, along with chance to put things right. The elaborate unveiling of his fucked-up life had been an emotionally cathartic experience; a clearing out of all the skeletons from his closet. He felt strangely like he had been sort of redeemed.

Tariq's old Opel Zafira was waiting for him when he was released, driven by a sheepish Tariq. They had asked him not to discuss the debrief and they had refused to confirm or deny whether his cousin was involved; he had been briefed on the implications of what they called the 'circle of knowledge', the less people knew the better it was for them both. Both men had been supplied with all the correct paperwork after being released without charge. One of the branch guys handed him his iPhone and larger separate envelope and said, "Put this safely in your bag now, this is from Tim and Ahmad, they said keep safe."

Tim and Ahmad had emphasised the need for him to always have his mobile on him and charged. It had a feature that they had added, if he dialled in his normal PIN code, no problems, if he dialled in all the nines, 9999, it meant that he was in trouble and they would send some very hard boys to sort it out and get him back — that was the final piece of reassurance that made things easier for him. He had seen and been at an ISIS interrogation and he did not to be on the wrong end of one.

When he got home he closed the door and opened the

envelope; it contained his normal looking Apple iPhone that had been encrypted, some numbers to memorise, and five thousand pounds in crisp fifty-pound notes with the passport they had taken from him. Imran smiled, his life had really changed. He was now a British spy; he would try to be a good one.

A telephone rang and jerked Imran back into the present; he finished his cigarette, threw it onto the path and ground it into the concrete with his foot. He quickly moved back into the office and answered the house phone.

"Yeah?" he said.

It was Mullah Rahman on the other end and he spoke in Bengali. "Is everything correct?"

"Yeah," said Imran "It is all there, checked, and I am now going to load it ready for the convoy tomorrow."

"No," said Rahman. "Keep the important items with you. They will not be going on the convoy. I cannot trust the Turks at the border, I want you to deliver them personally. I will tell you about the arrangements when I see you."

"OK, I will see you soon," replied Imran, and put down the phone. Imran smiled, another adventure, he would call Ahmad as soon as he could. He was excited; there could be a big bonus in this for him and if ISIS were paying to send him there. Result!

It was 0600 AM and Danny was asleep at the office accommodation in Baker Street, until he was rudely awakened by his mobile's ring tone, which was a stirring rendition of Wagner's 'Flight of the Valkyries'. He reached across and slightly groggily and unthinkingly answered his phone with the usual comic response usually reserved for close family and friends: "Hello, War Office, do you wanna fight?"

Typical Danny, thought Tim. "Hi Danny, it's Tim. I have some news for you, see you for coffee at the usual place at 0700."

"Great, I will get the brews in, see you then," replied Danny.

Danny was waiting for Tim with two hot Americanos accompanied by the obligatory Danish pastries as Tim opened the door of Baker Street's Costa Coffee. The store had just opened and Danny had managed to secure the bottom table where they could talk privately.

Tim had a spring in his step; he sat, sipped his coffee and quietly said; "Danny, excellent news, the kit is on its way, it will be where we want it to be in five days. It is actually better than that, one piece has been kept by the previously mentioned custodian."

Danny quickly realised the implications; the laptop left with Mullah Rahman was bound to increase their coverage. "Excellent news, Tim," said Danny with a beaming smile.

Tim continued, "Another piece of excellent news is that we also have a chance to deploy an asset to try and confirm whatever you pick up."

Danny smiled, "It looks like our project can move to phase two then, Tim."

Danny knew that the teams would have to deploy to organise the relay station for the bugged kit, he would send Sam and the team as soon as possible; they already had the relevant visas and clearances from the Kurdish authorities. Tim smiled and said, "Yes, Danny, I wholeheartedly concur. Let's go and get them back."

Danny sipped his coffee and placed some excellent vanilla Danish in his mouth. The simple and enjoyable act turned his thoughts towards the less fortunate, especially David Slater and the hostages, who he knew were in the midst of their suffering.

Danny had struggled to believe the data gathered from previously freed hostages, the reported brutality showed how quickly young men can descend into violent depravity when driven by an evil ideology, unchecked by conscience. The ISIS guys who had started their journey in Britain had seemingly lost any vestige of human decency.

Danny thoughts refocused on the job; he looked at Tim

and smiled. "Very good news, old chap. Let's get them out of that shithole, and hopefully inflict some retribution when we do it."

Tim responded by muttering under his breath, "We are coming to get you, David."

CHAPTER ELEVEN

THE CRADLE OF EVIL

Mosul, Iraq

The American hostage could never had envisaged the situation in which he found himself; no amount of preparation could have prepared him for the horror of his present existence. He looked around him; all three of them were enclosed in a large, dirty room, in a large, filthy house. The walls were once adorned with green patterned rich velvety wallpaper. It was now filthy, smeared with food that the guards had delighted in throwing at them. There were also smears of blood on the wall; David knew this because some of it was his.

He had assessed his chances of escape. There were two doors that led into the room. One was a thick, iron reinforced wooden one, with a small observation hatch that occasionally clanged open to allow the guards to spy on them. The other was a side door at the end of the room, constructed the same way with the same Arabic-style fretted ironwork. He presumed that this led directly outside to freedom. *It was probably a door on to the garden, a reminder of the house's happier times,* He thought.

David was suffering badly, but the two other hostages were in far worse state; *they had endured this shit for months.* The Dane had a serious leg infection, a raw suppurating sore. They had hung him upside down from the large chandelier that previously adorned the ceiling. The Dane's weight had torn it free but only after the

British guards had delighted in savagely beating him with thick electrical cable and while he was suspended from it, inverted, screaming and helpless. Before his painful release the dirty steel shackles that they had hoisted him with had scraped into the very bones of his ankles.

The Italian was a totally beaten man; *the poor bastard had been here for six long horrendous months.* He was mentally and physically finished, he talked constantly in mumbled Italian crying softly and muttering to himself. *Mostly about his young family at home,* surmised David, ascertained by his limited knowledge of Italian. The room smelt badly, it smelt of them. Apart from the time they had displayed them like trophies on video and they were hosed down and given bright orange jumpsuits to wear, they had been dressed in the same clothes they had been captured in.

David could smell his own body, it was a smell beyond body odour: a mixture of stale sweat, fear and urine. The guards complained that they smelled like baby pigs. Consequently all the barred windows of the room were open all the time so as to not offend their jailer's sense of smell. That was OK in the day, but as the temperatures dropped below freezing at night, it made the suffering a twenty-four hour thing.

Strangely though it also gave them a slight advantage as well, an early warning system, especially at night, as they knew when the bastards were near, they all smelt of cheap aftershave that they doused themselves in to protect themselves against the filthy kuffar. "You Kuffars stink," they would shout, hardly surprising when the prisoners had never been allowed to wash or change their clothes.

The most amazing thing was that they spoke English in a variety of strange English regional accents. It was amazing because the thought that any of them had been actually brought up or educated in any type of a liberal democracy was beyond David's belief. He had actually heard them on the phone, presumably to some place in England, asking for certain goodies to be shipped out to them. "The Kit-Kats had melted by the time they got here, just send some jelly babies and some Bovril, Mum." It was bizarre.

He also knew that they were bullying sadists of the worst type, because, as the only American he bore the brunt of the degradation and the beatings. He was, and always had been, a robust and physically strong guy. He realised though that with every lost meal and every beating he weakened. He therefore knew that with every day of confinement his chances of escape from this evil cradling lessened.

There was two types of violence that he had to face, the formal interrogations, which were conducted by the brainless little shit that the other hostages called Hassan, who laughingly called himself an intelligence officer who appeared to have the intellectual capacity of a child, which he coped with. Far worst, and far more dangerous, were the haphazard, unorganised, hate-filled lashing out that accompanied the British guards every visit.

Although David Slater was beaten regularly, he was far from a beaten man. He sort of knew where he was and he had picked up enough conversation gleaned from an intensive Arabic course he had taken before deployment to work out that he was somewhere in Mosul in Iraq. He also knew the guards struggled with their Arabic as well.

He also knew that the compound in which he was held was both near a boys' school due to very young voices he heard chanting the Koran, and also a very large mosque, a major mosque. *Something of Cathedral proportions* he thought, *by the volume of voices and vehicles he heard on a Friday.*

The call of the Muezzin calling the faithful to prayer allowed him to keep track of the time and the long monotone Friday sermons that seemingly lasted for hours, let him keep track of the days of the week. It also allowed him to play the 'Americans' game where he would count how many times they mentioned, cursed, or shouted the word 'Amerikee'; the last Friday sermon had mentioned it twenty-three times. He had been here now for one week, he reckoned that he had another week until they moved him to Syria. He thought that the Kurds were now beginning to close in on the 'Islamic State'; they would move them before they attacked. He had to escape by then, because he knew that they would be killed before his friends in the Pershmerga could liberate them.

If he could not escape, he would just take the opportunity to kill one of these scrawny little fuckers and hope they killed him quickly. One thing was for sure, if he got anywhere near a weapon he would take his chance. He had surmised that they were being held somewhere near the Grand Mosque from which Abu bakr al-Baghdadi had addressed his followers in July 2014, he knew he was in Mosul in Iraq.

He was scared, but not scared of dying, he had always lived a risky existence, base-jumping, climbing, and all the adventures on the road that had led him to this shithole. He was scared mainly of letting himself and his country down. He had decided that he would fight till the last, the very last breath; he would not make it easy for the fuckers. He knew that the thing that was nourishing him was his hate, he would try and harness that hate and turn that most negative of emotions into the thing that would set him free, one way or another.

Chapter Twelve

Debrief

Ahmad drove slowly along the Edgware Road. *This was a real melting pot,* he thought. He supposed that this was the closest Britain would come to a multi-ethnic society. Rich Arabs rubbed shoulders with poor Arabs. Iranians discussed business with Jews, and hard-working Polish workers supplied their services to all at a rate to undercut the locals. This was an ideal route to meet agent 'KEN' on, the newly recruited agent number 2030. The 'KEN' was Tim's idea for a codename, a little bit of wordplay on Imran's youthful 'Barbie' nickname.

Ahmad and Tim were quite pleased with his progress, he had phoned in regularly with some very interesting information that was now being cross-checked with other agents to check its veracity. In quieter times, all agents had a sort of trial period where their tradecraft could be improved and their loyalty tested. This time though they had a very tight deadline, so such professional niceties were on hold.

'KEN' would play the game or the ultimate sanction of thirty years would crush his world. It was a difficult juggling game with agent handling, you had to make them like you, you had to appear worried about their scary fucking world, while also maintaining some discipline or they would take the piss.

Ahmad also had some excellent technical help. The iPhone they had given Imran, which appeared exactly like his old one in the same black faux leather case and cover, not only gave them his precise location when he had it with him, but also listened in to all his conversations. So far he was playing the 'great game', the intelligence game, well; he had been truthful and it seemed that he wanted to please.

Ahmad's modified Tom-Tom GPS bleeped; there was 2030 right on time, a green dot appeared and indicated exactly where he was on the heads-up display. Ahmad then heard the confirmation in his earpiece from the cover car.

"That's Ken, black on blue at 200 your side."

Ahmad slowed the Toyota with the standard taxi sign that he had affixed to it when he changed the plates, and indicated to move into the inside lane.

Ken was walking towards the pavement; he was dressed in normal 'about town' clothes: a black short parka type jacket and blue jeans. The Edgware Road was safer for him because there were lots of different types of brown faces, but he still felt he was out of his comfort zone. The pickup route that had been explained to him had seemed to work like clockwork. He had to leave Edgware Road tube station at about 2pm, he had to start walking at 2.05pm, he had to buy a paper at a certain paper shop to confirm that he was OK for pickup, if he saw anybody he remotely recognised or if he felt he was being followed, he would ditch the paper and the pickup would be aborted. He recognised Ahmad and hailed the taxi with the rolled up newspaper. Ahmad pulled in and Imran moved into the passenger seat as he had been instructed.

"Hi mate, how are you doing?" said Ahmad in a very relaxed manner.

"We speak only English, yeah, fucking linguists are costing us a fortune bruv and this debrief is recorded. You don't mind, do you, mate?"

"No, that's cool with me," said Imran.

Ahmad turned towards him. "Thanks mate, it is hard to use a notebook when you are driving but I like to be upfront with you. Have you got anything really important before we start?"

Ahmad talked as he maneuvered the car into traffic. London traffic was a godsend to him, you could debrief a whole fucking ISIS battalion by the time you moved a couple of miles.

"Yeah, well, I told you about the laptops and the cash and passports, yeah, and you know that I am going on a mini-break don't you?"

"Yes, excellent work, we are impressed. How long have you got now for a chat?"

"I need to meet the fat Mullah at five," said Imran.

"Great, mate, loads of time. Now I will need to see you again after he has told you about the trip, we need timings, vehicles and routes. We will meet on Paddy's OK, midday tomorrow, start your walk at 12.10, is that OK for you?"

Imran understood straight away. Paddy's was the code word for another pickup route in Kilburn, a bit further down the Edgware Road. "Yeah, that's OK with me" Imran replied.

Ahmad gunned the car smoothly through the traffic as the car very slowly made progress towards Marble Arch and then said, "OK, what have you got for me."

Ahmad was impressed, this guy was smart and noticed things. Ken had memorised the plates of the key vehicles moving out on the convoy along with some ISIS recruits that were not coming back; they would change passports with some senior ISIS guys. The passports would then be doctored and they would come out on rotation for a spot of R&R. He gave Ahmad their full names and London addresses, and even let him know which vehicles they were travelling in. Imran also explained that he would not be with the main convoy but would drive from Dover to Calais in an earlier one, with another British 'clean skin' called Sayeed who had blagged a job with Save the Children and therefore had all the proper paperwork to cross the Turkey-Kurdistan border.

The second mini-convoy would leave earlier; it would consist of three VW transporter vans carrying medical supplies. In Imran's vehicle, however, they would also have hidden the IT stuff he mentioned, the Apple stuff, one of which the fat Mullah had acquired, and 50,000 Euros in cash to finance ISIS operations in Europe. The Mullah was also going to pick up five real British passports from the Qatar Embassy for some top guys to get back into London via Ireland for future operations.

Imran talked for about an hour and was only halted occasionally by Ahmad to check or to clarify a point like, "What does he look like?"

"What car does he drive?"

"What's the registration, mate?"

"Is that the same guy who used to live in St Albans and went Jihad last September?"

After a full hour in London traffic, the debriefing concluded and Ahmad said, "Ok Imran, you have done very well, mate. I will need to see you again tomorrow on Paddy's after your final chat with the fat man, OK?"

"Yeah, I can do that," he confirmed.

"I need every detail of the journey, we want you to get to where they want you to go, if we get the details of the vehicles and timings, we can make sure that you are not stopped going out or coming back. I will also need the details of your travelling partner, Sayeed, this guy that has the driving job with Save the Children. It is important we get his current mobile number and the number of any phone that the company might give him; this is for your protection. We are also very interested in the guys that ISIS are holding at the moment, and there is a huge bonus for you if you can find out where they are, obviously though, without putting yourself in danger."

Ahmad looked across at Imran and made eye contact. "Well done, mate, excellent work, but just to check, what reason are you going to give for being seen in a taxi on the Edgware Road?"

"I have that covered," said Imran. "I visited my uncle who lives near here, and I have no car at the moment."

Ahmad nodded. "We will work on getting you a really nice

one, mate. Make sure you get a taxi back, this should help," he said, as he handed him a small envelope. "Don't flash this cash around, mate, next time we meet we will talk about putting your wages into a savings account, open it now and leave the envelope."

Imran removed a thick wad of a variety of bank notes of various dominations.

"There is £500, Imran, to pay you for your time, and there will be double tomorrow if you get me what I need."

Imran smiled.

"I am going to drop you off now, keep safe mate." He depressed the send button while he said it, so the cover-car could hear, and Ahmad immediately heard a response his earpiece.

"Roger you're last, dropping in 200, and it is all clear."

Ahmad indicated left and pulled towards the pavement. Imran opened the passenger door, moved around the front of the car to the driver's window as he had been instructed. Ahmad opened the window and Imran handed him a twenty-pound note. Ahmad fumbled around for change like taxi drivers do when they are expecting the client to say, "keep the change," and then handed him one ten pound note and two fives.

"I must get this taxi service more often, I like your prices bruv," Imran said softly under his breath with a smile.

"We aim to please," said Ahmad, as he hit the switch to close the window, he then checked his mirror and pulled the car smoothly away.

That was a dream job, he thought, *the source was on time with good tradecraft and he provided excellent information.* 2030 also had a good sense of humour. *He might need it in Iraq*, thought Ahmad.

He pressed the send button. "Hi all stations and Zero, this is Ahmad, drop off complete"

"Roger that." He recognised Tim's voice. "Good job, see you back here for debrief."

"Roger that, boss," said Ahmad.

Chapter Thirteen

In or Out

The living room of the safe house was crowded. Danny was holding court with Ken and Tim in attendance, with all three guys sat on the large, brown leather Chesterfield settee. The team sat on the remaining armchairs facing them. It was evening time and the three art deco style lamps perched on three suitable art deco style pieces of furniture accentuated the lines in Danny's thoughtful-looking face.

"Guys, you have a choice to make," he said. "You have my word that any decision you make will not affect your future work with this company. It will also not in any way affect our personal relationship, in my world, mates are always mates, even if we go in different directions. The operation is now going to enter a far more exacting and dangerous phase, and I need to make sure that you are fully conversant with the risks."

Danny halted and looked around the team trying to catch any perceptions of doubt. "This next phase, in all possibility, is going to end up with a hostage extraction under fire. It will be very dangerous, very bloody, and carries an element of risk that all of you will not have experienced since you were in the Army. We are going to leave the room so you guys can chat. We will be back in ten."

Danny then led Tim and Ken out of the room and closed the door.

Sam brushed her hair backwards with her fingertips and removed a lipstick from her bag and lightly applied some. She then turned towards the four guys, who were looking at her wondering when she would finish her makeup and say something.

"Well guys, I'm in. Let's get this lad back to his dad."

Taff said, "Yeah, fuck all else to do until the next Rugby World Cup, I'm in too."

"Roger that," said Scotty, "I have another two months leave and it's all good." Scotty was on a career break as a contract officer with the UAE Special Forces, he would tell his wife that the London job had extended. He would not tell her where it was extended to though.

Pat looked all around the other three. "I am definitely in, guys, the long haired Sergeant Major (wife) has the decorators in at the moment, if I go back now she will expect me to help out and I would sooner shoot bad guys than do DIY. If you think ISIS is extreme you should try mixing it with the 22 SAS retired guys' wives club, that's a real terrorist organisation." The team shared a group giggle.

Finally a smiling Jimmy chimed in, "Guys, I have the trouble and strife's mum, 'her that must be obeyed', visiting next week, I would pay you fuckers to go."

The team had another chuckle until Sam spoke. "Excellent, but hey guys, let's make sure there is a decent insurance package in place first."

When the management re-entered the room, Danny turned towards Sam, Taff, Pat, Tommy and Scottie.

"Well team, what do you think?"

The three guys looked towards Sam. As team leader she was subliminally voted spokesperson by all.

"Yeah, we are all in, but we will need a substantial insurance package tied to a large cash payment on death or serious injury especially for the married men."

Danny smiled and said, "We have negotiated that with the client, £500,000 on death or serious injury, and there is a £100,000 completion bonus. The wages are £10,000 a week. Does that sound reasonable?"

Sam looked around the others to gauge their reaction; the smiles confirmed what she thought but Sam also knew that the team would also need to be substantially augmented to achieve the aim.

"OK, Danny, we are in, can you assure us that any other friends that I and the guys bring in with us for this job will be on the same package?"

"Yeah, exactly the same deal," said Danny.

"OK, you have got yourself a hostage rescue team," said Sam.

Tim then stepped forward and stood next to Danny. Danny gave everybody a very thoughtful look and then very clearly and concisely said, "OK guys, now that I know that you are with the project, I would like to let you know about how far the planning phase has gone, what we know so far, what we have in place, and how we see things happening in the future."

"Firstly, can I introduce a gentleman that you will probably have a very close working relationship with during the next two phases. May I introduce a colleague of Tim's that will provide an unofficial liaison for your deployment to the autonomous region of Kurdistan, Iraq. Team can I introduce this man who will play a crucial role in your deployment and operation; this is Ahmad."

Ahmad stepped forward from behind the door where he had awaited his introduction, he was nervous, he had thought long and hard about what he was going to say. As a covert agency his training as a MI5 officer had been a bit light on public speaking. He also realised that the guys he would be speaking to were veterans of the Afghan War and might have preconceived issues about his ethnicity. He knew this because he was an Afghan veteran.

Ahmad was dressed casually in jeans and an expensive-looking light fawn-coloured Kashmir blazer. He was a lightly built guy with an upright military type bearing, with a neatly trimmed beard, short black hair and slightly receding hairline; he looked more like an Italian or Spanish tourist than an Asian agent handler.

Ahmad moved into the room with a casual, "Hi, guys," and stood with Danny. "It looks like we will working together on a particularly dangerous project, so I wanted to take this opportunity to introduce myself and quickly run through my CV to let you know how I actually got involved in this operation. My name, as Danny said, is Ahmad; I am Kurdish on my father's side and Iranian on my mother's. Both my parents fled to England as refugees during Saddam's time and I have been here since I was three."

Ahmad paused and looked around the room; these guys were a tight group. They knew each other, they trusted each other, and he knew that he needed to gain their trust before he could complete his part of their mission. He also knew that the effects of an unchecked radical Islam had alienated and coloured the views of many of his fellow countrymen. He had felt the impact sometimes; the hard stares he received on the street, especially when dressed in his Punjabi Ops kit, they were sometimes a cross between scorn and outright contempt. As a guy who had fought for his country and had actually been 'downrange' in Helmand, this is something he understood, but it also pained him deeply.

Ahmad continued, "Britain gave both my parents and myself a home, I consider myself British, and a Muslim, although, like the majority of people who have gained the protection of being British in similar circumstances, I have no split loyalties. Like many of my Kurdish friends, who live in England, we don't do the radical Islam crap that infects our country at the moment. Our Islam is a fairly relaxed way of thinking about things, I do not spend hours bettering my head on the carpet, and I also like the occasional drink."

94

Ahmad detected some smiles. "I am also very proud to have served in the British Army. I joined in 2005, I was studying Modern Languages at Leicester and then I dropped out and joined the Int. Corps. I served in the British Army as a Corporal in Two Royal Anglians Intelligence Cell on Herrick 7. I ended up as the go-to translator for the 'Head Shed' (Battalion HQ) because my mother taught me Dari. I also speak Arabic, and of course Kurdish. I also speak Punjabi fluently because of my current job, but that is a more recent acquisition."

"I have worked for Tim for the last two years. Our unit, made up of both MI5 and MI6 officers, specialises in infiltrating Islamic State operations in London. I will deploy to Kurdistan on a task that will have significant crossover with yours. Tim has authorised me to support you, whenever, and in whatever capacity I can, within certain parameters of course, and on a strictly unofficial basis. My consideration at all times will be guided by the need to protect my source, but be assured that this will not interfere with our need to protect life, especially yours and David Slater's. I will do all in my power to help you. I fly to Erbil soon to prepare the way with the Pershmerga and the Asayish. Tim will give you my contact details in Erbil at the end of his presentation."

"Gentleman, and ladies of course," Ahmad smiled at Sam, "has anybody got any questions?"

Sam looked towards Ahmad. "What are the capabilities of the Pershmerga and the Asayish, and what are they like to work with, Ahmad?"

Ahmad looked towards the team. "The Pershmerga are brave guys and they are very good, actually, considering their lack of resources they are excellent. They are the only ones hurting ISIS at the moment and the only people taking ground from them."

He then beamed a huge white-toothed smile. "As for the Asayish, very well trained and experienced, and funnily enough, my cousin Tommy actually runs the counter-terrorist section. As you know guys, in the Middle East, blatant nepotism sometimes has distinct advantages," Ahmad said with a gentle chuckle.

Sam spoke. "I think you and the team are going to get on, Ahmad." Sam looked around the guys who nodded in agreement. "It is very nice to meet you."

Danny then stepped forward and spoke. "Right guys, now you are in, I will now give you a full update on both our progress and how we get this cracked."

Chapter Fourteen

The Mission

Sam was back in Helmand. It was hot, and the filthy dry dust stuck to her sweat and seemed to permeate her whole being. She was scared, almost petrified, her mouth felt as dry as the sand she was lying on as the incoming bullets kicked up dust peppering the ground all around her. She was scared to move. She had clearly seen the Taliban gunner carefully slide in behind the low wall, slowly and carefully adjust his RPD machine gun and get himself comfortable in the lying position, almost in slow motion.

She had seen him push the butt of the weapon into his shoulder and take careful aim towards Taff's back who was firing in the other direction. She tried to shout a warning, but nothing came out, just a dry gagging sound. She then tried to point her HK53 towards the Talib but she was unable to move it. It seemed like an immense, invisible force, held it in place, and the harder she tried, the more she felt weak, feeble and powerless. She had no strength, no control, she felt defeated.

The black-turbaned, heavily bearded Talib looked towards her, and smiled, displaying brown, nicotine-stained teeth. He looked directly at her; his eyes burnt into hers with a thousand years of hatred, he then smiled again as he slowly prepared to squeeze a five-round burst into Taff's unprotected back. Sam screamed and her screaming jerked her back to consciousness.

There was a hard knocking on the door. "Sam, Sam, you OK?" She immediately recognised Taff's worried voice.

"Sorry, Taff, I was dreaming."

Sam quickly left the bed and opened the door to let Taff in. She felt the concern in his voice and half expected Taff to launch himself through the door. Taff opened the door and looked at Sam's shapely, lithe body dressed in a short nightgown framed against the early morning light of the bedroom window. She looked beautiful, upset, and strangely fragile.

"You OK, kid?" Taff said gently.

"Yeah, now I'm awake," muttered Sam.

"Was it the same dream?"

Sam's voice quivered slightly as she spoke.

"Yeah, but variations on a theme, I think I am losing it, Taff."

Taff moved forward and held out his arms, Sam stepped towards them and she let herself melt into them. In that instant Sam felt content and valued, but also strangely vulnerable, and within that short embrace she found her bearings again and pulled back.

"Hope you are not taking advantage, you chancer!" Sam said with a giggle.

Taff smiled. "Not at all, Sam, no time for that, we have a plane to catch at ten."

"Yeah, that's right," said Sam. "So why don't you give a girl some space, I have some girly things to do before Heathrow."

"Roger that, kid, I've very manly shit to do as well, see you at eight downstairs."

Taff softly closed the door and walked back to his own room in the safe house. The last time he felt like this he was a schoolboy, and maybe this was not the time to be distracted he thought. He knew he loved her, but it was almost like there was an invisible barrier between them. Maybe it was the officer-other ranks thing or maybe it was just the admiration and respect he had for her. He loved her but he could not tell her, what if she did not feel the same way?

Sam stripped to get into the shower; she did this after every bad dream. She felt she was washing away all the dust, grime and memories of Helmand. She thought about Taff, she had always respected him, and she also knew that there was a loving bond of comradeship tying them together, but for her it was becoming something deeper. *How can I let him know? What if he doesn't feel the same way?* She had been hurt in the past. She didn't need rejection again.

Danny drove Taff and Sam to Heathrow deep in thought; he felt both excited and sad, elated and depressed. He never liked asking people to do something that he wasn't going to do, it rankled him. He just hoped that all would go well and all his people would make the return journey home. Taff and Sam also seemed buried in their own thoughts. There was always a nervous doubt that accompanied any sharp-end deployment. Combat experience was a great advantage but also sometimes managed to fire an odd warning shot from the past. You had to be brave to go back once you realised how fucked-up things could get when they went wrong, and you also had to come to terms with the fact that you might not be coming back.

Taff broke the silence. "What's this shit you have on, Danny?"

"That's Classic FM, you Welsh heathen, and that is Vivaldi, 'The Four Seasons, Winter'"

Taff laughed. "Well, like winter in Wales, it is fucking depressing mate, put on a bit of Heart FM, or we'll have slashed our wrists by the time we get to Heathrow."

Danny leaned across and hit the tuning button on the radio and some old Tamla Motown drifted from the speakers. "There you go, Taff, it's too late to educate you mate, as you are a typical one dimensional bootneck oik," Danny replied, and then was amazed as both Sam and Taff joined in the chorus of the Martha Reeves and the Vandellas' golden oldie 'Jimmy Mac', with an instantaneous slight variation of the words, "Danny Mac, Danny Mac, when are we coming back?"

Danny was secretly amazed how they could be so much on the same wavelength; they even seemed to think like each other.

Chapter Fifteen

Kurdistan

Danny had outlined the plan and dished out the visas, the team would deploy separately on different airlines at different times, but would all be in place in three days. The operations kit and equipment was now accompanying Ahmad on a Hercules flight from RAF Brize Norton to Erbil airport in Kurdistan, and was being supervised by an Erbil-bound British Army training team. Packed into five large reinforced plastic storage containers were all the weapons, ammunition, explosives and communications equipment that the team needed to get the job done. Ahmad also carried a separate briefcase containing fifty thousand dollars in cash to ease their way through any red tape or bureaucracy they might encounter.

As the Hercules slowly droned and rattled its way towards a war, Ahmad thought about what he had to do to make things happen. His final meet with Ken had supplied all that he needed, he had known the departure time, and when Ken would separate from the Save the Children convoy, and he also knew the final destination of the laptops. *If all goes to plan*, he thought, *they would start to come online tomorrow.*

His people were following the laptops' progress as they made their way towards Mosul. Once they were safely delivered Ken would let him know, he would then not only be running an asset inside ISIS who was actively looking for the hostages but he could also feed selected intelligence from the source and the laptops to the CIA and the Kurdish Asayish. All in all, an excellent bargaining chip.

Once the MacBooks were plugged in and activated, he hoped the London end would be flooded with their email traffic and voice intercepts. The only nagging doubt constantly bothering him was the reliability of the source. He had been fine so far, but they had cut corners on his training and his trial period. They would usually have a lengthy period of time to check his reporting against other sources and technical means before they would think about putting him back in the mix. The risk was the danger of a reversion to type once he was back in ISIS. He knew that agents also tried to do a double to protect themselves, Ken was still an unknown quantity and that worried him.

However the real ace in the pack were the bugged computers which Ken was in the dark about, which meant that he could use their technical input to check on the veracity of his information. Ahmad knew that in their London office they now had twenty mega-smart technicians and analysts to instantaneously sift the incoming traffic as soon as they came online.

The C130 banked steeply and pushed him against the four-piece harness on the uncomfortable nylon seat, sharply snapping him from his thoughts. A Para sergeant caught his look of concern. "Don't worry mate, it is just the pilot getting ready for Iraqi airspace. We will be there in another twenty minutes, have you been to Kurdistan before?"

"Not since I was three," said Ahmad.

The big Para smiled, realizing the connotations of the remark. *This guy's family obviously fled from Kurdistan*, he thought. "A lot has changed since then, mate, it is probably the only place in Iraq that is a significant upgrade on Turkey. They are a great bunch of people, my guys love working there — it is the only place in the Middle East that does not depress the shit out of me."

"Yeah, I am looking forward to it," said Ahmad, cutting the conversation short.

The Para then replaced the earpieces from his iPhone into his ears and got back into his music. It was never a very good idea to get too inquisitive with the spooks that they sometimes travelled into and out of Iraq with. You never knew what the fuck they were up to.

Sam felt the cold chill of Kurdistan in mid-January as the winter sun flooded into the plane and the plane door finally opened at Erbil Airport. When she had left Iraq the last time it was September 2006 and the temperatures had reached 50C. She had nearly melted on that tour, she remembered, physically and emotionally. It had been a really hard six months, working as a junior intelligence officer attached to G Squadron SAS. Her tour coincided with an all-out Special Forces War against Al Qaeda in Iraq, masterminded by US General Stan McCrystal. American and British Special Forces were smashing a different enemy compound every night, and if the intelligence teams were not debriefing an operation, they were sifting through seized documents, computers and phone intercepts to prepare the target pack to attack another.

They were called Task Force Black and they operated from a Baghdad bunker that the guys jokingly called the 'Death Star' as the attrition rate against the main enemy, 'Al Qaeda in Iraq' or AQI as it was termed, was off the scale. She also had responsibility to sift through the huge amounts of HUMINT (Human Intelligence) or agent reporting, that was being produced by the British DHU (Defence HUMINT Unit) handlers as well. It was only by the constant comparison between the vast amounts of intercepts hoovered up by technical means and these agent reports that a discernible intelligence picture slowly emerged from the opaqueness of Iraqi tribal politics. It was a twenty-four hour job, with little or no respite; against the background of the awesome, personal, responsibility for making sure that no SF guy's life was wasted due to a lack of research.

Then there was the long, coffee-soaked vigils during the night hours, manning the desk while the guys went on task, sometimes on two assaults a night, and then either subsequent elation associated with a good result or the disappointment attached to a bad one, and sometimes, the worst thing, the heartbreak of knowing that one of the guys she knew and had briefed on the target just an hour before was coming back already in a body bag or with a life-changing injury. Sam had not realised how tired and exhausted she was until she closed her eyes on the RAF VC 10 and arrived seemingly instantaneously in Brize Norton.

Taff moved down the steps after her, she looked back at him and smiled. He was so obviously a soldier, with or without his beard. He dressed like one and walked like one. Taff beamed a smile back. Sam was sometimes amazed that someone who could blend in and pass close-up inspection as an Afghan farmer, albeit a particularly burly one, could look so much like a military type pretending to be a civilian when he was dressed normally. Therefore their cover story had to reflect the way it was. Sam looked again at Taff; she had never really felt as close to anyone since her dad died and she hoped that she would one day be able to tell him.

They were arriving in Erbil as employees of one of Sir Ian's oil companies, Claymore Exploration. Taff was on the security and protection side, her visa said she was on the production side. Any decent cover story had to have its foundations in fact, and it was far from unusual to find ex-military types working in the oil industry.

Oil companies appreciated that certain specialised soldiers had the skill sets needed to operate across a variety of hostile environments, whether that was related to an extreme geospatial location in the middle of the desert, or the geopolitical challenges of the task where people are trying to kill you. Therefore ex-military security consultants usually found themselves in countries with extremely dangerous political backdrops, such as the Yemen or Libya, Afghanistan or Iraq. Sam had met these types in some very strange places in the past, never thinking at the time that she would be doing the same thing. Sam glanced back at Taff again, he was big, bearded, and dressed in the standard security circuit garb of the polo shirt, beige cargo pants, and lightweight-hiking boots. He was pretty obviously ex-military and arriving on a security task in Iraq, which in actual fact, he was.

Not that you could relate Kurdistan to the rest of Iraq in 2015, thought Sam, it was leagues ahead. The Kurds had made hay while the sun shone and made the most of the brief outbreak of peace, whilst since 2005 the rest of Iraq tore itself apart in an orgy of sectarian violence. The Kurds she had met had always been fiercely independent people, and likewise the Kurdish areas had always done things their own way. Kurdistan's stability had attracted investment, and the current instability in the rest of Iraq had attracted it even more. She remembered from her last Iraq deployment some of the SBS guys compared a deployment in Northern Kurdistan as like being stationed in Switzerland.

Sam knew that Erbil Airport was one of the results of this investment. It was strange for Iraq, it was clean and efficient, and it had been designed by a British company and built by a German one. It had a full size runway and every refinement that you would expect in Europe. Sam and Taff joined the queue for immigration and waited patiently behind a lengthy line of returning Kurds from Europe, all with hand baggage that would have collapsed a pack-mule. They had prepared themselves for a long wait when a big, smartly dressed, bearded guy in a suit, with a clipboard held aloft with Claymore Exploration clearly emblazoned, quickly identified them.

"Hi, I am Talal Scott, and you must be Samantha and Taff. Danny sent me, I am your fixer for your stay in Kurdistan. Danny says you guys should start listening to some decent music."

Both Sam and Taff recognised the phrase that Danny said he would give the in-country fixer but they had expected a longer wait.

"Hi Talal," said Taff. "What's next?"

"Just follow me, guys, give me your passports and visas, I'll get them sorted. Your bags are already loaded, we are going to the company's house in a place called Ainkowa. It's ten minutes away, and welcome to Kurdistan."

Talal spoke in flawless English. He was a big man, maybe six-two, with a close cropped slightly greying beard, burly bricklayer's shoulders *and hands like Taff's*, thought Sam, like proverbial shovels. He shook Taff's hand firmly and then turned to nod and beamed a big smile at Sam. Even in this more relaxed area of Iraq, it was still not good manners to shake a lady's hand without being invited. Sam extended her hand half expecting the macho death-grip that both men had just subjected themselves to, but he shook her hand very politely and gently.

"I am very pleased to meet you, Sam, and pleased to meet you Taff," he said, turning to Taff. "I hope you enjoy your stay, and I hope your business trip here is both rewarding and successful. Follow me, guys. The car is in the car park, we can chat on the journey."

He quickly turned and waved to one of the red-bereted presidential bodyguards that looked after security at the airport and made his way to one the automatically opening door of the terminal marked 'VIPs only', with Sam and Taff in his wake. Immediately outside the door was parked a new white Lexus Land Cruiser with a driver behind the wheel. Talal opened the rear passenger door on the driver's side and waited while Sam and Taff climbed in. There were two small bum-bags lying on the leather of the back seat. Sam smiled as she noticed that the nylon bum-bags were color-coded, a maroon like pink for her and dark-blue for Taff.

Talal moved around the Lexus, opened the passenger side door and got in. "Guys, this is my brother Mohammed but we call him Mad Mo. Don't worry, he got that nickname from the war and not for his driving."

Mo turned around and said, "Welcome to Kurdistan, guys."

Mo was a younger version of his brother minus the beard. "You might want to put your seat belts on, the way people drive here is the most dangerous thing about this part of Iraq."

Both brothers laughed, but Sam and Taff knew from driving in Baghdad that was probably not far off the mark.

Talal turned towards his passengers while he placed his seat belt on. "The two bum-bags contain your personal weapons, they are brand new Glock 19s, recently liberated from ISIS. They have been test fired this morning and they're loaded. You have three magazines with each, and there are thirty rounds in each mag. In each pack is your personal company ID and firearms license."

Sam noticed that Talal used the British name for this piece of kit; the Americans she had worked with called them the very dubious-sounding 'fanny packs'. *Two nations divided by a common language, as Churchill said*, she thought.

"This kit is yours for the duration of your stay; the other kit will be delivered to your place tonight."

It was a ten-minute drive to the Claymore house. The Lexus travelled quickly through the busy traffic. It was obvious to Sam that Mo was a trained close protection driver. His road positioning was good, he kept the correct distances while constantly checking the rear view mirrors for hostile surveillance, and they had seen that he had performed an anti-surveillance loop as the Lexus left the airport.

Sam was also looking, glancing in the mirrors occasionally, more through habit than intent, and she noticed a similar silver-coloured Lexus about two cars back in the traffic. After two changes of direction the car was still with them, she wondered whether Mo and Talil had noticed it.

"Hey guys, have you seen the silver four-by-four behind us, two back, with two guys in it? It's been with us for a while."

Talil gently chuckled and explained. "Yeah, couldn't miss them Sam, they are Tommy Talibani's guys from the Asayish and you will find that they will be following you a lot. They have been told by Tommy to keep you safe. Tommy will visit you at the house later to introduce himself, we consider you very important visitors."

"His concern is greatly appreciated Talil, that's a well-known name over here, wasn't Jalal Talibani the President of Iraq?"

Talil smiled. "Yeah, Baba Jalal or Uncle Jalal in English, his family is huge, powerful and everywhere, along with his old political adversaries the Barzanis. You will find that those two families just about run the place. Tommy is related, but was brought up in England and only returned to fight with the Pershmerga in 2003."

Sam remembered Tommy Talibani was Ahmad's cousin. *He will be an interesting guy to meet*, she thought, *I wonder how much he knows about the project?* Sam was always worried when the circle of knowledge slowly blossomed, although she accepted that without support from the Kurds, the job was unworkable.

Sam looked towards Talal's bulky form; he looked kind of familiar she thought. "What about your name Talal, Scott is an unusual surname for a Kurd."

"That's because our father was a British soldier who stayed here after the World War Two, converted and married my Mum, he ran a bike shop. I have a British passport and I have visited Scotland, I love it. I think the Kurds and the Scots are very similar, as you say in Britain, very crazy," Talal laughed, "I like single malt whisky, Scottish of course, but don't tell the Mullahs."

CHAPTER SIXTEEN

AINKOWA

Sam took in the change of scenery, so different from the clutter and occasional squalor of Baghdad. The snow-capped mountains silhouetted against the bright blue sky contrasted with and merged into the verdant green of the surrounding countryside. The Lexus sped past the everyday life of the Kurds. Laughing children skipping back from school, hijabed older women bartering at the local shops, a guy in traditional Kurdish dress with baggy trousers and his large sashed belt and turban, chopping wood outside his low, mud built house.

Sam was impressed, everything appeared so peaceful, so normal, and she thought, *I suppose this was what could be achieved if you had a breathing space from war.* She also quietly reflected on how bad things were in the rest of Iraq, of what she had seen in Bagdad, and she was suddenly sad.

The company was situated in the small Assyrian Christian enclave of Ainkowa on the outskirts of Erbil. A number of private commercial companies occupied the area, mostly concerned with various infrastructure projects associated with an expanding economy. The Claymore house itself was a large, two storey, six-bedroomed villa, set in its own gardens enclosed by a two metre security wall with security cameras dotted at each corner. Claymore had its own security detachment drawn from the local area, mostly older ex-Pershmerga guys. They were situated in a secure compound within a larger security zone protected by another private guard force.

As the Lexus arrived at the outer security barrier, Talal muttered some Kurdish into his hand-held radio and two green-uniformed security men armed with the ubiquitous AK 47s opened the double gates of the villa. An elderly man dressed in traditional Kurdish attire, stood at the ornate wooden front door framed by two imposing white marble pillars.

Talal leapt out of the passenger side and opened the door for Sam and Taff. "This is the Villa guys, and this is Polad the house manager. He will get you settled in, and we will be back later to see if you need anything, we will get your luggage to your rooms."

Polad smiled and extended his hand, "Welcome to Claymore House," he said. "I will show you your rooms and then show you around the house — your other three friends will arrive later. Supper is at eight and you have Mr. Talibani and Mr. Ahmad arriving as guests."

Sam and Taff followed Jalal up the large central staircase to the bedrooms.

"What do you think?" asked Taff, when they were finally on their own.

"It's good," said Sam "I like the way things are organised so far but I will feel much better when we are all together and we get the kit we need for the job."

"Yeah, roger that," said Taff. "I wonder how much people like Talil and Mo know?"

"I think they might have an idea, they're smart guys and they have obviously been trained well. My guess is that they must be in the loop to some extent, we will know more when we meet Ahmad and the Asayish guy," Sam replied.

Taff looked pensive, again worried about who knew what. "I think maybe that Talil and Mo are part of the system over here. If they're not Asayish guys at the moment, I am pretty sure they have been in the past."

"Yeah, I think you could be right," said Sam. "I just don't like wondering who knows what. Maybe we will get an idea later."

At six that evening, Jimmy was the first to arrive, wheeling a large reinforced black plastic container. He warmly greeted Sam and Taff and then busied himself unpacking the box like a man possessed.

"Guys. I will need some help setting this shit up." He removed a small Apple MacBook, which seemed to have sprouted various black and silver boxes from its frame. He quickly laid out the interior of the box on a desk in the downstairs office and proceeded to link the various different pieces together. He then attached it all to a separate HDTV monitor he had carefully removed from the box. He then removed an elaborate-looking aerial, which when assembled from its four separate pieces was about a metre long. The final attachment was what looked like a small six-inch computer dish that protruded from the end.

"Can you give a hand here, Taff, I am trying to rig up my latest reality TV show, 'Nasty Bastards are Us' or 'We is ISIS'. It will probably be littered with porn, but it should be an interesting show."

He then turned to Sam.

"Sam, when this monitor is set up I will need you to be manning it."

"Roger that," Sam replied.

"We will probably need to get this high on the southern side of the house, pointing somewhere towards the bad guys for an optimum signal."

Jimmy made the final connection to the HDTV and a simple pie chart appeared on the screen.

"Sam, this is dead simple, at the moment that pie chart is red, as we move the aerial outside it will start to go green incrementally as we optimise the signal. Take this, kid."

Jimmy then handed Sam a small handheld radio.

"Give us a running commentary Sam, as soon as it's all green, we are good to go. Once we have a strong signal we can transfer the data instantaneously to London."

Sam glanced towards Jimmy with her quizzical 'tell me more' look. "Will we have access to the data here?" she said.

"No Sam, in theory we could access some of it, but the main problem is the sheer volume of data this system can hoover up. It will need a lot of dedicated operators to process this information. We are expecting to hack all their communications systems, mobile phones, Facebook, email, file transfers, the whole shebang. The London office assures us that the kit is being handed over soon, what ISIS does with it is another thing. In theory they could just lock it away and not use it, and we will be back to the smoke pretty soon after that. Everything depends on them taking the bait, let's hope they do."

Taff and Jimmy then went to requisition the Villa's very dodgy-looking bamboo ladder, to hopefully scale the outside of the house and fit the aerial. "Good luck with that, lads," she said with a giggle. "It looks like I got the best job," as she gazed at the TV monitor and turned on the radio handset. Sam's expression changed and she looked pensive as she quickly made an assessment of the chances of getting this guy back. There were aspects she did not like. Firstly she did not like not having access to the data, although she now understood why. Secondly she also distrusted the ever-expanding circle of knowledge, because the more people in the loop, the more chances there were of traumatic compromise. Mostly though she disliked the uncertainty surrounding their key technical asset, the pieces of kit that everything depended on. She wondered what was happening to the laptops now.

Chapter Seventeen

Barbie's Back

It had been a long trip for Imran, agent Ken or 2030. The driver of the vehicle, the so-called 'clean skin' was a poor travelling companion. His name was Sayeed, and he was an ISIS wannabe that talked non-stop shit for a straight seventy-six hours about how committed he was to killing the kuffar and on the magnificence of the Caliphate. He even talked about volunteering as a suicide bomber. Added to this shit, his driving was also pretty abysmal and he had nearly accidently sacrificed both their lives on several occasions, normally by being half-asleep on the wrong side of the fucking road. Imran smiled. *Probably safer as a suicide bomber*, he thought. It also pissed off Imran that he could not even tell him he was talking shit, because wannabe Jihadists like him would be the first to shop you in to the religious 'Thought Police' for lack of commitment.

They had arrived in Mosul in the evening time just as the call to prayer echoed from the main mosque, with seemingly endless echoes from smaller mosques throughout the town. The VW transporter van was stuck at the main ISIS checkpoint on the way into town, as everything stopped for prayer. Imran knew that this was not a good time to flout convention, so he quickly tried to explain who they were in his underused Arabic.

The checkpoint commander seemed just as unsure and answered in the Chechen version of Arabic, as he was a big European looking Chechen. Imran knew that the Chechens

112

were scary fuckers, but this guy was very scary-looking indeed. He was one of the biggest guys he had seen, maybe six-eight and about as broad across. He had a Russian RPD machine gun strung across his chest that looked like a child's toy in comparison to his bulk. Fortunately, there was also a German convert on the main barrier that spoke English, so in the end both Imran and Sayeed took their own prayer mats from the van, and then joined the checkpoint guards in ritually preparing for prayer.

Imran was worried; he was returning to an organisation that he had effectively done a runner from, although the protocols of such an occurrence were fairly loose amongst the foreign fighters. It was fairly often in such a fluid social grouping such as ISIS, whose members reflected the global nature of radical Islam, that the odd rich Saudi's or Qatari so–called fighters arrived at the beginning of one month only to fuck off the next, once they had ticked their Jihadi warrior box, and they, or more often their fathers, had made a substantial contribution to the Caliphate.

To be honest, the majority of the actual guys doing the fighting were quite glad to see them go, they were usually stuck-up, holier-than-thou types, very spoilt and precious, and because of this, they were pretty shit at fighting. He remembered all the brothers being very relieved when one of the wankers fucked off home, after his usual three firefights against nobody, and his two hundred 'me defending the Caliphate' photos on Facebook.

Imran joined the guys in washing his feet, one in turn, right foot first and then the left. He then rolled up his sleeves and held out his arms palms upwards as the driver poured bottles water over both in turn, he then proceeded to wash his arms to the elbow as he then helped the driver go through the same routine. All the time he went through this almost mechanical ritual, he wondered what were the chances of anybody actually knowing him here in Mosul, after all he had been part of the killing in Tikrit.

Imran thought the chances were slim; all the Brits who knew

him were dead. After all he had done his time in Syria, far more than those spoilt wankers from the Gulf States. He would say that he had been allowed to leave by his Emir, Abu Khalaf, who had very conveniently been killed by a US airstrike not long after he fucked off. Abu Khalif also had responsibility for ISIS strikes against the 'far enemy' in Europe; he would imply that he had been sent home to work in London if they questioned why he left.

As he knelt onto his prayer mat, he ran through every question they would ask him. Ahmad had reminded him, and he knew from experience, that they would be suspicious. They would search him and the driver thoroughly, they would take all their property, iPhones, cameras, and examine them for bugs. They would cross-check their travel paperwork to make sure it checked out. They would definitely go through the donated laptops with their tech guys. He just hoped that Ahmad and his new gang had not been stupid enough to try and bug them. Still, he thought that was the fat Mullah's responsibility and he still had one of them, *the greedy bastard,* thought Imran.

As all this was running through his mind he continued to go through the mechanics of prayer, he got to the part where he was looking at the upturned palms of his hand in the pale last light of the winter sun. He remembered what his dad had told him about this part of the prayer ritual. His father followed a far more gentle form of the Hanafi strand of Islam; he had almost disowned Imran when he went Jihad. "Look at your hands, son, look at the individual creases in them. Allah has made all our hands different and yours uniquely for you, look at your palms in wonder and realise that Allah is all powerful and we are but insects compared to God." Imran studied the individual uniqueness of the palms of his hands, and an image of them being cut off flashed into his mind. He had seen it happen in a market place in Raqqa to a guy who had been caught smuggling cigarettes. *Fuck knows what they will do if they find out I am working for MI5!* he thought.

Imran knew that he was going to have to be smart to survive the next twelve hours, but he was not scared, it was part of the game, and he also knew that he did not scare that easily. He never had a problem being brave; it was that in the past he had been brave for the wrong reasons and for the wrong people.

Chained to the wall in a building only 500 metres away from where Imran was considering his chances of survival, another struggle for understanding was taking place. David and the other hostages had also heard the call to prayer; to them it meant a half an hour respite from their tormentors, when you knew the little fuckers would not barge their way into the room. The hostages had been aware that something was being planned.

The previous day had brought a more senior ISIS figure, a tall, slightly built, bearded man in his fifties, dressed in the religious regalia of a senior cleric. His name was Mullah Mohammad Al-Rafdan and he now hated Americans and the West, but it hadn't always been that way. He had once been a fiercely secular man and had not only once been a fanatical Iraqi Baathist but also a senior member of Saddam's 'Mukhabarat', his feared secret police. He changed when the Americans had imprisoned him in Camp Bucca for his resistance work, the prisoners ran the prison and associated freely, he had met Ubu Bakr al-Bagdadi there and sensed a change in the political wind, and ever the pragmatist had quickly reinvented himself not only as an Islamist but as an Islamic scholar. In Mullah Mohammad Al-Radfan's world, *it doesn't really matter what you believe, it's what other idiots 'think' you believe that counts.* He walked into the room with an air of religious serenity, until the appalling stench disturbed his concentration.

David had studied his face and detected how the stink of the room assaulted his nostrils; he removed an immaculate white handkerchief and held it over his face. He could see his reaction to both the condition of the room in which they were held, and the very poor condition of them all.

He seemed especially concerned with the Italian. His

previous injuries had suppurated and had been infested with maggots. David had been unable to help as he was the only prisoner that his jailers kept permanently chained, but he had advised the Dane on how to dress the wound. He tried to explain that the maggots were probably saving the guy's life by eating away the infection.

David had heard snippets of Arabic, he was not well enough versed in the language to understand everything, but he knew enough to work out that even though the Mullah guy was speaking quietly, he was angry with the guards. He also knew enough Arabic to pick out words like 'shabak', meaning prisoner, and 'dufah' meaning payment. He also thought he heard the phrase 'Muqabil hafha' which he thought meant payment for this, or something similar. David was helped by the English guard's poor Arabic, as some words were repeated several times when they seemed not to understand. David definitely knew that he heard the word 'Raqqa', and he also knew that once they were moved to Raqqa, escape was more or less impossible. He knew that he had to do something soon, and if he died doing it, so be it.

After prayers, the big Chechen and the German convert came across and escorted the two new arrivals over to where the VW van was parked. Standing by the van was another slightly built guy, who was dressed in standard black loose shameer khameze and the black shemagh headscarf of ISIS. Imran knew straightaway that he was a Brit, he noticed his very expensive black Nike trainers and his G-Shock watch, which when he left, was the British volunteer's calling card. The Nike trainers alone would take an Iraqi working man a month to save up for.

The big giveaway though was the expensive 'Blackhawk' chest webbing and the ex-Iraqi Army short-barrelled M4 strung across his chest. The British lads generally got the best kit. ISIS thought that they brought extra kudos to the caliphate having arrived from a country, which the rest of the Islamic world was dying in droves trying to reach, just to secure a better life for their families. If you came from a place like Britain where people had the advantage of free health care and free money from the state, you had to be a committed Islamist.

"Hi mate," he said. "I'm Hassan and I'm the security officer here."

He looked at Imran and a faint hint of recognition appeared in his eyes. Hassan had a Yorkshire type accent, probably Barnsley or Dewsbury, thought Imran.

"We appreciate your efforts guys and we had been told you'd be arriving, but you no doubt realise that we have to be careful." He glanced at the big Chechen for backup and then carried on. "Big Ivan here will be looking after you while we debrief you, first of all, I want you to remove your clothing and shoes and put these on."

He handed Imran a large box containing what looked like a bundle of clothing and two pairs of flip-flops.

"And put all your clothing, phones, wallets and every piece of personal kit into the box. I'm sorry, lads, but this is necessary. You and your kit are going to be thoroughly searched. The van and its cargo will be quarantined until we have gone through that as well. I think you know what we are looking for, any sort of bugging device — it's for your protection as well as ours."

Imran and the driver were then led off to the kitchen of a nearby house, closely escorted by Ivan and the German. Imran was secretly a wee bit impressed; the security procedures had improved a lot since he had been with the brothers. The two newcomers were thoroughly searched by a guy who seemed to be a medic of some sort, and the search was intrusive to say the least. Meanwhile the guards searched their clothes, checking the seams and testing the stitching. They spent a lot of time examining the driver's shoes and Imran's HiTec boots. Another guy then took the clothing and footwear away; Imran assumed that they would be x-rayed. Hassan asked for their mobiles and put both handsets into a separate plastic ziplock bag. *That's my lifeline gone*, thought Imran.

"Right guys," said Hassan. "Now I want you to write down the access codes for your mobiles, so we can check out who you have been speaking to."

The two immediately complied.

Imran thought, *should I put 9999 down? Maybe this was a chance to use the duress code*, but then thought better of it. *No*, he thought, *I don't feel I need that yet, this is just a thorough security check and the way that the US predator drones, are taking them out a daily basis, I cannot blame them.*

The two travellers were then separated and moved to different rooms in the house. Ivan and Hassan stayed with Imran. He was led by Hassan with the big nasty Chechen walking behind him into a large, white painted room that only had four pieces of furniture. A simple wooden desk had three cheap white plastic chairs around it. On the desk was a small voice recorder that Hassan clicked on. Hassan then sat down behind the desk and motioned to Imran to do likewise. Ivan sat behind him, Imran felt his menacing presence and he knew that was the intention. Imran noticed a dried pool of blood in the extreme left hand corner of the room, he sort of smiled inwardly as he realised that this was a ruse that the security guys had used when he was in Raqqa to make the interviewee a bit more on edge.

"Welcome back to the Caliphate, Barbie" said Hassan. "Have you anything you want to share with us before we start to chat?"

Imran felt that old familiar sinking feeling, he felt a bit shaken, but he knew that they had found nothing so far. He had also been at a few interrogations himself and was fairly confident in his cover story, and he knew that there was nothing in his clothing, belongings, or on his phone that could compromise him.

"Thanks," said Imran "It's good to be back with my brothers, but you know it's only for a short stay, I have another mission now," he answered confidently.

The next four hours seemed like a lifetime; Hassan talked, cajoled, half threatened and constantly double-checked his story. They knew about his previous time in Syria and they knew about his involvement in the fighting in Tikrit. Imran was also asked about names and numbers they had obviously taken from his mobile phone. Over the period of the interrogation Imran though slowly realised that Hassan actually did not know half as much as he thought he did, and he also realised that he didn't actually know some of the places under discussion. He wondered how the driver was coping with this debriefing when he heard a shout and a sort of strangled scream coming from another room in the house. *Maybe not so good*, he thought.

"OK, let's take a break," said Hassan.

Imran was left with the ominous presence of the big Chechen who occasionally rocked back and forth on very flimsy Chinese-made chair, murmuring lowly as if silently chanting a song or a prayer, Imran thought he had been involved in maybe one battle too many, he had seen it before, a sort of PTSD shell-shock thing, he was some scary fucker.

Hassan broke the silence as he returned carrying a large plastic sealable box containing what looked like his clothes.

"OK, Imran," said Hassan, in quite a friendly manner, "we are happy with you, you can get your old clothes on now, you can have your mobile, but we do not want you to turn it on, here is a replacement for while you are here."

Hassan handed him a simple Nokia handset.

"This is only for us to talk to you, it is hooked up to Yello, the encrypted walkie-talkie system we use here, and it is the only system that we allow."

Hassan paused for effect.

"I repeat, do not turn on the phone at any time, we'll know if you do."

Hassan then handed Imran the remote locking key for the VW van.

"It looks like you will be driving on your own from now on mate, your driver didn't make the cut, so you will be driving that back in when the Save the Children convoy leaves Iraq."

Imran was genuinely surprised.

"What do you mean?"

"It seems that your friend had some strange numbers on his phone and no way of explaining them, it also seems that he could not explain his movements well enough, it looks like silly Sayeed might be working for some part of the British security services. We will soon find out who." Just as Hassan said this, a long scream pierced the silence.

"That's us finding out now," he said with a smile. Imran thought of Ahmad's requests for Sayeed's mobile numbers at the last debrief, maybe that was why they found compromising numbers on his phone. *Is that why Ahmad said, "It was important for your safety"?*

CHAPTER EIGHTEEN

TOMMY TALIBANI

Ahmad and his cousin Talil were at that moment driving towards the Claymore house to meet the team from London. Ahmad was lost deep in thought. He reflected on the strangeness of the situation, here he was in his father's country, which was now effectively at war with ISIS, with a cousin who he had grown up with in London, who was now a Colonel in the Kurdish Security Services. Ahmad and Talil were close friends; they had a sort of invisible bond, the product of the extended Kurdish family structure, reinforced by the cultural ties that come from being brought up together in a fairly rough area of London.

Talil, or 'Tommy' had more often played the part of an older brother and had weighed in on his side when he needed it. It was also usually Tommy that would be sent to make sure that he came in from playing football to do his homework after school. In Ahmad's and Talil's small part of South East London, football bound the communities and families together and jointly supplied them with a group identity, and in South Bermondsey, in that rather insular part of London, just to the East of Tower Bridge on the south side of the river, the football club was Millwall.

Growing up a Millwall supporter in London was a bit like being the Kurdish Nation in the Arab world, thought Ahmad, surrounded by enemies who wished to do them harm and for them to fail. Adversity applied by enemies had likewise bound the Kurds closer together as a nation. The Kurdish attitude in the

Middle East had therefore always somehow replicated the same attitude reflected in the famous Millwall football chant: "No one likes us, no one loves us, and we don't care."

Ahmad's thoughts drifted back to his present concerns. The last contact with Ken was just as the agent had crossed into Kurdistan. Since then Ahmad knew that his phone had been activated in Mosul. He suspected that this might have been as part of the inevitable security screening that he knew he would receive. Because of this activation, the techs in London now knew the current GPS coordinates of the phone and the fact that the memory had been trawled for data. He still did not have confirmation that the laptops had been delivered; he needed agent Ken to get in touch. He also knew that some agents went rogue once they felt safe again with their erstwhile comrades.

Ahmad's thoughts were broken as the guards opened the double doors to the Claymore house and Tommy Talibani stopped the Lexus outside the front entrance, where Sam was waiting for them. Ahmad knew that the next meeting would be crucial to the success or failure of their interconnected tasks. He knew that without Tommy's help the rescue mission was dead in the water. Ahmad beamed a broad smile and extended his hand towards her and after a polite handshake gestured towards the Lexus where Tommy had just closed the driver door with a slam and had emerged from the front of the vehicle.

"May I introduce my very good friend and cousin, Tommy Talibani."

So here he is, thought Sam, the famed head of the Asayish and the guy they would have to work with to get things done.

Tommy was a burly guy, a head taller and much broader than Ahmad. He was wearing a well-cut, expensive dark grey suit with a roll-neck cashmere sweater. Sam was pretty good at making an assessment at first sight; it is often the small details that make a decent intelligence report, and she also had that inbuilt feminine insight that allowed her to make a fairly accurate assessment of most men fairly quickly.

He looked fit and his hair and close-cropped beard were well groomed; he was late thirties or early forties. She quickly glanced at his dark brown swede shoes, they looked like Loach's, probably bought in London, on his left wrist he wore an expensive, but not overly ostentatious Rolex Sea Master sports watch. *This guy was dressed well, and knew how to dress,* thought Sam. Initial impressions were good, but Sam also knew that it took more than a decent suit to make a decent man.

Tommy offered his hand to Sam for a gentlemanly handshake.

"I hear you are from London," said Sam.

"Yeah, South London, 'Deep South'," which he deliberately pronounced as a long exaggerated "Saarf", surprisingly delivered in a broad cockney accent.

"We moved to London when I was ten and I came back to Kurdistan in 2003 and joined the Pershmerga before it kicked off over here. I worked with the American Special Forces during the war and I've been here ever since. I still get to 'the smoke' to see my mates sometimes, hopefully when I can also get to see my beloved Lions play, but we've been a bit busy over here for a while. And I think, with your help, we might get a bit busier," he said with a slight smile.

"Let's go meet the team," Sam said and led the way into the house.

The house itself was a hive of activity; packing material of every type littered the front hallway. All the guys had arrived now, Pat and Scotty had arrived business class on Turkish Airways into Erbil only an hour earlier, and were now fully occupied unpacking the large shipment containers that had arrived with them, delivered by the incoming British Army Training Team. *They look like demented kids on Christmas morning unwrapping presents,* thought Sam.

Every possible combination of Ops kit that had been quickly

gathered from the wish list they had brainstormed with Danny and Ken at their pre-deployment meeting. Sam had never worked on a project with such an unknown quantity of kit and equipment. The team would not really know what was available until every box was empty, because everything was put together so quickly.

Pat was helping Scotty to unpack the weapons from their black reinforced plastic boxes. Pat examined a Colt MI8 assault rifle. He pushed down on the releasing pin behind the working parts of the breach and slipped out the receiver and breach block, he then examined the barrel by holding it up to the light of the window.

Scotty was applying some WD40 and working his own particular technical magic on a British GPMG machine gun.

Jimmy Cohen was opening a large packing case and removing various pieces of technical equipment for his inspection, and responded visually with either an instant scowl or a muttered "Fuck it", when he looked at something that wouldn't work, or a radiant smile when he picked up something that would.

Taff was removing what looked like foam rubber packing material from another box and was arranging them in piles. The box was marked 'High Explosive' and Taff was the demolitions and 'explosive entry' expert. Sam instantly recognised that part of their wish list had come through. Taff was unpacking various lengths of what was called Explosive Cutting Tape, or ECT. This tape was about four inches wide and half an inch thick and came in various lengths up to three feet long. It had a thin V-shaped strip of high explosive imbedded into the centre of one side, which effectively acted as a shaped charge along its whole length. It was stuck onto a surface with a film of one-sided sticky tape. Once attached and connected to a detonator it could cut through anything from wooden doors, to walls, or steel structures. It would be used for the door charges they might need on the operation. With ECT and a skilled operator, they could get anywhere they wanted to go.

The guys stopped as Sam and the visitors arrived.

"Lads, this is Tommy Talibani who is here to chat on how we can work together."

The guys waved to their new visitor with rather grimy hands and smiled.

"Let's take a break in the front room and chat to Tommy and Ahmad, I think they might have some news for us and you could probably do with a wet anyway," Sam said with a smile.

Chapter Nineteen

Logistics

Ahmad and Tommy sat down on the settee amongst the previously abandoned crates that littered the lounge. Small piles of equipment were stacked in various places on the carpet throughout the spacious, high-ceilinged room. The team was obviously trying to put their very diverse kit from London into some semblance of order. One pile was reserved for ammunition, *a lot of it,* Ahmad thought. The guys stood in the ankle-deep confusion of open crates and boxes as small piles of equipment started to take shape. There were boxes and boxes of ammunition of all types with long belts of machine gun ammo strung aimlessly in every direction.

Ahmad instantly recognised some other gear he knew about. He could also see the unmistakable outline of a claymore mine. *Now that is a scary piece of kit,* he thought. He had once attended a seminar on this fiendishly effective weapon. It was a concave dark green box, about nine inches long and two inches in depth and weighed about three and a half pounds. It could remotely fire a directed explosive charge packed with 700 small ball bearings towards an enemy up to about a hundred metres away and with typical American forethought and clarity, embossed on the dangerous side was written: 'FRONT TOWARDS ENEMY'.

He remembered what an SBS instructor had said after a demonstration while he was at the fort. A single claymore had left the targets completely shredded and neatly peppered with

700 small holes. The SBS guy had said, "You see guys, just like a really big bar of chocolate, every fucker gets a bit."

Usually considered a highly effective ambush or defensive weapon; Ahmad thought it was an odd choice for a hostage extraction.

Tommy surveyed the scene of organised chaos and said to Sam.

"It looks like you're planning a real party, are we invited?"

Sam smiled. "Yeah, more the merrier, to be honest we had hoped you guys would tag along."

Sam continued, "The truth is that we have no idea what kit and equipment London has been able the supply at short notice. So this is really an exercise in reverse planning. We've got to see what tools we've got before we can decide how we're going to get the job done. You and your guys are very much the make or break of this planning phase."

The team now entered the room and sat where they could find space for an impromptu briefing from Ahmad.

Ahmad stood next to Sam by the framed portrait of the Kurdish leader Jalal Talibani that hung in pride of place on the living room wall alongside a picture of Her Majesty the Queen. Ahmad looked quickly around the team, who all appeared to be crouched forward and listening intently.

"Right guys, I think you'll want to know if I've any definitive news on the task or the hostage situation. Firstly, let me tell you that I'm presently light on facts, and at this stage a bit heavy on supposition. As you know, supposition is the 'mother of all fuck-ups' so I'll only tell you what I actually know."

Ahmad paused and looked around the room and continued.

"The laptops still haven't been properly activated. We do know, however, that they have been delivered. All have been briefly switched on in the Mosul area, possibly while ISIS techs attempt to security check them, therefore we have been able to get a GPS lock-on reference their present location. We do have an agent in place, but he's not yet been in contact. I do believe that he will though, when it's safe to do so, but that again is purely supposition."

Again Ahmad paused to let the information filter through.

"Confirmed information from other sources however indicates that ISIS intends to move the hostages. We also believe one hostage might be released soon; we believe that the Italian authorities may have paid a sizable ransom, although again this cannot be confirmed at the moment. The same source confirms that the remaining hostages will be moved to Raqqa, and that the American hostage is still in fairly good health. I also have some good news, but for that I will hand over to my friend here Mr. Talibani."

Tommy Talibani looked around the room; he could see that he was dealing with a very experienced team. The majority of his guys were either teenagers or in their early twenties. Tommy was the oldest guy in his Police Commando, these guys looked much more experienced.

"Hi guys, my name is Talil Talibani, but call me Tommy, I think you all know who I am and what I can do for you. Let me first tell you that you are safe working with my guys and myself. I am the senior officer of the Asayish Special Police Commando, which is a unit of 150 men, which are trained and equipped by the US Special Forces, and we would like to help."

Tommy was obviously used to briefing people, he spoke carefully and enunciated clearly, but always with a discernible cockney accent.

"First of all guys, my name, for you Afghan vets, it's Talibani not Taliban, so don't forget the final syllable, it's a fairly well-known name out here, my Uncle Jalal on the wall beside me was the first Kurdish President of Iraq. I lived in London until 2003 when I left to fight with the Pershmerga in 'Iraqi Freedom' and I have been fighting Arabs ever since, I see these wankers in ISIS as no different. I have pledged my support to you and your efforts in the hope that any joint operation will hurt them more. You might have guessed that to me this is more than just politics, I have seen what these guys are capable of and I want them removed from existence."

Tommy's eyes seemed to burn with hatred as scenes of ISIS carnage flashed into his mind.

"To me guys, this is personal, I have some possible timings for you. My unit must supply a diversionary raid on Mosul within the next week to aid a general advance in the Syrian sector towards Raqqa. It is my earnest hope that we can integrate our plans with yours to free our American friend and his fellow hostages."

The team instinctively looked towards Sam for her reaction. They had all expected some level of support from the Kurds, and especially the Kurdish Secret Service, but this was a whole new level of military cooperation that brought with it a somewhat double-edged advantage. To Sam, this was yet another bombshell, the operation was once again being bracketed by circumstance; it had been effectively been given yet another deadline. The operation had once again expanded outside their very strictly controlled parameters and the circle of knowledge had now exploded exponentially outwards.

"When will you know the timing of this attack, Tommy?" she said.

"Within the next couple of days," replied Tommy.

Sam inwardly digested the new information as her brain raced for a solution. That meant, she thought, *that the whole operation needed to be planned and implemented within 48 hours.* They desperately needed a confirmed location for the hostages. She needed to speak to London.

At that precise moment an audial bleep sounded in the right ear of one of the Arabic language specialists employed in MI5's London office. The bleep meant that one of the bugged laptops had come online and was sending information. The translator sat up as an image initially flickered and then became solid. The operator saw a white bearded older man wearing thick glasses looking straight into the screen. The GPS flashed up the location as Whitechapel in London, as a confused-looking Mullah Rahman tried to decipher the Apple operating system.

The MI5 technical operator informed his controller; it appeared that the first laptop was transmitting.

Mullah Rahman looked deep in thought; he was wondering how he could phrase the important email that he needed to send to Mosul.

The technical operator knew that any message would firstly bounce through his receiver. It was important that all messages from this guy were screened before they reached their intended destination, lives were at risk.

Mullah Rahman prepared to tap out his message; he would then put it in his draft message box. The guy to whom he sent his important emails would then simply log onto a shared email address and read the draft. The ISIS tech guys thought this procedure improved the security of his email system because he never actually sent the message; it was retrieved by the addressee and then deleted.

He had to let them know in Mosul two important pieces of information. Firstly that the ransom had been paid for the Italian and was now in the ISIS coffers, and secondly and perhaps more importantly, that the American hostage was not what he seemed. A friend at Al Jazeera had told him that the American hostage who was posing as a journalist was actually called Connor Cameron, and he had once served in the US Rangers.

Chapter Twenty

Connor Cameron

As Sam was thinking about talking to London, elements of the London office were thinking of coming across to her. The company researchers had turned up some interesting and quite worrying anomalies, while preparing an in-depth information file on David Slater. It was not that there was a lack of information, just the reverse; it seemed like some of the information gleaned from Google, Facebook, and other elements of social media were possibly too complete. The other real worry was that the profile that they had laboriously compiled actually differed significantly with the information supplied by the client.

The David Slater they had researched was born in a different place, went to school elsewhere, and had graduated from a completely different high school and university. Danny had sifted all the information and compared and contrasted the inconsistencies. Kenny had repeated the process and eventually both arrived at the same conclusion. The person they were contracted to release from ISIS captivity was not who he seemed. The information on the US journalist called David Slater that the researchers had compiled seemed to be a very professionally put together legend, the sort of legend that would pass initial background checks — in other words it was like a very elaborate web-based cover story.

Kenny had seen the same technique used by MI5 and MI6 to protect agents. Both men did not doubt that the man was Sir Ian's son, he had positively identified him, but they also knew that key elements of his background had been changed. But why? They needed to meet Tim and they needed to get instruction from their client, they had put a team in harm's way and now needed clarification before they proceeded.

Tim's phone was on answering machine and Danny left a message, he said, "We seem to have some problems with your credit card details, sir, please ring back."

This was the prearranged code they had agreed on for use in case of unforeseen circumstances.

Within ten minutes Danny's encrypted number rang. "Yeah, it's Danny."

Tim's voice was calm and relaxed. "Hi Danny, I think I know what this is about and I can understand your concerns. I have a meeting with Sir Ian tomorrow at six at Stansted Airport, he would like you to attend."

Danny shot a perplexed glance towards Kenny. "Roger that, we need to speak, but why Stansted? I presume we're going somewhere?"

Tim took his time to respond. "Yes, Danny, we are flying into Erbil tomorrow, there have been some developments that we'll need to manage at close quarters. Sir Ian is determined that he needs to be there as things start to happen."

"Roger that, Tim, I'll see you at the airport. Where's the RV?"

"We're meeting at the private jet terminal at Stansted at 0600, bring your passport and a toothbrush if you want to come with us."

"See you at six," confirmed Danny.

"Well, that solves a problem," said Kenny, while picking up a small backpack that was lying by his desk. He handed the small black reinforced nylon pack to Danny.

"This is the last of Jimmy Cohen's wish list, it has just arrived. We were going to have to send someone with it on a military flight, but this is a much quicker fix, you can give it to him personally."

132

"Sounds like a plan," said Danny. "But what the fuck is it?"

"Believe it or not," said Kenny, "it's a camera drone, but a lot smaller than the ones we were using in Helmand and we have just borrowed it from MI5, so tell Jimmy not to lose it. It is state of the art, and called the PD 100 Black Hornet, made by a Danish firm called Prodynamics. As I understand it, the little drones are especially designed with very quiet rotors that emit very little noise, and they are coloured and shaped so they are hard to see. It should give the team the ability of conduct an aerial survey."

Danny smiled. "Even an often-confounded technophobe like me can appreciate how useful that could be, Kenny."

At five in the morning next day, Kenny gunned the Mercedes slightly as he sliced through London's early morning traffic. Danny fumbled with the music system trying to rustle up Classic FM, as Kenny deliberately confounded his efforts by retuning with the button on the steering wheel. It was great fun for Kenny but would only be truly funny when Danny finally found out that you could control the radio from the steering wheel; he had been doing it now for about six weeks. Danny gave up muttering about "fucking new-fangled gadgets", and then addressed the subject that was worrying them both.

"So, what do you think Ken, where does this leave us?"

Kenny looked thoughtful, by nature he was a careful man and liked to make his situational assessments incrementally, in stages, based only on facts.

"It leaves us no different to where we were before Danny. We still need to know what's going on, and I think that we're only getting told a limited amount of information on a need-to-know basis. This needs to change before we commit our team. We must have all the facts. My guess is that our client's son is a bit more committed to Uncle Sam than we thought. It looks like he once served in the US Rangers for starters; our media assets also have reservations reference his press credentials as a photojournalist. Some of the places he claims to have been to just don't check out. I think he is a spook, maybe CIA. The point is, if we can find out, others can to, and if that happens his life isn't worth shit in Mosul.

"Let's hope their people are not as thorough as ours then mate," replied Danny. "We need to find and fix where he is and get him out sharpish, or he will end up in the latest ISIS snuff movie."

The Mercedes moved smoothly up to the private terminal and pulled up outside. Danny quickly shook hands with Kenny, exited the passenger door, opened the rear door and grabbed his grip bag and the small backpack containing Jimmy's kit from the plush leather of the rear seat.

"I'll see you when this is done mate, at the end of operation piss-up."

"Yeah, roger that Danny. Best of luck, old mate."

Danny slammed the door and made his way into the terminal.

He wondered how Sam and the guys had settled in, the full team had only just arrived in country and it looked like things were going to start to move very quickly.

Chapter Twenty One

Planning for War

Sam wearily pulled back the duvet and attempted to arrange her thoughts. As she sat perched on the edge of the bed, the enormity of the challenge continued to race through her mind. She had not slept properly, her mind had raced with a thousand different possibilities and their various negative and positive permutations as she tried to brainstorm a workable plan. Sam had a wealth of experience in planning high-risk intelligence operations, in high-risk areas, but this was different. A strong element of this plan would be an all-out military assault. She needed surprise to be on their side, she needed solid intelligence, she needed advice, and she needed the guys.

Pat, Scotty and Taff had actual live experience of a coordinated house assault. All the lads from the units based in Poole and Hereford specialise in what they call the 'Black Role' and each Sabre squadron will spend countless hours and expend thousands of rounds honing their room combat skills. By the time they actually get to conduct a live assault, they have developed an almost spooky muscle memory for the application of controlled firepower. Sam resolved to convene a brainstorming session. To be successful, she thought, they would have to be unconventional. The plan must reflect the modus operandi of the opposition; they had to think like the enemy.

Sam's mind raced as she quickly showered and dressed. By the time she had stepped out of the bathroom, she had the semblance of a workable plan.

As she entered the main sitting room, Jimmy Cohen was busy compiling a checklist of all the equipment that had been neatly assembled and laid out. By that morning, only at the beginning of day two, the majority of the kit was neatly laid out in rows, completely covering the large Arabic style carpet in the front room. Jimmy looked up from his iPad and gave Sam a big smile and a cheery, "Hello, gorgeous."

Sam looked around the room and it was obvious that the team had made progress with the equipment.

"Looks like you guys have sorted it all, but you should have given me a shake to help."

"Taff and the lads did not want to wake you too early, you looked like you needed a good kip."

Jimmy Cohen had taken responsibility for being the unofficial QM (Quarter Master), it made sense as he was the only guy who understood some of the more complex technical kit.

The weapons were laid side-by-side; there were three short-barrelled US Army M4s along with three slightly newer Colt M18s. These were both extremely effective assault rifles currently in use with the American military and also by ISIS since they had seized huge stockpiles of American supplied weaponry after the fall of Mosul. There were also some slightly older weapons including eight MP5Ks, a very short-barrelled machine pistol made by Heckler and Kock, which had been the preferred tool for covert carry and room entry in the mid-nineties. There were also eight Glock 23 nine-millimetre pistols with their magazines and holsters.

The heavier weaponry had also been neatly placed next to the wall. There were two of the latest Para Mini-me .556 light machine guns as used in Afghanistan by the US and British Special Forces, next to an older and heavier British GPMG Medium machine gun made by FN. There also seemed enough ammunition of various types to start a small war. Finally, sitting on its biped legs, newly cleaned and oiled was the menacing shape of the awesome USA made Barrett .50 caliber sniper rifle.

The explosive cutting tape was nearby, similarly laid out neatly in its respective strengths. The light eleven-grain charges were cut into eight-inch lengths to be used as door charges for explosive entry. At the other end of the spectrum the twenty-seven-grain could be used to destroy a decent-sized bridge or cut through a steel wall. There were also five claymore mines laid out, side by side, each with their respective 'clacker', or hand-cranked firing mechanism, placed with each.

Jimmy had laid out eight different sets of military equipment, including combat clothing, chest webbing, magazines with a variety of sights and ancillaries for the assault rifles and eight individual sets of body armour. The combat clothing was of the old US type, the same type worn by the Pershmerga.

That's good, Jimmy thought. He knew from personal experience that the middle of a firefight is not the place to stand out from a crowd.

The weaponry and equipment was initially intended for a minimum of an eight-man team. It seemed like a combination of the current fluidity of the situation and the ever-tightening deadline might not allow this to happen. The extra personnel had already been contracted by London from a short list of preferred contractors approved by the team, and should already be on their way. Sam thought it was doubtful that they would arrive in time for the actual operation. It seemed that circumstance had contrived to rush the team headlong into more like an 'immediate action' than a carefully thought out plan.

British security contractors or the 'Circuit' as it is sometimes called, is like ISIS in one respect — it is a global phenomenon. Sam had just received a text from Doc Doughty, a friend of Scotty's from the Royal Marines, saying that he had just boarded a flight from Spain. Two other guys were in a similar situation on inbound flights from the UK. One of the volunteers, an ex-Marine called Mac McCallum who was a personal friend of Taff's, had only just boarded his flight in New Zealand, and he would not arrive for at least thirty-six hours. An ex-Four-Five Commando Royal Marine sniper for the Barrett called Eddie Warden was arriving from the USA. Sam gathered her thoughts, *what I need is the combined experience of the group to craft a workable plan. I need to get all the guys together. I'm sure it can be done, but we need to think outside the box on this one.* She needed Danny's advice.

CHAPTER TWENTY TWO

LONDON TO AINKOWA

Danny boarded the small executive jet pulled up by the private terminal at Stansted. There was only time for brief greetings to be exchanged as the passengers strapped in, and Sir Ian's personal Lear Jet 75 immediately lurched forward onto the runway. The two Pratt and Whitney engines purred powerfully, seemingly in a hurry to get airborne. The jet was like flying in a small living room, thought Danny. It smelt of opulence, that same mixture of fine leather and wooden trim that you would experience in a Rolls Royce.

There was room for eight passengers but only Sir Ian, Tim, and Danny were on board as Sir Ian's security team had flown ahead the day before. There was a nervous anticipation in the air, there was a need to know who knew what, and the trip was an ideal opportunity to find out. As the jet levelled out at 15,000 feet, Sir Ian pressed a button on the teak and beige leather cabinet next to his seat and a tray with a decanter of whisky with three crystal whisky glasses appeared.

"I seem to remember that a decent single malt is your favourite tipple, Danny, I always think that this always a civilised way to start an in-depth discussion."

"There's no better way," Danny replied. He then relayed his concerns. "I'm a wee bit concerned, as I do not think we've been told everything. This could have severe repercussions for my team on the ground, and I think as an ex-military man you can appreciate my concerns."

Sir Ian poured the decanter and handed the glass to Danny.

"Until yesterday I was in the dark as well. I think maybe Tim can address your concerns, and that is why I asked Tim to invite you. It is a bit too late for petty secrets. As you may have surmised, I am on this flight because I think my son, without our direct intervention, might only have a finite time to live."

Both men looked towards Tim. He looked pensive, almost pained as he addressed Danny directly.

"OK, Danny, I am going to forget all about any pretence of secrecy and tell you what I know. I think it's exactly what you have worked out, though," Tim calmly stated.

"I think my guys picked up the problem of the inconsistencies with David Slater's online profile at about the same time as your guys did. I double-checked some biographical data with Sir Ian and I think we came to the same conclusion, that is, his profile had been changed significantly to protect both his true identity and his employment. In other words, an online legend has been spun around his past, 'a bodyguard of lies to protect the truth', to use a Churchillian expression — a professionally invented past to protect his very perilous present. We therefore believe that he works for the US Government, although this has not been confirmed or denied by our friends from Langley."

Tim paused for effect and sipped some single malt. "Now Danny, the most important thing about this information is not whether it is true or not, it's whether the terrorists think it's true. We have picked up chatter from sources within the Arabic media, especially Al Jazeera that says they are ready to 'out' our man as a CIA agent. Once that happens, he will be dead within hours and they will, of course, deny any responsibility for the disclosure."

Danny immediately realised the implications, the deadline for extracting the client's son had just tightened and therefore the odds for a successful conclusion had just correspondingly shortened.

Danny lifted and looked into his glass, as if he was trying to use it as a crystal ball. The horrific image of the caged burning Jordanian pilot seared into his mind. He knew they had to act, and that time and circumstance was conspiring against them.

"We have no choice, we will have to reorganise quickly and go as soon as possible. As soon as we have a fix, we must get him out of there," said Danny.

Sir Ian looked directly at Danny, and then glanced towards Tim. "Now we know precisely where we are, my son's time is running out and you are the only people that can help him."

Sir Ian looked out the window as the Lear Jet banked slightly to the left altering the flight path to towards Turkish Airspace and onwards to Kurdistan. He now knew more about the son who he had been refused any contact with after a typically acrimonious American divorce, where he had witnessed two sets of lawyers fight over the carcass of their brief marriage like rabid dogs. He had often thought of his young son and had been racked with guilt over his inability to compromise with his mother.

He had been unable to arrange a custody agreement and in frustration he had adopted his preferred coping strategy, of just blanking the whole episode from his increasingly busy life, but there had always been that painful nagging doubt that he could have done more, fought harder for his son, *this is my chance to do precisely that,* he thought.

Tim had described in detail what his American contacts had told him. David Slater was Connor Cameron, he had left home at sixteen, dropping out of his Ivy League college and had joined the US Army and had served in its Elite Ranger Units. He had then spent almost ten years in the US Military in its Special Forces, possibly in Delta, or so Tim thought. He had then been attached as a contract soldier to the CIA, subcontracted from a company called XE, which used to be called Blackwater.

As Tim explained, this made his son, Connor, under his protective CIA nom de guerre of David Slater, a deniable CIA asset. A shadow warrior, a highly trained Special Forces soldier but a mere pawn in the CIA's covert 'war on terror' and an extremely expendable one at that. He looked down at the vast expanse of cloud and earth and realised the enormity of the task. Somewhere down there was his son, who was suffering, his flesh and blood. *I will get him out*, he thought, *even if I have to do it myself.*

CHAPTER TWENTY THREE

THE DEATH HOUSE

First of all, things had seemed to improve for the hostage named as David Slater, whose given name was Connor Cameron. The visit from the senior ISIS Mullah-type guy had initially brought about some improvements in the hostages' living conditions. The Italian had been taken away on a stretcher to receive medical treatment, an ISIS medic-type had examined and had seem to catalogue the remaining two prisoners injuries. The Dane was suffering the worst, the unrelenting months of brutality and neglect had shrunk his once healthy frame into a wizened husk. The American recognised in his fellow hostage all the symptoms of advanced malnutrition, combined with a mass of infected sores and lacerations caused by the constant filthy conditions and daily mistreatment.

He had heard the guards discussing the situation in hushed tones. They had been severely admonished for their treatment of the hostages, not through altruism though — from the gist of what was being said, the Mullah, although understanding of their disgust at the kuffar, thought it was just bad business sense to kill a hostage by mistreatment and neglect just before they had secured a juicy deal to release him.

Therefore, the last twenty-four hours had been almost like a holiday. The food was now edible and untainted; his chains that previously pinned his arms to the rear had been removed and replaced to the front so at least he could wash. He had been supplied with washing water, soap and a toothbrush. This had allowed him to try and help the Danish guy who was now at least able to lie down on an improvised foam rubber mattress.

The water ration had also improved and they were now supplied with bottles of water instead of the usual brackish stuff from the taps that had caused stomach problems. The beatings and verbal abuse had stopped and something had changed. In the evening, just before the call to prayer the guards and the medic arrived again. They carried a stretcher and carefully lifted the injured Dane onto it and carried him away. In that instant, when the door slammed shut and he heard the key turn in the lock, he was alone with only the mournful sound of the call to prayer for company.

It finally meant that he was responsible only for himself; he did not need to think about the repercussions that might be suffered by the other hostages if he resisted or attempted escape. He knew his time was running out. Sooner or later they would find out who he was and whom he was working for, he resolved to escape knowing full well that any escape could lead to death.

He was rested and fed, only his left hand was now shackled and the thick manacle and heavy chain would make a fine weapon. He would take the next opportunity to change his situation. Even if he only had a chance to kill one of these skinny little fuckers before dying he would do it, even better if he could take a couple of the pathetic little fuckers with him.

Within one kilometre of where Connor lay chained, Imran had been making inquiries; he had fairly free reign to walk around the streets adjoining the accommodation they had provided him, although asking too many questions here could severely endanger your health. So, as in all things, he was careful. He tried to chat at the market and pick up snippets of information. He talked to some of the other British volunteers; they varied from the newbies, ultra-dreamer types, to the more hardened older guys who had been around when he was in Iraq.

A lot of these guys were thoroughly disillusioned with the whole thing, but more or less marooned in ISIS between a rock and a hard place, but on the ISIS side by the increasingly harsh penalties for desertion. *They do not fuck about with human rights under Sharia law,* thought Imran, and they would receive an inevitable prison sentence if they ever made it back to whatever shit place in UK they came from.

Imran had lived long enough in Arab areas to realise that one of the best ways to pick up information is to keep your ears open while you take tea. The other way is to ask the kids. He had managed by using both methods to find out that there were some kuffar held near the school on the other side of Mosul's main market, in what the locals called the 'death house'. Imran walked across the main market square with the Great Mosque behind him.

The square was busy with all manner of traders and hawkers vying for business from the permanent and improvised market stalls, scattered in amongst a sea of black robed women, all with the obligatory and very bored male family escort, all trying to make ends meet like housewives the world over. Imran also noticed some of the prices; some were particularly eye-watering and strangely, the only currency used was dollars. *You might as well get your veggies shipped in from Harrods*, he thought.

In the middle of the throng there were two ISIS guys standing by a Russian four-barrelled ZPU-4 anti-aircraft gun. This was an awesome weapon that Imran had actually been on the receiving end of when he was in Syria. It fired a four-barrelled blast of heavy 12.6 machinegun bullets and was designed to take down aircraft. It could be towed by a trailer or was sometimes mounted by ISIS onto a Toyota truck. This one was dismounted and in a sandbagged emplacement. One guy was seated on the small seat that extended from the chassis and seemed to be scanning the airspace above the mosque with binoculars. Ahmad looked to the left and then to the right.

There were three such weapons pointing out from the crowded market area, outlined against the sky and positioned facing towards the south, *probably to react against helicopter incursions*, he thought. Imran knew the ISIS rationale, which always placed such weaponry in the middle of the local civilians in case of drone or air attack. It was a win-win situation for them; it protected the weaponry and the operators with a cloak of innocent civilians, while also ensuring international outrage if droves of them were killed in a US air strike.

He also knew that they would only site and man this type of prestige weapon permanently if they were protecting something special. They were facing south, he thought, so he decided to explore to the north. On the north of the square he was just in time to see a deluge of excited kids pour from a newly opened door of what seemed like the boys' madrassa, or religious school. The madrassa had another ZPU-4 anti-aircraft gun manned by two guys on the roof. About twenty metres from the school, there was a heavily fortified large white single story building.

As Imran observed, there seemed to be a guard changeover in progress. He knew that simply looking at security arrangements in an ISIS area could get you killed, so he decided to walk towards the activity. He walked to within talking distance before a black-robed guard levelled his AK47 in his direction.

Imran swallowed hard. "Hi, brother," he said in Arabic. "I am looking for my cousin who is with the brothers, his name is Tariq Al Britani."

"You should not be here, brother, this is a restricted area," replied the guard in thick, Chechen-accented Arabic. "Try leaving a message at the mosque, the British have a notice board there, but you must leave here quickly or we will both be in the shit."

"Many thanks, brother," replied Imran.

Now that is interesting, he thought, *Chechen's only guard high priority targets. I think this is the place the anti-aircraft guns are trying to protect*. Imran quickly made his way back to the square as the crowd suddenly parted to allow an ex-American Humvee to press through it. It was now painted black with a large black ISIS flag hanging limply from the rear of the vehicle.

He followed the slow progress of the vehicle until it parked outside of the double doors of the white single-storey building. Then Imran got the break he was after; from the protection of the edge of the market he observed the double doors of the house open and three ISIS guys struggle out carrying a stretcher. The call to prayer sounded loudly from the minaret on the Grand Mosque as they carried the loaded stretcher towards the black Humvee. The casualty on the stretcher was hooded and tethered to it by straps, but Imran could clearly see the very dirty GITMO orange jump suit the guy was wearing. He had identified where the hostages were being held. Now he needed to let Ahmad know.

After prayer, it took Imran just ten minutes of fevered negotiation and one hundred dollars to hire a Thuraya satellite phone from Mosul's thriving black market. Five minutes after that he was on top of one of the buildings behind the Mosque protected from prying eyes by the gathering darkness. This was also common practice in Iraq where sometimes the phone signal was only accessible from the roof; it also gave you the advantage of knowing that nobody else was listening in. He dialled the number he had memorised on his first meeting with Ahmad with the added 0044 prefix, an English voice answered.

"Hello, this is Fortnum and Mason customer complaints, how can I help?"

Imran recognised the coded reply, he had phoned in directly to the MI5 source line.

"Hi, this is Imran for Ahmad. I have the house, I need to speak to him."

"OK Imran, well done. I have this number now and Ahmad will phone you in fifteen minutes, get somewhere where you can talk."

"OK, in fifteen minutes," said Imran.

The duty controller at Box immediately flashed up the file for Agent 2030. He read the file updates and immediately understood the urgent nature of the contact, and within five minutes Ahmad had a number. Fifteen minutes after his call Imran's phone rang.

"Hi Imran," said Ahmad. "Excellent work mate, now listen carefully, I need you to describe the target house as clearly as you can in relation to a known location."

Ahmad then conducted a telephone debrief trying to extract every last piece of detail he could. He hit Imran with a seemingly endless series of questions.

"How far from the Grand Mosque?"

"How many paces from the Madrassa?"

"Can the ZPU-4s engage from the roof to ground level?"

"How many guards?"

"Are there bars on the windows of the target house?"

He finally finished with, "Well done mate, excellent work. Give me a missed call as soon as you need to speak, meanwhile, this is what I want you to do..."

Imran listened intently.

Imran then made his way back to the busy throng of the market square. As he pushed his way through the gathering crowd reinforced by worshippers leaving the main mosque, he detected a change in the atmosphere. There was a sort of nervous excitement in the crowd with people seemingly rushing to get somewhere.

"What's going on, son?" he asked a boy of about ten who almost collided with him.

"We have found a spy," he said.

Imran immediately surmised what was going on, he had seen it before. There was about to be a public execution.

Three Toyota pick-up trucks illuminated a triangle of light in the middle of the square into which a hooded figure was pulled. His head was covered with what looked like a hessian sack as he was dragged screaming by his manacled arms. He was then placed on his knees in front of the expectant crowd. The hushed murmuring subsided as a white robed Mullah stepped to the side of the kneeling figure.

Mullah Mohammad Al-Rafdan loved to preach; it was his town and he got a positive buzz from being the focus of its attention. He was the senior ISIS man and was again relishing the opportunity to talk. Leadership was all about selling an idea to motivate people and he was enjoying it. He was speaking loudly and passionately in Arabic, but he was going a bit too fast for Imran to pick it all up. He caught some words, 'jasoos' meaning spy and 'murtadd' meaning apostate. It was apparent that this guy, who was at that time shaking in fear facing the crowd, was about to get killed. Imran felt a sort of collective frenzy building in the crowd. The crowd's anticipation increased as the long sermon from the Mullah reached its peak. The audience seemed to be mostly black-robed women, with the mandatory male relative. Imran spotted the occasional child trying to wriggle its way through the throng to get a better vantage point.

A black clad and masked figure was immediately to the rear of the kneeling man, his left hand resting on his shoulder seemingly keeping him in position. The kneeling figure rocked slightly as he seemed to murmur some prayers. The Mullah was suddenly silent as the man in black pulled off the kneeling man's sandbag hood to show him a short black combat knife. The kneeling man screamed and shouted a long, "No — please..." as the knife was drawn strongly across his throat, biting deep into his neck as his executioner sawed the knife through the toughness of the trachea.

The sound that half-escaped and half-screamed from the victim's windpipe still shocked Imran. Like many of the British fighters, he had never experienced the ritual halal slaughter of animals until he reached the Middle East. His mum had always got her halal meat from Tesco's and the suffering of the animals had initially really worried him. He suddenly thought of the butchery that he had been involved in at Tikrit, and realised that a butchered man sounds very much like a butchered sheep or goat. Imran felt a deep shame flow inwards from the scene, almost to his very soul.

The killer continued the butchery, seemingly enjoying the suffering and almost like he was trying to prolong it. He held his victim's hair with his left hand as continued to saw and slice the small knife vigorously though the spinal region of the neck. The crowd excitedly shouted, "ALLAHU AKBAR! (God is great)"

As the head was finally completely severed and held aloft for their inspection, Imran was genuinely shocked as he recognised the ashen face of the bloodied head. The starkly terrified dark brown eyes, protruding and seemingly frozen in their final moment of terror. It was his old travelling companion, Sayeed.

"Poor fucker," Imran mouthed silently.

The still kneeling and bleeding carcass of the rest of the butchered Sayeed now slumped heavily onto the dirt of the marketplace as the bloodied black clad executioner calmly placed his severed head onto its back. *Not quite the glorious end you had in mind, old mate*, thought Imran.

He wondered again about the numbers they had found on Sayeed's phone, maybe that was the way that Ahmad hoped to draw the suspicion way from him. Either way, it was hard to feel sympathy for such a fucking idiot. After all, it had turned out a good night for Imran, but a particularly bad one for silly Sayeed.

At that particular time, just ninety miles from the horror Imran and the crowd had just witnessed, Ahmad was elated. His source had come through, come up trumps and done a thoroughly good job, and he raced to file an interim report to Tim and London. He then phoned Kenny on his London encrypted phone.

"Hi Kenny, listen mate, we have had a break. We should

have a general location for the task; I expect to have a technical lock-on by this evening. I need to speak to Danny as soon as he lands. I have also arranged detailed air photography of the area. It looks like we can get started, mate, and I'm phoning Sam and the team now with an approximate grid and description of the target house."

Chapter Twenty Four

The Plan

The team sat down in the living room in amongst the newly organised kit and equipment for the job. Sam looked around at the assembled troops; there was probably a century of combined military experience between them. British contractors like Taff, Scotty, and Pat had cut their teeth in Iraq and Afghanistan and had probably as much combat experience as any guys in the world. Jimmy was probably the world's leading expert on gathering intelligence by technical means. Their combined skill-sets covered just about every eventuality.

Their operating procedures had been shaped and amended over hundreds of high-risk operations, and now they were gathered to attempt one more. It was only by tapping into this wealth of experience that a workable plan could be brainstormed. Sam sat with her back to a large whiteboard and held a bunch of board markers in her hand. She handed each guy a different coloured marker. In a conventional army unit, the officers devised the plan and the troops executed it under their leadership, however in their very unconventional parent units, this was the way it was done.

"OK, guys," said Sam. "We have an approximate location and we have air photography arriving for detailed planning and orders tomorrow. What I suggest we do now is try and brainstorm a plan that will work. I have also done some rudimentary research on Google Maps and that's loaded onto the projector."

Sam placed another whiteboard and propped it on a chair next to her, it had a rudimentary sketch map outlined in black marker.

"This is based on source information guys, it shows the location of the hostage holding facility in relation to the main square behind the Grand Mosque in Mosul. The target house is a protected building, which is located next to a boy's madrassa. It has a guard force of approximately twelve; we believe these guys are Chechens. We hope to have more detail from both air photography and Google Earth tomorrow for detailed planning.

First of all let's just talk about timings. What do you guys think is the best time for an extraction? I think it should coincide with prayer timings, what do you think?"

Each of guys looked towards the board and tried to make their own individual assessments. Taff was the first to chime in.

"I think it is a straight choice between the classic dawn attack just as the guards have adopted flying carpet mode on their prayer mats, or the evening equivalent, just at last light, to allow us the cover of darkness on the extraction."

Scotty then added, "Yeah, it worked for us like that a couple of times in Iraq, although it also has the disadvantage of them all being awake after the call to prayer."

Pat then offered, "It's going to have to be a silent approach and a walk onto the target. How far is this from the ISIS front line? We will obviously have to mount from where our Pershmerga guys have secured their FEBA (Forward Edge of Battle Area). We also need a really good diversionary attack elsewhere, to try and draw these guys away once we are ready to go."

Sam flashed up a PowerPoint slide from Google. "This is the Pershmerga FEBA guys. It is approximately ten clicks to the target, that's a long walk in. We could mix it up and go for a covert drop off and infiltrate the last couple of clicks on foot. The FEBA itself runs on a front that intersects both the main Highway 1 and Road 80."

Sam pointed to a spot on the projection of the map with a laser pointer. "This is the final Kurdish position, and this is the first ISIS checkpoint, the main motorway here is a sort of no-mans-land, which both sides try to patrol. It means by skirting around the main ISIS checkpoint on Highway 1 we should be able to be dropped about three clicks from the target for a walk in." Sam then looked at the board and then wrote 'Dawn Attack' in marker pen. "OK guys, what are the advantages?"

After a free flowing exchange of comments, a quick list of advantages appeared.

Less activity on target
Approach target in darkness
Facilitates the use of covert approach
Less people on the route

She then wrote 'Last Light Attack' and repeated the procedure.

The team then discussed each element again. The subjects were presented by following the basic military planning format of ground, situation, mission, execution, service support, command and signals, until the bones of a workable plan began to emerge from the seeming chaos of free thought.

By the time they broke for coffee, each element of the plan had been discussed, Sam knew how they could do it, and also how they would do it, and she had enough information to start detailed planning. Sam then nominated each guy a specialist subject to research and also a part of the operation to prepare. The next task was to see what support the team could hope for from Tommy Talibani's guys. Sam needed the mother of all diversions, at exactly the right time, delivered with split second timing on the main ISIS checkpoint. Taff, as the explosives man, was tasked with giving them a really loud wake up call.

Chapter Twenty Five

Kurdistan — Wednesday Morning

Danny was unsure about the whole idea of the client being so closely involved, not only in the mechanics of such a dangerous operation but he was also equally unsure about the wisdom of Sir Ian even being in the country where the operation would take place. He realised however that as with any commercial enterprise outside the neat military world that he was used to, *that he who paid the piper called the tune.* It was Sir Ian that had insisted on being in the country when things were happening and he was a difficult guy to dissuade; he was, after all, paying the wages.

Danny was deep in thought as he gazed through the cabin window. He had never been involved in an operation where the goalposts moved almost constantly. The latest escalation in the threat to the hostage had further accelerated and condensed the planning stage. Once the news about the American was received in Mosul, they might just execute him straight away. Ahmad and his Kurdish cousin would be meeting him at the airport. It looked like they would have to go very soon. He hoped that Sam had managed to sketch out a workable plan. Once that was in place they could coordinate any action with the Pershmerga.

He was still thinking of all the things that could go wrong as he caught his first glimpse of Kurdistan as the plane descended. It was a remarkably green country, he thought, very reminiscent of Scotland, and like Scotland in the winter the surrounding peaks had a heavy frosting of snow. It was a complete contrast to the dirt and dust of the Baghdad skyline. It all looked so calm and tranquil in comparison. It was somehow hard to imagine that only ninety kilometres to the west of where they were landing was the sizable Iraqi town of Mosul in the grip of the Islamic State. Danny's mind turned to the hostage, what was he thinking now, what condition was he in, was he aware of the extra danger he was in?

Don't worry son, we will get you out, he thought.

The Lear Jet touched down and taxied towards the area of the airport reserved for VIP and military flights. As the plane stopped and the cabin crew started to prepare the door for disembarkation, a small convoy of vehicles drove towards the plane. Sir Ian's security team arrived in three white armoured Land Cruisers. Tommy Talibani's silver Lexus followed them with Tommy driving and Ahmad in the passenger seat. The whole entourage was shepherded front and rear by two airport security vehicles. *This guy travels in style,* thought Danny. As Sir Ian descended the steps he was swiftly guided towards his car by his security team and spirited away.

Danny lifted his grip and the small rucksack that he had brought for Jimmy from London and descended the steps of the aircraft. He was met by Ahmad who was standing by the silver Lexus. He extended his hand in welcome and swiftly introduced his cousin Tommy.

"Danny, this is Tommy Talibani from the Kurdish intelligence service, we grew up together in London."

"Hi, Danny, welcome to Kurdistan, mate," said Tommy in his heavy cockney accent.

"I am very pleased to meet you, Tommy. I have heard a lot about you."

"I have heard some good stuff about you as well, mate, and I am very impressed with your team."

Danny opened the rear door of the Lexus and slid into the

rear seat, carefully placing the black backpack alongside him. He threw the grip into the rear of the vehicle. The door slammed as Tommy drove towards the terminal.

"We will get your paperwork done on the way home Danny, there's no time now, because, mate, me and your guys are going to dish out some payback to the Daesh very soon."

Danny noticed that Tommy used the Arabic and more derogatory term for ISIS.

"Because in forty-eight hours' time I will be rolling into Mosul and kicking some serious Daesh-bag arse."

Danny thought of all the repercussions of Tommy's statement. His team had just two short days to plan and implement the extraction if they wanted to take advantage of the Pershmerga attack. Tommy and Ahmad took the time it took to drive from the airport to explain the progress being made.

He firstly explained that the laptops had been activated but not used. He thought that Mosul was not their intended final destination, perhaps it was Raqqa, in which case they could still end up even more useful when they did finally start transmitting. This had been a major setback but not a total disaster because they still had one asset in the area who had not only been able to locate the hostage holding house, but was also in a position to place a locater device to give the team a precise lock-on. Jimmy's work with the laptops had also already paid its way; the London end of ISIS's operation had been breached and was already feeding vital information on their whole London fundraising set up.

The team also now had an accurate grid and description of the target house, and had implemented the research phase of the operation. Sam and the team had furnished a long list of items that needed to be purchased locally including Arabic clothing.

Ahmad summarised, "In short, Danny, it looks like your team is good to go."

Danny smiled and replied, "Yeah, it is better than we could have hoped, the last team members should arrive this afternoon."

Tommy then carried on the quick debrief. "As far as my guys are concerned, we are to launch a diversionary attack on the main ISIS checkpoint outside Mosul at Dawn on Friday."

Tommy paused for effect. "We will be able to cooperate with you in any operation you might mount then, but this timing is not flexible as it's supporting actions elsewhere on the Syrian front. I can't change the timings, so it's a one-shot deal"

Danny looked pensive. "OK, Tommy, at least we know where we stand."

At that point the Lexus arrived at the first checkpoint before the Claymore House. The barrier lifted and the car pulled up outside the gate.

"OK Danny, we will be in touch if anything else happens. I have an urgent meeting with Tim now. Let me know when Sam is going to give operational orders, I want to be there if possible"

"I need to be there as well," added Tommy as he hit the release button for the rear door. "See you later, mate."

Danny retrieved his grip from the rear of the Lexus and carefully lifted the black rucksack containing Jimmy's present.

"See you later, guys," said Danny, as he made his way to the front door of the house.

Sam had heard the doorbell and heard Danny's cheery voice in the hallway. She was showered and dressed and still pouring over the detail of the developing plan. She felt tired and physically drained, as she had suffered yet another sleepless night. The awesome weight of responsibility seemed to be sapping her of her confidence. She had stayed up until the early hours of the morning, planning and re-planning. Making initial assessments, adjusting them, thinking again, and then discounting them. Each phase of the plan threw up more problems than answers. She realised that any plan she had put together before was devoted to subterfuge and generally keeping out of trouble. The planning process only covered offensive action in case of compromise but this was a different ball-game completely; they were actually going in close and personal, people were going to die, and she did not intend that it would be her guys. When she finally dozed off, fully clothed on the top of her bed, she had also realised that her relationship with Taff had changed.

She had initially tried to distance herself from the deep feelings that she had slowly felt developing, the tingle in the pit of her stomach as she brushed past him. The time she spent just looking at him hoping to catch his eye. These feelings now seemed to lie at the very core of her being and Sam was beginning to realise that she loved him very deeply. She had also realised the negative effects of this, and how it could affect the team; she had realised that she had developed an almost primeval urge to protect him.

She therefore found that she had tendency to completely block out those feelings. She now could not even share the usual moments of shared comradeship with him that she so valued. She had lain awake on her bed in a restless frisson of sexual tension, feeling it slowly grow within herself, knowing that he was in the room next door. Her inner feelings of loving need had in turn triggered quite graphic thoughts and desires, all of which were far from comradely. She had really never felt like this about anybody, she found herself thinking about Taff more and more, it was not just love; the cocktail of feelings was increasingly being laced with good, old-fashioned lust. As Sam descended the stairs she resolved to try and park this stuff until she got this job over with. They both had to be on top of their game over the next forty-eight hours.

As Danny entered the house, he recognised a scene he had witnessed a hundred times during his army service, British soldiers preparing for a scrap. As each team member busily occupied themselves about their allotted tasks and their individual piece of the plan. Sam beamed a smile as she seen her old mentor walk through the door, she knew that some of the pressure was off her now. Danny embraced Sam in a fatherly hug. "Hi Sam, how's it going?"

"It's good, Danny, we are just treading water trying to keep up with developments, but we think we have the bones of a plan," she replied.

"I am really pleased to hear that Sam because the goalposts have just moved again. I have just chatted with Mr. Talibani and our Box and Six mates, Tim and Ahmad — you will need to get all the guys together for an update, we need to go on Friday morning if we want to save this lad."

Danny surveyed the scene; the whole house was covered in kit and equipment that was slowly beginning to be packed, repacked and adjusted. Pat and Scottie were preparing the weapons for a trip to the firing range at the Pershmerga camp. Each weapon came with its individual sighting system that had to be zeroed to the individual. Taff was preparing small door charges from the ECT (Explosive Cutting Tape), carefully cutting the pieces of foam padded explosive into eight-inch lengths, wiring them up and then stowing them carefully away in a canvas bag.

Jimmy was assembling the body armour, inserting the high velocity plates into the special compartments at the front and the rear. The HV plates were the latest type and were made of a lightweight, polymer-type composite material.

"Here you go, Jimmy, a new toy for you, compliments of the British Army. Please do not break it."

"Excellent," said Jimmy. "I didn't think it would get here on time, this will make things so much easier."

Jimmy carefully unpacked the bag and removed a tan light canvas pouch designed to hang around the operator's neck. Jimmy placed the equipment around his neck, he flicked some press-studs with both thumbs and the front dropped down and opened suspended on two canvas straps to reveal a small tablet computer. Danny watched seemingly fascinated as Jimmy checked the equipment, removed the light brown control unit and switched it on.

"Watch this," he said as he opened the front door and moved

through it into the main courtyard of the house with Danny and Sam immediately following in his wake.

"We should have enough battery for a demo," he said, as he checked the power level light. He held the control module in his left hand, which looked pretty much like any gaming type piece of kit. He then reached into one of the other two pouches to the left-hand side of the tablet display, pulled the press-stud that clicked forward to reveal a small grey-black Nano-helicopter, a literally tiny piece of kit that was about the same size as a small sparrow.

"This is the business end of the system, it has three different cameras at the front, including a thermal imaging one for night."

Jimmy turned the front of the tiny drone towards Danny and Sam and continued, "Each one has the resolution to pick out really minute detail. It flies pretty much like a small helicopter, with one important difference — it's very quiet and it's designed to be hard to see. The whole drone weighs only 18 grams and it will fly through almost any weather."

Jimmy held the tiny, toy-like drone until its rotors started to hum and then released it from his forefinger and thumb, gently tossing it into the air, much like he was releasing a small bird back into the wild. The small craft soared high over the house and then soundlessly hovered with Jimmy making small adjustments with his thumb on the joystick.

"You cannot hear the rotors at all when the black hornet is at twenty feet, and look at the picture, it's high definition with amazing clarity."

Danny looked in fascination at the tablet's screen as he got an airborne view of Claymore house.

Jimmy then took the tiny drone on an airborne reconnaissance of the house, visiting each door and window in turn. He hovered the craft momentarily at each.

Danny could see through the front room window. Both Pat and Scotty were busily packing kit and weapons for their trip to the range, oblivious to the little drone within spitting distance of the window.

"That's pretty amazing technology," said Danny.

Sam was also extremely impressed, when they had last seen hand launched drones used in Helmand they were more like quite large toy aircraft and they were generally used on IED clearance operations or route clearances. They also could not hover and they were noisy and easy to see.

Jimmy continued. "Because of its manoeuvrability and its size, you can effectively do a very detailed CTR (Close Target Recce) of anywhere remotely without putting anybody in harm's way."

"What's it limitations, Jimmy?" Sam said. Sam knew that new technology always had problems and limitations.

Jimmy answered Sam while pressing a single button on the remote control that recalled the drone to its original launch site. As the tiny, fragile-looking Black Hornet obediently retraced its route back to its launcher, he turned and looked at Sam over his shoulder and answered, "The main limitation is range and distance, you have to be in close to use this, maybe within three clicks. You only get twenty minutes on target, that means I will need to get within range tonight if we want to use this, kid. You need to get me to within two kilometres of the target and we need to do that tonight. We are also going to have to get a detailed look at the main ISIS checkpoint near the target house as well."

The small drone then returned to Jimmy's outstretched hand.

Danny turned to Sam and Jimmy. "If Jimmy and the guys are up for it, I will talk to Tommy Talibani and Ahmad and see if we can get the clearances and permissions to patrol forward tonight. We will need a good look at the target if we are going to launch the operation on Friday."

Jimmy looked at the tiny drone and chuckled. "Looks like we are going to do work tonight, little fella."

CHAPTER TWENTY SIX

THE MEETING

Danny had phoned Ahmad and quickly arranged a meeting with Tommy Talibani. He not only needed to arrange a reconnaissance patrol that required his complete support, but he also had an ulterior motive; he wanted to get to know him a bit more. After all, this was the man that held the fate of his guys in his hand. He knew that without Kurdish help the extraction was a non-starter, but he did not want the team's efforts to become a diversionary attack for the Pershmerga either. His team's lives were on the line and he needed to know that he could trust him.

Tommy arrived at Claymore House within the hour, this time dressed in sweat-stained and dusty US military combat dress, with a green patterned shemagh (scarf) wrapped around his neck. He wore his red Pershmerga SF beret and displayed the rank of Lt Colonel on his shoulder epaulettes. It almost seemed to be a different looking, more serious Tommy than the well-dressed Londoner he had previously met. He had left his body armour and weapons with his driver but had obviously just returned from patrol.

Danny met him in the front courtyard, the team had just left to zero their weapons at the Pershmerga base and they were alone apart from the house staff and the guards. The two men shook hands.

The ever security conscious Danny furtively scanned the surrounding areas for any listening ears. "Let's walk towards the rear of the garden and chat. I do not really know how much English the staff understand, but it's best to be on the safe side." Once safely out of earshot and screened by the walled garden that skirted the property, a worried-looking Tommy explained his concerns.

"I have just got back from having a butchers at the forward Daesh positions…"

"And..?" Danny said.

Tommy carried on. "They are stronger than I thought, they have been reinforced. It looks like they are preparing themselves for a push against our positions."

Tommy looked around, seemingly scanning for listeners.

"Our sources tell us that they are preparing their usual signature tactic of a coordinated suicide bombing assault. They have four vehicles, including a truck, but they are just waiting for the brainless cannon fodder to arrive to drive them,"

Danny paused in thought then replied, "That could be a massive problem if they decide to attack at the same time as us."

"Yeah," said Tommy. "My guys are fairly well dug in and have fucked up several such attacks easily in the past. The last time they managed to take out the car-bombers with the Dushka (DShK, Russian heavy machine gun) as they left their lines. My main problem is the ultimate nightmare scenario of our assault being caught in the open by them, that could be a real cluster-fuck."

Danny paused and adopted his thoughtful pose; his chin cupped in his right hand. "I think we have some kit and people who can help you. We have two excellent pieces of equipment that will make things safer. Firstly we have a PD 100 Black Hornet surveillance system that can supply you with a live feed to check on the enemy and identify targets just before the attack. Secondly, we have a Barrett 50 Cal sniper rifle and a guy flying in who can use it. Our guys arriving in-country will probably be too late for the orders and rehearsals for the Op but they can join you and act as our liaison officers. What do you think?" Danny concluded.

"Excellent, fucking bang-on mate," Tommy replied enthusiastically. "I can't wait to start culling these Arab Daesh-fucks."

The response, with its racist undertones, quite shocked Danny. In the British Army you are of course always trying to kill the enemy but it's on a businesslike basis. And although sometimes hate had slowly crept into the equation, as it had to some in Northern Ireland and in the 'Ghan', it was never expressed quite like that.

"This is personal to you, isn't it, mate?" said Danny.

"Oh yeah, you bet," said Tommy.

Danny detected a flash of zealous hate in Tommy's eyes.

"It is ISIS now, but it was Saddam before, they are all the same fucking people."

"Arabs are Arabs, they can't help it."

"We have a Kurdish folk tale that we are told as children that sums it up. It's about a toad and a scorpion, want to hear it?"

"Yes of course, especially if it helps me understand," Danny replied with a smile.

"OK, there is a toad who is sitting on a hill after a flood just getting ready to swim to his house when a scorpion crawls up to him. 'Brother,' says the scorpion, 'Can you help me, I am far away from my home and if I try to get there I will drown. Can I get on your back as you swim across this water?'

The toad considers this for a minute and then says, 'Yes, I will help you, but remember that if you sting me, we will both die, because if you sting me you will surely be drowned.'

'I wouldn't be so stupid,' says the scorpion.

He then climbs on the toads back and starts to be taken safely to dry land. After they have gone halfway the scorpion deliberately stings the toad. The frog gasps in pain and says, 'Why did you do that, brother, we were nearly safely home and you gave me your word!'

The scorpion simply replies, 'I can't help it, I'm a scorpion.'"

Tommy looked at Danny. "The moral of the story is simple, thousands of years of fucking other people and their own over has ensured that you can never trust an Arab, and the West needs to learn this. We have been under the cosh from these fuckers for centuries, surrounded by them and used by them. Saladin from the famous Crusades was Kurdish, we were their strong back because they were such weak fuckers, and it hasn't changed much. We are still trying to carve out somewhere of our own to give us some distance, but the so-called liberal democratic West is too involved in the oil business with the people in Saudi, Qatar, and Turkey who jokingly actually finance these ISIS fuckers to do anything to help."

Danny was jarred by his frankness; Tommy's blatant mixture of racism and hate was a reminder that war in this part of the world is total and a no-holds-barred affair. He had known this reaction before, where hate slowly encroaches upon common humanity and finally snuffs it out like a candle flame. He had seen it in Kosovo, in Bosnia and in Ulster – you hate your enemy so much that you dehumanise them, and they become animals. It was totally wrong but also totally understandable, especially in such an animalistic struggle. ISIS had initiated it, he was sure that the Kurds would eventually finish it, but it would not be pretty, he thought.

Danny turned towards Tommy. "You don't think the West is doing enough to help, do you?"

Tommy smiled. "We've had many promises, some kit, a small British Army training team and some weapons, but we are still on our own, mate. We are losing young lads all the time, they cannot be replaced, we need more help. We will help you as best we can and try to kill as many of these fuckers while we do, like in all business in the Middle East," Tommy said gravely. "The enemy of my enemy is my friend. Added to that, Sir Ian has not only helped us as a nation through his oil industry investments but more importantly the guy who was snatched was working

166

with us. In short, Danny, we owe him, and a Kurd never forgets a friend. So what can I do for you and your guys?"

Danny pulled out a neatly folded map from the side pocket of his trousers and then knelt and picked a single blade of grass from the garden lawn. He then used the blade of grass to indicate a grid reference somewhere in Mosul. "I need to get some of my team to within three clicks of this place near the Grand Mosque."

Tommy looked at the map. "OK mate, this might be difficult at short notice but consider it done, I will make the arrangements. It will probably be the two Scott brothers, Talal and Mad Mo. They know the area like the backs of their hands and they often do a bit of recce stuff for us, they can lead them around the Daesh checkpoints. I will check and let Sam know the score when we have a jumping off time."

Tommy's mobile phone bleeped and he quickly checked his messages. "I have got to go now, old mate, there's a fucking war on here but you and your team are heartily welcome to our bit of it."

Tommy readjusted his dust-stained red beret and threw his shemagh back around his neck. He then extended his hand warmly towards Danny. The two men exchanged a quick look and then smiled almost simultaneously; they understood each other. As Tommy made his way back to his car Danny quietly reflected on the meeting. His long experience of working with both the frailty and strengths of human nature had finely honed his interpersonal skills. He could almost instantaneously detect deceit. It was a valuable and essential skill that he had developed over twenty-five years of agent handling from Belfast to Kabul. It had kept him safe, and he had now made another assessment: Tommy Talibani was, without doubt, a man he and his team could trust.

Jimmy had two hours to prepare for the patrol. Taff would be his backup and the Scott brothers would get him to within working distance of the target. They would be properly Hajiedup. Orders were a hasty affair, just a cursory look at a possible route on Google maps, some ERVs (Emergency Rendezvous points) pulled off the map, and the allocation of arms and ammunition along with some discussion of the correct 'Actions On' in the event of compromise and on the target location. Sam had been unhappy with the very short notice, but had understood the urgency and need to compromise on preparation to use the Black Hornet operationally.

Talal and Mad Mo arrived at the house driving a black, dusty and very beaten-up looking Toyota Land Cruiser. Talal quickly dismounted and opened both passenger doors and beamed a confident smile.

"Welcome to our new ride guys, recently confiscated from the Daesh. We have even got the black flag in the back. It looks beaten up but in really good mechanical order, apart from a little bit of blood on the back seat."

As Jimmy climbed into his seat he noticed a fresh smear of blood on the rear of the front passenger door.

"Not very hygienic," he said to Taff.

"Yeah, I have heard of quick recycling procedures but you guys have kicked the arse out of this one."

Mad Mo beamed a big smile from the front driver's side.

"Sorry, lads, no time, we only got this an hour ago with the previous occupant still in it. Tommy's guys slit his throat as he was sleeping on that back seat. It cheered the boss up though, as a 'Mad Millwall' supporter, as the sleeping shithead was a Brit and wearing a Luton Town strip under his ninja shit."

"Yeah," said Jimmy. "When you snooze, you fucking lose."

Both Scott brothers laughed. "I love Brit expressions, I must remember that one," Talal laughed. "But, hey guys, we have covered the rear seat in blankets as you'll notice, it shouldn't bother you too much. Here is another blanket to cover up your kit," continued Talal as he handed a brightly-coloured blanket to Taff from the front seat.

Taff laughed quietly when he read the bold Arabic script emblazoned across it. 'Iraq has a bright future', it said.

Those were the fucking days, he thought, *where hope ruled over logic and the Arab world.*

Taff placed his FN Minimi .556 machine gun with a 100-round box magazine attached beside him. It was a weapon he was familiar with, this version had first been developed for the US Special Forces and he had used it to great effect in Afghanistan. He patted it reassuringly as he checked the safety, he had only just zeroed it that day, and it was bang-on.

Jimmy had opted for the Colt M18 assault rifle with an adapted 100-round box mag attached. Both guys were also carrying Glock 23 pistols under their clothes and each had an MP5K machine pistol slung around them suspended on a bungee cord over their left shoulders. It was a reassuring reminder of the unwritten rule of their respective parent organisations: if you need to go armed, go fucking heavily armed.

In a separate bag was the chest rig for the Black Hornet containing the whole Nano PD 100 system. Jimmy had worked hard to readjust its parameters, and he now thought he had probably increased the battery life to nearly double the range. *We will soon find out tonight*, he thought. He only had two heli-drones, so he would get two chances to get it right. He might also have to use the kit to check on ISIS movements and locations on their route.

Jimmy knew their normal operating procedures; they minimised movement on the roads in the day because of the deadly combination of US air surveillance and aircraft. Any permanent, or semi-permanent checkpoints were sited in the midst of civilian areas for obvious reasons. ISIS generally either patrolled in four-cab Toyotas or Fords mounted with ZPU-2s. The Iraqi Army generously donated the Fords as they fled Mosul along with hundreds of US armoured Humvees. The ZPU-2 is a highly effective 12.6 mm Russian made heavy machine gun, which was really meant for use in the anti-aircraft role, which meant that it could rip a vehicle to shreds in seconds.

Mo turned around from the driver's seat and said, "The fun starts here, guys."

The Toyota pulled away from Erbil towards Highway 1 and Mosul. Taff half opened the window to try and flush away the acrid smell of petrol and blood. *Thank God it isn't the height of summer*, he thought.

The usual mixture of local traffic lessened and the tension increased as they drove towards the Islamic Caliphate. The vehicle was waved through several Pershmerga checkpoints after Talal muttered some Kurdish into his handheld radio and received the appropriate reply. Taff assumed that they used a simple password combination.

Taff had worked in and around Mosul with the SRR; it was a difficult place to blend in then, and possibly a lot worse now. It used to be a fairly integrated city of two million souls. It spanned both sides of the Tigress. Al Mawsil in Arabic literally translated is Junction City. It was then a city that was once considered a successful melting pot between Iraq's intersecting religious beliefs and cultures, now with ISIS in control the Christians and Shia and Kurds had fled and only one million inhabitants remained.

As the Land Cruiser moved along the road towards Kalak on Highway 80, the terrain subtly changed from a sort of desert plateau to a barren alluvial steppe. Although the winter rains had coloured the roadway green with a variety of grass types and shrubs, it was rugged country. Sharp hills and mountain ridges jaggedly broke the almost level terrain, presenting an almost lunar landscape in appearance. Pershmerga key-points were silhouetted against the greying sky on these higher pieces of ground. Each loosely sandbagged position displayed a proudly fluttering Kurdish flag.

This barren wilderness had very recently been a fiercely

disputed front line, where a victorious ISIS had met and been fought to a standstill by the solid brave fighters of the Pershmerga. The refuse of war littered the landscape in between indicating a recent, very intense, and bloody battlefield. A black painted ISIS Toyota, a remnant of recent fighting, rested on its side. A black-garbed figure hung unceremoniously from the passenger window, it had been there sometime and swarm of crows circled at what remained. Such a site is unusual in an Islamic country, where the dead are gathered and laid to rest almost immediately; it signified the level of hate in the conflict. There was no mercy now on either side, ISIS had beheaded Kurdish women fighters and now the Kurds considered them as only black carrion crows themselves. The sights on the road seemed to mirror the Kurdish people's current struggle against ISIS. It was as the battle and battlefield had become, it was unrelenting and unforgiving.

Talal turned towards the guys in the back. "OK lads, this is our final checkpoint. We will wait here until we get a call on the route ahead from our sources, that will help us stay out of trouble."

The car slowed as it negotiated the chicane of low concrete barriers that started at about one hundred metres out from the permanent Pershmerga VCP (Vehicle Check Point). There was an uncomfortable moment as the Kurdish gunner of a British donated GPMG (General Purpose Machine Gun) mounted on the circular swing cradle of an armoured Humvee swung towards them.

He was a youngish guy who looked barely eighteen, but he levelled the machinegun towards the Toyota's windscreen with practiced ease. *Young guys are always the most unpredictable on the battlefield,* thought Taff; *they could be brave but also very fucking stupid.* The tension dissipated as the young man's face burst into toothy grin as he recognised Talal and Mad Mo.

"Baba Talal! Baba Mo!" he shouted.

Talal shouted back in Kurdish and then explained. "This guy

is my young nephew Tariq. He has been on the front line for two years now, my sister worries me stupid about him."

Both the brothers simultaneously left the vehicle for an affectionate reunion.

"Fuck me, these two have relatives everywhere!" Taff muttered quietly to Jimmy.

"Yeah, there must be an entire Scots-Kurdish Clan hidden over here," Jimmy said with a smile.

"Yeah, probably all Millwall supporters as well," Taff said with a chuckle.

"Yeah, Jock Millwall supporters, now that's a scary thought bruv," said Jimmy.

The checkpoint was the last permanently manned Pershmerga position before the front-line got a bit messy. It marked the furthest ISIS incursions into Kurdish territory before a mixture of US airpower and Pershmerga determination brought it to a bloody end. It consisted of a detachment of four US made armoured Humvees and two dug in and sandbagged emplacements on the high ground either side of the main road. On each of the defensive positions, two of the awesome ZPU-4 four barrelled anti-aircraft guns were silhouetted against the milky evening sun.

A long anti-tank trench was dug all around the position to protect against possible suicide attack and coils of barbed wire protected the slopes. The road ahead was also protected by a chicane of low concrete security barriers to ensure that the oncoming traffic slowed enough to check the occupant's identity and intent. Suicide bombing was the primary rue de guerre of the Islamic State and they had no shortage of volunteers to gain their prised place in Jannah, or paradise.

Taff was well aware from his Helmand days of the lightning calculations and instant decisions the defending machine gunner had to make as he scanned the approaching traffic weaving through the chicane towards him. Was anything unusual about the vehicle? Did it seem unduly heavy on its wheels? What was the attitude of the driver? Two large craters at the epicentre of what looked like huge explosions demonstrated their ability to detect such vehicles. What looked like the engine block of a very large truck lay upright and stuck into the ground about fifty metres from the crater. It was stuck, implanted in the ground at a strange angle, *like some weird piece of modern art*, thought Taff. Sam had once tried to drag him around some poncy modern art thing at the South Bank when they were doing a surveillance serial in London for the SRR. He was worried about Sam, she had been a bit distracted lately and not her usually cool professional self. He briefly wondered what Sam was doing now.

Chapter Twenty Seven

Eve of Battle

Sam was worried; everything was going at a pace now that was almost out of control. She had hated the idea of the last minute arrangements made to take Taff and Jimmy on the CTR. *It was the sort of plan that could have been written on the back of a fag packet,* she thought. It went against her highly honed sense of risk management, but she also knew that if a risk could not be planned out, removed or at least minimised, then it had to be accepted.

In this case the acceptance of risk was a bitter pill to swallow as it included Taff. Sam had increasingly begun to realise that she had really fallen in love with him. She also realised, as the boss that this was not an ideal time for this to happen. Sam knew, in the final analysis it was going to be the combination of her plan and the teams joint decisions and performance on the ground that would lead to either success or failure; to life or death. At the end of the Op, they would all be on the airplane celebrating in forty-eight hours' time or they would be dead, or at least mourning the loss of a friend, or in Sam's case, a loved one. It is a strange feeling known to all soldiers on the start-line. That time before action when you have to finally internalise and deal with that fear of death. You had to almost wrestle with it, to mould it to your will, in order to control it. They had all done it many times, but it never got any easier.

Ninety miles away at the ISIS death house, the now solitary

174

hostage tried to come to terms with his own chances of survival. Connor had now just about given up hope of any rescue. He felt vulnerable, lonely and abandoned. He had detected a change in attitude from the guards. There was still the taunting and the puerile, almost childish verbal abuse, but there was also a new element, they seemed more wary of him. The skinny little Brit had still pissed in his rice bowl that morning but he had made sure that he had two other guards with him. Something was happening but he didn't really know what.

There was a subtle change in the dynamics going on; the atmosphere seemed tenser, a new edge had appeared. Connor sensed that they knew more about him and were changing their plans accordingly. They now checked on him more frequently, a different guard every about half-hour. Connor assessed the timing by counting the seconds and then the minutes. He needed to work out if there was a pattern to their visits. The timings seemed consistent, every half hour with a difference of up to two minutes. That gave him about twenty-eight minutes to minutely explore his immediate environment. How secure were the window bars, how secure was the quite dilapidated looking door and ancient lock? How secure was the thick chain tethered to the wall?

He once again started thinking of escape, and of possible death, he wasn't finished yet. He must take his fear of death and shape it into a weapon. He had heard the baying of the crowd from what he thought might have been a beheading the evening before; it focused his mind. He needed to keep himself strong. He started to mentally rehearse how he could hurt them most. If he was to die, it would not be seen on YouTube, it would be very messy and not very photogenic, and perhaps one, or maybe two of these little fuckers would die with him. He would not let these fuckers use him as part of their evil propaganda. He would not let his friends, family or fellow Americans see a cowed hostage meekly submit to the knife. He thought briefly of the father he had not seen since he left, the only summer that he could remember being with him was that long, blissful one at the family house in the Hamptons before the divorce.

A smile briefly flashed across his face as he remembered that he was once loved and cared for. Where the fuck did things start to go wrong? His father was apparently some big-shot business guy then. He had sort of given up and left him with his very rich, but hopelessly alcoholic mother that had managed to drink herself to death in just five short years after that. He wondered whether his father ever really thought about him. Would he mourn him? Would he be proud of him?

Sir Ian was once again thinking about his son; he was in an almost melancholy mood. He felt no closer to the action even after his move to Kurdistan. He had used all his considerable influence to ask for assistance but that was just about all he could do.

Danny had given him regular calls and the London end of Hedges and Fisher had sent him an almost constant and continuous stream of intelligence updates. He was almost certain now that the scum that called itself ISIS, or at least the London end of it suspected or even knew his son's true identity, he was fully aware of the implications of that. Mullah Rahman was now banged up in Belmarsh High Security Prison in breach of his bail conditions on a previous conviction of incitement to terrorism.

Tim from M16 had acted promptly to protect Connor but could not say whether he had been able to send his message by some other means. The bugged computer had at least given the team some time and breathing space. Sir Ian knew though that if certain Arab media outlets in London suspected who his son's true employer was, then sooner or later the evil bastards who were holding him would find out.

Danny had told him that they would know if a hostage rescue was a realistic possibility within twelve hours and if so, the operation would go in within twelve after that. Would his flesh and blood last another twenty-four? He was a powerful man who had expended all the influence and power he could muster. He now felt almost helpless. He knew that the fate of his boy rested firmly in the hands of the Hedges and Fisher team. He also knew all about military operations; he had been in his share of them and was nearly killed in a few.

It was a simple equation but a difficult one to get right. You needed brave people at the right time, combined with unbreakable resolve and a simple workable plan, and more than your fair share of stupid, dumb-arse luck. The dice had left the shaker; the cards were dealt; now all he could do was wait and pray

CHAPTER TWENTY EIGHT

THE KALAK CHECKPOINT

The Kalak checkpoint was quiet as the guards took time to pray. Big Talal and Mad Mo lifted their prayer mats from the rear of the vehicle and both nodded to Taff and Jimmy as Talal casually said,

"Just going to check in with the 'Big 'Un', as Billy Connolly would say."

Both guys turned and joined the rest of the guard force in prayer as if it was the most natural thing in the world. Taff knew that it was a common held belief throughout the spectrum of Islam that shared prayers are more powerful than single ones, they sort of delivered a more powerful signal and therefore delivered more bang for the buck.

A sort of eerie silence descended on the checkpoint as everything stopped for prayers, with only the MG positions still manned.

It was a bit of a surprise to Taff, he did not consider either of them particularly religious. The laughing and joking of the half-Scottish brother had seemed to mask their faith in their own particular brand of Islam. It was a more considerate and gentle form, *but no less devout in devotion or faith,* thought Taff. Anyway, didn't the padres say that you get don't get many atheists in the forward trenches? Anyway, it was a dodgy operation and maybe they could use any help they could, practical or divine.

Taff and Jimmy prepped and checked their kit instead. Jimmy

checked that all the battery levels on the Black Hornet PD 100 were at optimal levels. Taff carefully primed the six grenades they had brought to the party. He removed and prepared the claymore mine he had also brought along and then replaced it back into its green canvas shoulder bag. He thought they might need it to cover the team bugging out. A well-placed claymore was ideal for slowing up pursuing troops. Seven hundred ball bearings coming explosively your way could be a serious deterrent to pursuit.

Talal and Mo returned to the vehicle and started to do their final preparations. They had both modified AK 47s, short stocky weapons of the type issued to Russian paratroopers. Each had fitted a circular 100-round box magazine, they looked a bit like the type you would get on a tommy gun in Al Capone's Chicago. They cocked their weapons and applied the side safety lever.

They removed their Glock pistols from their belt holsters, easing back the slide to check for the glint of brass that told them that they were ready to go. As the guys prepared their kit, Taff noticed that the crews of two of the Humvees also were also preparing their weapons. Talal then visited each tyre on the Toyota in turn to deflate them slightly. Both operators knew that this procedure was to ensure that extra bit of purchase on the four-wheel drive if they suddenly had to go off-road.

"Right guys," said Talal very casually. "This sort of trip is a regular gig for us. We will get you to within two clicks of the target but this is the best way to do it. In about ten minutes, a local guide with all the relevant ISIS paperwork will arrive here. We use him often and he has never let us down. He will be driving a white Toyota Corolla and he will front us into Mosul, and report back on ISIS movements via ICOM. The two Humvees go next to take care of their usual business of taking the Daesh-bags out, and we bring up the rear and try to skirt around any obstacles or contacts with the enemy. Any questions?" he said, looking at Taff and Jimmy.

"No it sounds pretty workable and straightforward. We will

need to access some sort of compound or cover for me, to operate the PD 100."

Talil smiled. "No problems, we can do that, thanks to these Daesh shitheads the majority of what used to be the Mosul Christian quarter is empty."

Taff's danger hackles sort of clicked in. "Are we going to talk about some sort of anti-ambush drills or action on contact?" he said.

Talal laughed. "We will just do what we usually do, get out of the car and shoot the fuckers. I will work with Mo, you work with Jimmy."

Taff was sort of satisfied with that; a simple action-on is sometimes the best. "Roger that," he said.

"Roger that," Jimmy said.

At that moment, Talal's phone rang and was quickly answered. A brief conversation in Arabic ensued. "Let's mount up, our guy is five minutes out. And get sorted, you will need these when we get to Mosul, guys," he said, throwing them two large black abaya garments with their accompanying niqab face veils. "You two will be the two ugliest women in Mosul," he said with a chuckle.

Taff and Jimmy placed the clothes next to them on the back seat.

The engines of the two Humvees burst into life and smoothly rolled out through the chicane and onto the road in front of the checkpoint. Talal's young cousin was again mounted as the gunner, manning his GPMG and scanning towards the front to cover the motorway and the high ground to the west. The other Humvee, armed with a US Army donated 50-caliber Browning heavy machine gun, similarly scanned the other side of the road to the east. Both vehicles quickly responded and directed their firepower towards an approaching white-coloured Toyota saloon car. Talil rapidly picked up his handheld radio and said something is Kurdish.

"That's our guide, guys," he said casually to Taff and Jimmy over his left shoulder. "This guy is really reliable — he is a tribal leader and his people have lived in Mosul for centuries. He leads a Sunni resistance group. He has all the right ISIS passes and connections to go through their checkpoints. He has worked for the Americans against Al Qaeda and now he works with Tommy and his guys. He will stay in his car, he does not want to advertise his presence."

The white Toyota stopped 100 metres short of the checkpoint, flashed its lights once and performed a slow three-point turn and then immediately started to drive towards Mosul and Highway One.

Talal delivered a quick brief. "Right guys, here's what's happening. Our friend will scout us in, the Humvees will follow to attack any ISIS patrols on the roads scouted by our friend from Mosul, and we will make sure that we can roll off the road to avoid any trouble. Any questions?" he finished.

"No, we are good to go," said Taff.

"Roger that," said Jimmy.

The two Humvees appeared to give the scout car about a ten-minute lead and then slowly began rolling towards Mosul. Taff noticed they kept a decent space between the vehicles and he watched in professional appreciation as the drivers rotated their weapons with synchronised precision, covering possible ambush points until both fighting vehicles became small dust clouds on the horizon.

"These guys know what they are doing," he said to Jimmy.

Talal turned from the front seat. "They should do Taff, they do it every day. This is the way they control the road."

Talal picked up his AK, checked the safety and placed it cradled on his lap. He then placed a light shemagh scarf over its bulky 100-round drum mag.

"To them, today is no different than any other day." He then turned towards his brother. "OK Mo, let's go, bro, let's hunt some Daesh."

Mo gunned the Lexus and the mission had begun.

Taff was momentarily lost in thought, *How will this turn out?* he thought. This was not something that he had not done before in the Marines or the Army but the stakes were higher now. It was now, as they say, 'shit or bust'.

Chapter Twenty Nine

ISIS Patrol

The Land Cruiser made good progress towards Mosul. Taff had always been quite impressed with the Iraqi road system. He knew it had been loosely copied from the American system after one of Saddam Hussein's early diplomatic visits to the States. Highway 80 was one of the main feeder routes into a web of fast highways that spread across the country. These highways had so far very much favoured the Daesh, whose unique combination of fast moving vehicles packed with fanatical fighters, combined with the use of multiple suicide car bomb assaults, had thoroughly demoralised a poorly trained Iraqi Army.

Taff had worked with the Iraqi Army before. It was a strange set-up. Some of their Commando and Special Forces units were really good, but as a general rule the regular Army was split along ethnic lines, with the Sunni troops unwilling to fight their own people and the Shia battalions totally unwilling to fight in what they considered foreign Sunni areas. It was a sad fact, he thought, that since the US invasion and the waste of billions of dollars of training money, a decent, fairly well commanded (by Middle Eastern standards), and secular army was riven with religious hatred and was a shadow of its former self.

During the speedy approach, the Land Cruiser only slowed to negotiate recent wreckage on the road. Some of this was from conflict. On one occasion they passed a burnt-out T72 Russian-made Iraqi Army main battle tank, whose turret laid upside down in the dust at a weird angle some ten metres from the rest of the charred hulk. Crudely scrawled Arabic script proudly proclaimed it as belonging to the Islamic State. A neat entry hole could be detected through the side of the armour just below where the turret had once been attached. It looked like a missile strike, probably an F16. *No one survived that one,* thought Taff.

Another wreck told a more tragic story, what seemed like a family car, a Toyota Camry, was intermeshed and seemingly fused with a cement lorry. The speed and ferocity of the smash was so intense that it was almost hard to see where one vehicle stopped and another started. Both had burnt out. Taff had seen this before, a heart-breaking sight. As if to emphasise the waste, a solitary broken little girl's doll lay twisted, broken, and dirt-covered, to the side of the road. He had once bought his daughter a similar present. It seemed a grim and fitting testament to Iraqi standards of road safety. Taff earnestly hoped that the small owner had survived, but he knew that this was just hope — kids were never strapped in. Iraqi men in general consider both safety precautions and seatbelts effete. They always used the risk management system of Inshallah. Taff was familiar with the concept: if it happened, then God willed it.

The four-by-four made good progress towards Mosul. The last downpour had been burnt off from the sun and now the rear wheels produced a cloud of uniquely fine Iraqi dust as they spun further towards danger. Both the Scott brothers had become tenser and more careful the closer they came to their enemy. The Kurdish music had been turned off, and instead Talil constantly monitored his handheld radio and mobile phone.

The battered black Toyota stopped at irregular intervals along the route to listen into both. Talil turned to explain, "It looks like our guy has reported back on some ISIS troop movements up front. We are going to pull over and wait for a while to see what the enemy is doing before we run into them."

Taff checked his GPS. *Getting closer,* he thought, but the team were still at least fifteen clicks way from being able to deploy Jimmy's Hornet.

The four-by-four pulled off the road, the flattened tyres crunching against the gravel as Mad Mo sought the protection of a rather tatty-looking palm tree for some overhead cover. Big Talal then retrieved another piece of communications equipment from a bag at his feet. He quickly attached a large plastic aerial to a slightly longer ICOM radio and opened the front passenger window and held it aloft. The radio crackled into life with a range of Arabic voices reporting from different areas.

"This is one of their radios," said Talal with a grin, "it belonged to the Brit guy who went to sleep forever on the back seat. The Daesh have spotters all along this road and they use these radios, there is no cell phone signal here now. Once we get to the populated areas they will use a smartphone network systems like Snapchat and Yello."

Taff and Jimmy listened intently to the transmissions and could just about make out what was being said in the very guttural country Arabic of the area.

"The Kurdish pigs are coming towards you — get ready, brothers."

And then another voice, lighter in tone, maybe a boy. "They're in two Humvees, one heavy and one light machine-gun"

Talal looked around and smiled. "They think they are setting a trap for our guys, but they are the ones that are trapped. Once my guys upfront have fixed where they are, the US Air Force will fuck them."

Talal talked quickly into the Kurdish handheld and relayed instructions. Although Taff was fluent in Dari and Arabic, the Karmanji dialect they spoke, very rapidly, remained almost incomprehensible to him apart from the odd word. He did however sense the urgency of the transmission; he surmised that the Kurdish guys in front had just been told that they were heading for contact.

185

Almost instantaneously there was a loud WHOOSH-BANG. The unmistakable sound of an RPG exploding one kilometre away was swiftly followed by a heavy exchange of gunfire. Taff could see the distant tracer stitching across the sky, green from the Russian weapons sometimes interlaced with the bright red from the British GPMG and the US 50 Cal. Talal quickly exited the Toyota and placed a large orange marker panel on the dusty roof.

"We stay here, guys," he said to his passengers.

Within what seemed like a very tense, long minute, a new sound filled the air from the rear of their position. The distant roar of twin General Electric Turbo fan jet engines became louder as Taff observed the fast moving speck on the horizon materialise overhead as one of the US Army's most sturdy and reliable ground attack aircraft, the Grumman Warthog A10. It briefly seemed massive above them as it passed very low over their position.

"Here's the Kurdish Air Force," said Talal, with a laugh.

Almost instantaneously, the unmistakable sound of the A10s nose-mounted 30mm Avenger reverberated through the air. The bullets from the multi-barrelled Gatling type cannon were unleashed so fast that it made a sound like a madwoman wailing.

WAAHHHHHHHHhhhhhhhh!

WaHHHHHHHHHhhhhhhhhhh!

Another long rip of 30mm cannon wailed again.

"I wouldn't like to be on the receiving end of that," said Taff.

"A fucking big roger that, bruv," Jimmy replied.

"Let's go," said Talal, as Mo swiftly reversed the Toyota back onto the median and drove towards the sounds of the contact. "We are going to go around them while they are busy," he continued. "As soon as Mo gets to the right-hand track, we will leave the road and take the back route into town."

Mo slowed the Toyota to a crawl and engaged the four-wheel drive, carefully negotiating the drainage system that ran along the side of the road. Once over the concrete and gravel, the Toyota started to follow a small track that wound its way towards Mosul.

"Hold tight," said Mo, as the four-by-four lurched forward at speed.

Mo energetically wiggled the steering wheel to the left and to the right to try and maintain traction over the more muddy areas. Taff could tell he had done this before, *probably many times*, he thought. He always seemed to choose the correct line for the vehicle; that is a skill in cross-country driving learnt by experience and not by instruction. The Toyota slowly made its way onto the higher ground on the right hand side of the road, they made good progress over the harder alluvial plain, the four wheel drive system straining sometimes at its workload but always overcoming its difficulties.

Taff looked out the left hand passenger side window; two palls of black smoke billowed from the area of the A10 gun-run. Talal looked over his left shoulder and explained, "The smoke is what's left of an ISIS technical and a tank, that was the idea, it's an American one, it's called 'find, fix and fuck up'. The scout found them, the Pershmerga fixed them, and the A10 really fucked them up. With the help of the US airstrikes we are winning this war now."

The Toyota now seemed to be slowly making its way back to the road, slowly, sometimes very slowly, picking the best route down from the high ground and back towards the road. The quite warm sun had dried the ground and Mad Mo needed to minimise the dust that gently rose from the mixture of rock and gravel as they made their way back to rejoin the main route. The Toyota stopped by a small shepherd's hut surrounded by some sparse-looking trees.

"This is the final stop before the road, you need to put on the lady- kit guys," said Talal.

Taff and Jimmy dismounted and quickly helped each other Haji-up.

Both operators were very familiar with the correct way to wear them; they had used them many times. *Talal probably does not realise how often we've used this trick*, thought Taff. Jimmy had once spent a full week in Gaza dressed in exactly the same way.

All four guys then ran a final check on their comms and weapons. Jimmy removed the PD100 Black Hornet from its bag and again carefully checked the cameras and battery life. The little drone had three forward mounted cameras that provided amazing clarity as well as a night vision capacity. Jimmy looked at his toy almost lovingly; *this is why I love technology so much*, he thought. *Twenty years ago, a CTR (Close Target Recce) would have been very up-close and personal.*

Talal then turned towards the two passengers. "OK, good news and bad news guys, the good news is, that we here we have your official ISIS documents," he said, handing them some very faded and jaded-looking folded cards. "The bad news is, they are not very good and will not survive a proper inspection. In other words, if we are stopped prepare to debus and fight through." Talal smiled. "From here on in, we're on our own, another ten minutes once we have hit the road and we should be in range."

Taff quickly checked his GPS. "We have another five clicks before we can get set up, mate."

"Roger that," said Jimmy. "But the closer we get to the target the more time we have on task."

"Let's see how it goes," Taff replied.

The Toyota made its way tentatively towards the roadway with Mad Mo coaxing the best out of the four-wheel drive. It then drove along the median to find a convenient place to break onto the highway. They followed the deep drainage channel along the road until they came to a bomb crater, possibly caused by an IED. The Toyota climbed the scattered rocks and within a minute they were speeding towards Mosul.

As they approached the outskirts of Mosul they were met with the first signs of the city, family homes, mostly squat two-storey buildings with flat roofs. Some had a stairway up the side of the house for access to the roof. The houses were mostly red brick built covered in a dust-coloured plaster, they seemed mostly abandoned now and were showing signs of disrepair. The plaster had fallen away in clumps, revealing the dirty red brick or grey naked breezeblock. Some houses had been burnt out and were just roofless shells.

"This was a mixed Christian and Shia area," said Talal "These were mostly Christian families who could not pay the 'Zakat', or religious tax for infidels, so their houses were burnt. You can see the houses marked with an 'N' for Nazerine, or Christian. If they paid 400 dollars Zakat a month they could stay."

Talal then pointed to another house. "This house is marked with an 'R' for Rafadile or Rejecter, this was the house of a Shia Muslim, they usually were not so lucky and hundreds were killed. The Tigress was clogged with their bodies for weeks."

Taff scanned for activity through the black fog of his niqab; he wondered how women in this part of the world ever coped. The Toyota passed another burnt-out building in the shape of a Christian church. Taff noticed the large stone church cross had been removed from the roof and laid smashed in the gutter outside. He read the Arabic script raggedly scrawled across the Church door.

'Owned by the Islamic State', it simply stated.

He lifted the niqab and checked his GPS, four clicks, they were getting closer but the area was changing for the worse and they were now approaching the centre of the city. Taff had done surveillance serials here before with the SRR and knew that the Sunni areas of Mosul were always the more challenging. The traffic was building up with the normal rush for home before prayers. It was the usual mixture of Toyotas, Hyundais and Kias, sprinkled with the odd old BMW or Opel. The Toyota was then temporarily stopped in traffic.

"Don't worry," said Mo. "This is normal, probably an accident up front — our guy says there's no checkpoints."

As Taff turned in his seat to scan to his left, he grinned under his face covering. "Jimmy, check this out," he said quietly. "Nine o'clock to me, mate."

Pointing in the opposite direction was an almost identical, black, dusty, and battered black Toyota Land Cruiser. Not only was the car the same, but two guys of a similar build also drove it, and they had two black robed women in the back.

"Would you fucking Adam and Eve it," said Jimmy in his best Cockney accent. "Now that's fucking bizarre, you can't say we don't blend in old mate."

Talal giggled from the front seat. "Probably another British SAS Team." Talal lifted his finger and pointed to heaven in the 'One God, One Caliphate' gesture favoured by the faithful, and the driver of the other Black Toyota responded in kind.

"Probably just as ugly as our Brits," said Mo, the team chuckled quietly. With that comic moment over the traffic started to move again.

Taff checked his GPS, this time having to squint through the mask. "We are in range guys. Let's go firm, we need an LUP (Lay-up Position)."

Mo turned right before the main square onto a back road. Taff noticed the black ISIS flags fluttering slightly from the majority of the buildings. The back street was not crowded, but far from ideal. There were some civilians, mostly men dressed in winter clothing and the odd black-robed woman with her obligatory male relative.

Taff spotted a black-clad and masked ISIS guy swaggering along the street, lording it, and waving them out of his way. He had the regulation ninja kit on, with a long religious beard, no moustache and baldhead. He had a US M4 assault rifle slung casually slung across his shoulder. "Doesn't look too good here," he said, exaggerating his broad Welsh accent. "There's a guy there with a bad-ass looking rifle and his head on upside down."

Mo laughed quietly. "Don't worry, just up here is the edge of the old Christian area, it should still be within range."

Within 500 metres, it was like they had entered a ghost town. All the buildings had the 'N' scrawled across them. The Toyota stopped outside a semi-derelict compound with two large double steel doors. Talal opened his door and got out. "Stay here, guys — this looks good."

With that, he gently closed the car door and with remarkable agility for a guy his size, quickly jumped up and over the wall. Within seconds he had opened the double gates of the compound and Mo quickly drove in. "Don't worry guys, this happens all the time in this area. It's usually the locals looting the buildings, this should do the job."

Taff checked his GPS. "We are two clicks from the target, Jimmy."

"Fucking ideal," said Jimmy as he started unpacking the kit. "Let's try and find our mate Connor, then."

Chapter Thirty

Close Target Recce

Within a half a mile of where Jimmy was preparing to launch his toy, Imran was sipping tea, the last before evening prayers, and considering how he could carry out his instructions from his handler. Ahmad had asked him to try and place his iPhone against the wall of the hostage house, next to the Chechen checkpoint. He was to ensure that it had a full charge and that he had hit his emergency code before he did so. Ahmad obviously wanted to double-check on the position and description that Imran had supplied. He was then to get as far away from the phone as possible. It was an easy task; the only problem was staying alive while he did it and, more importantly, staying alive afterwards.

He thought about a rudimentary plan, he would wait until after last light and then see how close he could get to the holding centre without being challenged. He now knew the full implications of failure; Sayeed's hideous execution had clarified things in his mind. His brief stay in the caliphate had confirmed all the reasons why he had left in the first place. Under the banner of religion there were some fucking gangsters making money on the backs of others. The caliphate was a house of cards propped up by Saudi and Qatari money. Rich Arab states were using the poor people of Mosul in the front line of the their sectarian war against the Shia. Like the gangsters at home, it was the ordinary people getting on with their lives that suffered under them. The senior ISIS figures were the ones with the girls, the cars, and the Swiss bank accounts. *Fuck all ever changes*, he thought.

He would try to place his phone tonight and he would get back to safety, and London as soon as possible; Inshallah. He resolved then to make it his business to put these wankers out of business. He had allowed them to ruin his life; he would try to stop them doing the same to someone else. He did not want any young lad to carry around the guilt that he felt; he would try to find a way to atone for his sins. He felt a sense of purpose about his future now; he could make things right again; at least he vowed to try. Common sense told him that once he had confirmed the target house, a rescue would happen within the battery life of his phone. He wondered how they would get close enough, the house was crawling with Chechens, and he hoped they had a decent plan.

Ninety miles away at the Claymore house in Erbil, Sam looked around the room at the new team members; each guy was a well-known character on the Circuit. Danny sat next to her to deliver the official company welcome address and get them to sign the contracts. Eddy Warden had been the last to arrive and had already picked up and field stripped the Barrett 50 and was examining each part in turn. Eddy was in his fifties and had been a sniper since his successfully completing the sniper course at Commando Training Centre at Lympstone in the early eighties. He had a sort of affinity with the Barrett, because as the wing Sergeant Major, he had not only run the trails that led to the Royal Marines adopting it, but he had also nearly been tagged with it in South Armagh in the nineties. Fortunately the zero of the weapon was off and he survived. The crack and thump of a Barrett was a relief when you were the target, because if you heard it you had survived it. Many a British soldier didn't during that tour.

Mac McCallum had travelled the furthest, he had arrived exhausted from New Zealand, via Dubai. The hectic run-ashore with his mate Dave Dubois on the way in had not made the journey any less stressful, but was great craic. Mac, Scotty and Doc, the other new arrival, had been friends for almost twenty years. Mac had claimed one of the M4s as his own and was busy putting together his chest webbing. Doc was just Doc. Doc had been a mountain leader in the Corps and despite breaking most of his bones falling off numerous climbs, had survived them all, to develop a reputation for both loyalty and reliability. Doc had picked up a GPMG and had stripped and cleaned it. He was now examining each individual part for excessive wear and reassembling it. The four guys were a ready-made, tried and tested team, and had conducted many dodgy Ops between them.

Sam was dressed in jeans and a t-shirt, her long blonde hair had been tied in her usual ponytail and she wore her favourite pink flip-flops. Her bright blue eyes flashed in welcome as she looked at the guys who had arrived over the past twelve hours. Some of them looked pretty old compared to the young operators she had worked with in the past, but they all emanated a sort of quiet confidence that comes with at least twenty years of high-risk jobs on the Circuit. Sam realised that were not a lot of things that these guys had not seen, they had been involved at the very start in Iraq, they had seen the Iraqi's hopes for peace confused and crushed since the 2003 invasion, and since that they had all seen the same thing happen in Afghanistan. She wondered how they would react to having a woman team leader and quite a young one at that. She needn't have worried; all the new team had been briefed on her reputation, especially with the 'Angel of Death' tag line, they had been told of her capability.

"Guys, welcome to Kurdistan and this operation," she said. "I will hand you over to Danny soon," Sam paused, "but I must just let you know that this is a high-risk operation and a war-fighting rather than a security-based task. Your part of this gig is to be our guys with a full-scale Pershmerga assault, however the money and insurances correspond with the risk." Sam paused and looked at the new arrivals, they all sort of gave her that sort of 'no shit, Sherlock' type of look that told her they understood.

Eddie spoke. "Yeah, we have talked Sam and know this is a proper Commando raiding task, we have done it before and we can do it again, and we all have our reasons for being here."

Eddie laid the Barrett across his lap, its vast bulk made the armchair he was seated on look small. "It's not just about the money for me or any of these guys, it's about a chance to make a difference, to just get one person away from these ISIS wankers."

There was a general murmur of agreement from all the new arrivals.

Danny stood up to face the new operators. "Right, guys," he said. "If we are agreed, I have your contracts here for you to sign. The second part of the contract is a non-disclosure agreement," Danny paused, "basically, it says what happens in Kurdistan stays in Kurdistan. If you agree to the terms, sign the individual documents and you are part of the firm."

Danny handed the contracts to the guys who like true professionals read them from page to page before signing and returning them.

"Welcome to Hedges and Fisher," Danny simply said. "Let's go to work."

The light was beginning to fade in Mosul as the populace readied itself for the mournful evening call to prayer. Taff, Jimmy and the Scott brothers, had busied themselves checking and rechecking the equipment. The smell of blood from the back seat had become pungent and oppressive, and the guys now sat under a lone tattered tree by a wall at the side of the compound. The windows had been wound down to try to reduce the smell, but it hadn't worked and the smell clung on, the last significant reminder of the Jihadi football fan from Luton.

The inside of the house smelt worse, the once impressive, richly-decorated home had been left open to the elements and had also been used as a toilet by some of its recent visitors, who had appeared to have wiped their arses on the rich brocaded curtains that flapped aimlessly through the broken windows. That was probably the only reason that they were still there. Everything else, including carpets, furniture, and light fittings had been stripped out. It was therefore an ideal LUP, everything that could be stolen had been stolen, and therefore the chance of looters turning up while the guys were there had reduced. Taff noticed the mark on the wallpaper left by a heavy crucifix that had once proclaimed the family's religious allegiances to all.

Jimmy had prepared the PD 100 Black Hornet for its job; he just needed to get the optimum lack of light to make it more concealable in flight. He had decided to fly it at last light, after the call the prayer, when the chances of it being spotted would be less. The blackish-brown, mottled colouring of the tiny drone could make it almost invisible in the right light.

The call to prayer began, the mournful sound of, "Allahhhhhha-Akbar" drifting from Mosul's hundreds of minarets as the guys got ready for the launch. The two Scott brothers had put their godly devotions on hold, and now stood either side of the Toyota armed with their AKs, each with its distinctive drum magazine. Taff listened for activity in the street outside and then prised the steel double doors apart very slightly to check up and down the street. "Good to go," he whispered to Jimmy.

Jimmy placed the harness for the screen around his neck and adjusted the straps for comfort. He then flicked open two press-studs and the heads-up display screen lowered in front of him. He then lifted the tiny bird-like drone, powered it up and let it go. It buzzed as its rotors reached full power and climbed into the sky. At about thirty metres it stabilised itself before becoming very still, seemingly watching and waiting.

At that height it could barely be seen or heard. Jimmy tested the cameras, all were working, he then tapped in the co-ordinates of the hostage holding house and the small, very fragile-looking drone buzzed slightly as it made its way there. Jimmy looked at its progress on the screen; it showed deserted streets with only the occasional latecomer worriedly making their way to the nearest mosque. Non-compliance with religion had become a very painful experience under ISIS. The only people not at the mosque would be the ISIS 'religious police', accompanied by the women of the Al Khansa Brigade, charged with upholding the strictest adherence of Sharia law. The drone made its way over the near silent Mosul, Jimmy kept it at the optimum height over the streets at about thirty metres, he adjusted slightly for a light easterly-blowing wind as the Black Hornet closed with its target.

Within ten minutes, the large dome of Mosul's great mosque hove into view. The little drone looked down onto the main market square and Jimmy started to film. The square was still deserted, but Jimmy noticed that the three ZPU-4s protecting the square were still manned by some bored-looking ISIS fighters. He mentally logged the time, an ideal time to take them out without civilian collateral damage.

Jimmy touched the control to the right and the drone complied, there was the main ISIS checkpoint protecting the hostage holding prison. It appeared to be busy, the checkpoint was manned by a lot of fighters — some were praying but all the heavy weapons were manned. The drone carefully filmed some vehicles parked to the rear of the checkpoint: a couple of four-by-fours, one black and one white, Four-runners or Surfs by the look of them, and a medium-sized civilian flatbed truck, maybe a Daihatsu. Jimmy flew the little Hornet in close; it was packed with what appeared to be cement bags and was very heavy on its wheels. Jimmy guessed that this could be a heavy truck-bomb, the little drone tried to get in closer to look but Jimmy spotted an ISIS guard manning a ZPU suddenly look upwards straight towards the drone, with a sort of puzzled face appearing over his full religious beard. The drone was seemingly attracting attention; he froze the forward pitch and slowly made the small shape blend into the night sky by lifting it upwards.

Jimmy then moved the Black Hornet towards the prison. It was a large one-story building with a fully manned ZPU-4, four-barrelled heavy machine gun taking pride of place on its roof. Jimmy systematically flew the drone around the house, first from thirty metres all around and then from twenty. It was getting dark now and Jimmy switched to the thermal camera. The screen moved into an eerie green light as Jimmy moved the Hornet towards the doors and windows for a closer look.

The windows were covered with irregular steel bars; the doors seemed to be of sturdy construction. The double doors at the front seemed to be the main entrance; they were constructed of heavy oak and reinforced with what seemed like old-fashioned thick riveted iron. *Let's try and find our man,* thought Jimmy.

The PD 100 then systematically visited the barred windows in turn. He switched on the IR laser attached to the thermal camera that allowed him to actually see into the rooms of the prison. The ghostly glow revealed a group of praying figures in the main room by the big front doors. The drone was then directed to the next room where thick bars were firmly attached to the outside of the wall. The Black Hornet's invisible stab of infrared light pierced the gloom of the interior and focused on what appeared to be an old bloodstain on the wall. The camera moved slowly down the wall and there was Connor, cold, shivering, and huddled against the cold.

The prisoner's face turned towards Jimmy on the monitor. The hostage had seemed to sense a presence in the room and looked towards the window. What was that slight buzzing noise? *Maybe the bastards are filming me,* he thought.

He had feigned illness on the last of their visits, he would gather up every ounce of his strength to resist once the time came.

So be it, if they are getting ready to move me, then this is the start of it. Connor gritted his teeth and repeated the mantra that he had constantly mentally repeated. *No dishonour. Fight to the death. Fight to the death. Fight to the death.* He had made a plan. *One or two of these ISIS fuckers are going to die in this room, I have managed to prise this chain from the wall, I can pull it out any time.* He envisioned revenge. *It's a good weapon and I am going to batter or strangle that skinny little Brit fucker with it, and try to kill anyone else who tries to stop me. Tomorrow this shit stops here.*

Sam and Danny were mesmerised by the pictures that had been instantaneously transmitted to the TV monitor at Claymore House. The CTR had been a complete success; the technology had delivered beyond their expectations. They not only had the layout of the Chechen checkpoint, but they also knew their routine at last light, and they also knew what vehicles ISIS were preparing for their next planned attack. They would run checks on the vehicles the drone had identified, the two four-by-fours and the truck bomb. The Black Hornet had also identified all the doors and windows of the target house, which would help with setting the breaching charges. The best entry point seemed to be the small side door that offered some concealment from the main square; they knew how the door was secured, that it was not reinforced, and that it opened inwards.

Jimmy and his favourite toy had even managed to gain a positive ID of the client's son. Although bathed in the eerie green light of the night vision camera, and thrown into shadow by the IR torch, the hostage, half-cowed and seemingly collapsed against the bloodstained wall, was definitely Connor Cameron. Connor's face, clearly discernible behind a matted blond beard and long unkempt hair, was undoubtedly etched in suffering. Sam thought she had also seen something else though, a look of resolve, and also a sort of defiance in Connor's eyes.

"We are coming to get you, son," said Danny.

"Right, let's do orders for the rescue as soon as we have

debriefed Jimmy and Taff," said Sam. "I have just worked out how this can be done. It will have to be a simultaneous assault on the checkpoint timed with the hostage extraction, and I think our last chance is tomorrow at last light."

"Sounds like a very workable plan, Sam," Danny replied. "Let's get the troops together for a chinwag and crack on."

The leash constraining Danny and Sam's 'dogs of war' had loosened. The covert hostage extraction had by necessity morphed into a full Commando attack.

Sam felt sort of liberated, it was all so clear now. The only plan that would work would be the one that allowed the maximum application of controlled violence where it would hurt the enemy most. The countdown had begun, what they needed now was a way to take out the Chechen checkpoint at the start of the assault. *How would ISIS do it?* she mentally asked herself. *They would use a suicide bomber*, she subconsciously answered.

Chapter Thirty One

Plan of Attack

Sam had waited nervously for news of Taff and Jimmy's successful extraction from the CTR; she needn't have worried too much. Jimmy's little toy had clicked into its return to sender mode as soon as it's batteries were depleted, and had more or less flew into Jimmy's outstretched hand. The Scott brothers had then simply reversed the procedure of the insertion without the aid of the Pershmerga, and simply drove as fast as they could in their very smelly Toyota to the Kalak checkpoint and safety as the scout pronounced the road clear.

Talal had then surprised both of the Brits when he had produced a small hip flask of of whisky from the front glove compartment of the vehicle and announced a toast.

"Scottish and Kurdish by birth, British by law, and Highlander by the grace of God; death and confusion to the Daesh," he said, drinking a large slug of whisky. He then allowed the flask to be passed around the occupants. Mad Mo had two large gulps.

"We don't worry about drink driving out here, lads, it only improves Kurdish road manners," he laughed.

Talal continued, "It's haram to drink alcohol, the Mullahs say, but not when it's a decent Scottish single malt with my mates," he giggled.

Jimmy and Taff laughed. Both operators had worked with the best of the best in the SF world, and they knew that for cold, hard, calculated courage, the Kurdish Scott brothers were second to none.

Sam waited anxiously at the door of Claymore House. She knew the guys were safe, Tommy Talibani had called that in, but she had sought of felt a nagging void in her chest since Taff had been on the Op. She knew that this was unprofessional behaviour, but she didn't care. She had to hold herself in check, she had even inwardly plotted how she could actually leave Taff out of the Op all together, but as the burly form of Taff stepped down from the Toyota she knew that he would never allow it. She felt like just launching herself at him, kissing him, but she still had a job to do.

"Well done, guys," she greeted both operators. "Orders at 1400 hours for the main Op." She paused, "The other guys are here, so we have a full team."

Talal leaned out of the passenger side window. "You have a fuller team than usual, Sam, Tommy has just asked us to help you get back in."

Sam was impressed, she had intended to ask Tommy for the Scott brothers for the second insertion. "That's great, guys, I hear that you two know the way pretty well."

Talal laughed, "Yeah, you could say that," he said. "My Dad, ex-British Army, ran the bike shop in Mosul and had the franchise for Raleigh push bikes." He looked towards Taff and Jimmy. "We were less than a mile from his old shop today, lads," he said.

"You two coming in for a brew?" said Jimmy.

"No thanks, Jimmy, we have got to see Tommy. We will be back for orders."

With that the Toyota reversed and with a wave the guys left the compound.

The hallway to the house resembled a small military reunion as Jimmy and Taff met the rest of the guys. The constant buzz of conversation resounded about the house; unanswered and half-answered questions abounded.

"What did you do after that dust-up on Route Irish in Baggers, Doc?"

"I thought you'd got tagged in Sangin with Forty, Taff?"

"What happened to that job with CR (Control Risks) in Africa, mate?"

Once the conversations had partly subsided, Sam intervened. "Right, guys, let's chat about the job over a wet." Sam subconsciously used the Royal Marines term rather than the Army one, a brew. When she was growing up with her dad it had always been a wet.

"Danny and I need to pick your brains, guys, I have an idea of how this is going to work but need some advice on weapons systems and big bangs."

The extended team then moved as one, and seated themselves in the main lounge of the house. They were draped over the various pieces of furniture and equipment and faced towards where Sam and Danny were seated on the brown leather Chesterfield settee.

"Right, we need to synchronise the main attack on the Chechen checkpoint with a room entry to free the hostage. Both things have to be simultaneous if we hope to get Connor out alive. We must coordinate this between our two assault groups: Mac, Doc and Eddie with Jimmy working his magic with the Black Hornet, and the extraction group, which is me, Taff, Pat and Scottie."

Danny added a comment "What we need guys is a fucking big bang to start things off. ISIS would start such an attack with a suicide vehicle bombing, not suggesting that, but would it possible to remote one? Taff, you are Mr. Demolition, what do you think?"

Taff considered the question for a moment and answered,

"There's no control with a remote vehicle, if we are to get accuracy in the timings, somebody's got to push a button. Have we access to an armoured-type vehicle?" Taff queried.

"We could ask the Pershmerga," said Sam. "They might have a spare Humvee."

"That could be the answer," said Taff, "A sort of Trojan horse-type scenario — ISIS use Humvees a lot, a paint job and a black flag and we could get in close. As for the big bang, I could put three or four claymores onto the front bumper of an armoured Humvee, they would be rigged to go off simultaneously and throw a couple of thousand nasty little ball-bearings at the Chechens when the other team is ready to breach on the extraction. If all goes well, the shaped charges on the claymores will be travelling in the Chechens' direction and the guys inside will be unharmed and could still join the fight."

"How would they be operated together?" Sam said.

"The claymores could be rigged to go off when a single clacker (firing device) is activated. It's a simple device, we have used it on ambushes in Helmand with Forty Commando."

"Right, excellent idea, let me get on to Tommy and his guys," said Danny.

Sam was pleased, the final piece of the jigsaw had nestled into place — but who would drive the Humvee?

It was dark now in Mosul, really dark — there were no streetlamps because there was nothing to power them. The only light seeping through the darkness came from some solar street lighting with very battered looking panels, bearing the odd bullet hole, that ironically had been supplied by US Aid during the 'Heart and Minds' phase of the American occupation. The odd set of car headlights also sometimes danced across the main city square, illuminating Imran and throwing his shadow into dark relief. On those occasions he froze, and slowly tried to blend into his surroundings. It was dangerous to move at night, there were very few people about because the Islamic State had an undeclared curfew, and the only people moving were ISIS fighters and their mobile patrols.

He examined his emotions, was it fear he felt or was it

excitement — what made men do dangerous things? What possible reward could outweigh the very real chance of being publicly executed?

Things had changed for him now completely. It was like a dark, oppressive hood of twisted thinking had been lifted from his eyes and he could see for the first time. It was simple, it was good against evil.

His mission was also simple; he would mark the hostage house by leaving his activated iPhone as close to the hostage as he could. It would then take him ten minutes to get to his VW transporter van, and then with the full approval of both MI5 and the much-vaunted caliphate he would return home to London. He guessed that this final mission was a type of test that would properly qualify him with Ahmad, but he did not care. He would get the job done and be out of there.

Back at the Claymore House in Erbil, the Thursday morning was a busy one as the late arrivals all had to complete the thousand and one things that you have to prep before action. Doc and Eddy had booked the thousand-metre range at the Pershmerga Camp to zero the Barrett and the other longs. Sam had to pick up four Osprey 40 silencers for the Glock 23s and six Flash-Crash grenades for room entry, the only guys with these in the country were some SAS advisors with the Pershmerga. Tommy had organised it, but in typical British Army fashion, Sam had to sign for them. Danny accompanied her for top-cover and to organise an OOB (out of bounds) box for the Op.

Mac helped Taff with the claymores. Both had experience of fabricating steel and had borrowed the cutting and welding tools from a friend of Talal's, who was the local blacksmith. Tommy had supplied a battered looking but mechanically reliable old US M114 Humvee. The armour looked good but the front covering of this model was still made of a light fiberglass. They had to fashion a thick steel bumper for the front of the Humvee, thick enough to deflect the blast outwards, and then fashion three enclosed steel frames for each individual claymore mine.

Talal and Mo were fully occupied gathering and supplying a list of Sam's requirements from the Erbil market and local businesses. There were some bizarre requests written in Sam's own precise handwriting.

A locally purchased Toyota or Hiace side-opening van in
excellent mechanical condition. Dark colour preferred.
A baby's pram (old sprung wheeled type if possible)
A small rucksack
Bicycle type bungee cord (twenty metres)
One small black abaya and full niqab (worn-looking if possible)
High velocity plates (2)

Talal was still busy bartering with a stallholder over a very decrepit looking old style pram when he heard the distinctive crack of a 50 calibre round. He looked towards Mo.

"That's the guys at the range," he said in English. The locals carried on unperturbed, seemingly used to the loud bangs that occasionally came from that direction.

Eddy and Doc were on the Pershmerga 1000-metre range at the 650-metre point. Eddie made sure he was totally comfortable behind the bulk of the Barrett as he prepared to fire again. He hooked a magazine of ten heavy 50 Cal rounds securely into its frame and checked that it was securely housed. He then smoothly jerked the cocking handle towards him with his right hand to slide the big round into the breach. He then placed the weight of his shoulder against the Barrett's butt and pressed his weight against the biped legs. The cross hairs on the BORS (Barrett Optimal Sighting System) optic scope perfectly intersected the standard British Army Figure 11 target 650 metres away. Doc was lying beside Eddy with both hands cradling a pair of high power binoculars, staring intently for the fall of shot.

"Ready?" said Doc.

"Yep," Eddy replied, as he gently paused his breath, slowly squeezed the trigger and shouted, "SHOT!"

BANG!

But not just any bang, it was a huge, resounding bang, distinctive almost of a small explosion, known to any who have been under fire from a Barrett 50 Cal.

"Fuck," said Doc, "I'd forgotten just how loud this fucker is."

"Yeah, but where did it go?" Eddie said calmly.

"You are about six inches high and a foot wide mate," Doc replied.

Eddie carefully clicked the zeroing ring on the standard bors sight, there were some audible clicks as the adjustments were made and Eddie was then ready to take another shot.

"OK, standby Doc," Eddie said as he again took up first pressure on the trigger and shouted, "SHOT!"

BANG!

"How's that mate?"

"It's bang on, mate," said Doc.

"OK," said Eddie, "let's try three rounds rapid, buddy,"

"Roger that," said Doc.

Eddie shouted, "SHOT!" and then the Barrett fired.

BANG! BANG! BANG!

"What's that like, mate?" he enquired.

"Bang on, Eddie, an excellent three-round group, bang centre," said Doc.

"I am not going to waste any more rounds, Doc, I am going to save the rest for the Daesh."

"Yeah, mate, good idea. Now let's get my M18 on target."

"OK, mate," Eddie said with a smile.

Taff and Mac had worked away at the Humvee; they had mounted the claymores to the front and mounted the GPMG in the gunners ring mount. They had then painted the thing an ISIS black and Taff had roughly painted the appropriate ISIS slogans in white Arabic script once the black paint had dried. ISIS had luckily supplied an endless supply of propaganda videos to make sure that it looked authentic. Finally, they had taken the black ISIS flag that had been donated by the sleeping victim of the Toyota, and had mounted it to give it its final aura of authenticity. Danny inspected the result and was suitably impressed.

"How does this work?" he asked Taff.

"Like all good pieces of kit, mate, very fucking simply," Taff said. "The three Claymores are firmly fixed to the reinforced steel bumper; the outer two are slightly angled outwards to give a good spread. All three devices will fire off a single firing button on the driver's side. There is another firing device, which is an original Claymore clacker on the passenger side just in case the button does not work. Each firing device is wired separately, so it doubles our chances of getting a timely detonation," Taff smiled.

"Who is driving this invention, Taff?" said Danny.

"That's a million-dollar question, Doc Doughty has volunteered, the mad bastard, but he only speaks a little bit of Arabic. We'll need a fluent Arabic speaker to get close, although it's a Chechen checkpoint, it still needs somebody fluent. I talked to Talal, and him and his brother said they would ride shotgun with Doc. Sam will know before orders. I pity those Chechens, two mad half-Kurdish Jocks and a mad ML will be attacking them. They will be dropping off Eddie and Mac with the Barrett on the way in."

Taff laughed and then looked suddenly pensive. The enormity of the challenge had suddenly loomed large in his consciousness. It was all very dangerous, but this part was especially dangerous, and he could have invented the instrument of his best mates' demise. It was a suddenly a very sobering thought. Taff continued, "I am keeping the other Claymore to cover our extraction. I have a good idea on how it can be used, I'll chat to Sam about that before orders. To be honest, mate, this is not an ideal scenario, we could have done with a timed air strike on the position but the extraction needs to be coordinated between the strike team and the extraction team, and a team member pushing the button is the only thing that can guarantee doing that."

Chapter Thirty Two

Orders

At 1400 hours, the library room of Claymore House was full to the rafters with expectant operators. It was a large, high-ceilinged room, lined with mainly leather-bound books that filled the room with a smell of ancient leather, omitting a slight musty odour. The room had been hastily packed with white plastic chairs that reinforced the expensive leather armchairs. Tommy Talibani sat in the front line of seats with Talal, Mo and three of his senior officers. All were dressed in the uniform of the Asayish Special Commando and all were English speakers. The two Hedges and Fisher teams were separated according to their nominated tasks, extraction or assault. The room combat team of Scottie, Pat and Taff were to the left of Tommy's guys as Mac, Doc and Eddie were seated to the right of the Pershmerga designated as the assault group. Jimmy stood next to Sam to explain the Black Hornet video footage. Sam stood in front and to the left-hand side of a PowerPoint projection screen. In front of the screen was a medium-sized table with a scale model of the target house, checkpoint, and the Madrassa.

All attending knew that orders are important; they at least gave a framework to the murderous mayhem of warfare. Sam had given orders many times, but never when the stakes or the potential for disaster were so high. She looked out at the guys, all the expectant faces knew what she knew — this was a high-risk operation and some people might not get back from it.

Sam felt a little nervous, although this was generally a good thing before an Op. Apprehension sharpened perception, intensified intent, and therefore helped out when working out the 'what ifs'. A good set of orders should not only show the easiest way to achieve a military aim but it should also consider all those situations that could happen by chance. What if we have a break down on the way to the target? What if there is a contact with the enemy on the way to or from the target? What about casualties?

The next two hours passed in a flash; Sam imparted a continuous download of information, all given in the tried and tested formula that starts with Ground, Situation, Mission.

Sam had Jimmy talk through the Black Hornet over-flight video and constantly compared the latest IMINT (image intelligence) pictures that were streamed and displayed on the PowerPoint projector. She also constantly used a laser pointer to indicate some point or other on the accurate scale model that lay on the table below the projector.

The operation was complex, the assault group and extraction group would have to attack simultaneously with split second timing to gain any chance of success. The Pershmerga forces would only deploy after the room assault and attack had been initiated. The approach of both teams would be totally covert until the last moment. By the time Sam reached the end of the orders sequence and asked, "Gentlemen, any questions?" followed by the synchronization of watches, everyone knew every piece of the plan and how he or she featured in it.

Sam, Scottie and Pat had worked together to Haji-up. Taff was now ready for the Op. He was dressed in Iraqi Arab winter clothing, which was an odd mix of traditional Arab and Western dress. He had clipped his full beard in the Iraqi style and a green sleeveless utility jacket, the sort used by keen anglers, hung loosely over his knee length brown dish-dash top. Both garments more than covered his weapons and his body armour and his ammo cache.

The ISIS documents supplied by Tommy Talibani named him as Mohammad Al-Ubaid, from a large Sunni tribe local to Mosul, so a traditional black and white shemagh scarf completed the subterfuge. A white and red scarf would have made him a Shia, and that would not be a good thing on this Op. Scottie had helped him hang the MP5K around his right shoulder with bungee cord; it now hung comfortably under his utility jacket.

He tapped gently on Sam's bedroom door to help her Haji-up.

"Come in, gorgeous," said Sam.

"Fancy going to a fancy dress party?" said Taff with a broad grin.

"Yeah, I suppose I'm going as the UBO (Unidentified Black Object) again."

"Yes, you know it makes sense," Taff replied. "This thing can make you disappear in an instant from Kabul to Cardiff!" he said in an exaggerated singsong Welsh accent, handing Sam the worn dirty looking black abaya and full-face niqab, which had been newly delivered by the Scott brothers.

Sam was dressed in her normal comfortable jeans, a long sleeved t-shirt and KSB boots, her hair tied as normal in a golden streak of a ponytail that hung momentarily over her left shoulder as she wrestled with her body armour and weapons cache.

Taff looked down at her boots, they seemed so small and petite, like a small girl's. He watched the girl he loved calmly prepare for action, unperturbed and focused, a real warrior in a pretty woman's body. He looked at her hands, small delicate with perfectly shaped nails busily adjusting her shoulder straps. Standing close, he caught the light scent of soap and the warmness of her body.

Slowly at first, and then with increasing intensity, Taff felt an almost painful feeling of dread, of fear welling up from the very core of his being. It seemed to seep from deep inside him, an awful feeling of nagging, aching, internalised emptiness. Taff had never really been scared of anything in his life, not growing up, not in the Marines, not in the SRR, not on operations, but he had known fear. Fear was the thing that made you quicker than the other guy; it was controlled fear that soldiers shaped and moulded into calmly delivered violence. It was controlled fear that provided that turbo-boost of adrenaline when you needed it. Taff realised that the fear that was welling up inside him was different; it was actually the fear of loss. He suddenly realised that this girl he was going to help get dressed for battle was more important to him than anything he had ever known in the past. He knew he loved her, and he also knew, in that instant, that he could not bear her loss.

Sam sensed a change; she stopped what she was doing and looked at Taff. Taff felt Sam's deep blue eyes search his face.

"You OK, Taff?" she said. Sam noticed that Taff's eyes were watery, a small tear escaped and rolled slowly down his face.

"Sam, you don't need to go on this Op."

He continued and blurted out the first thing that came into his mind. "I love you, and I can't do without you. I can't afford to lose you."

Sam looked at Taff and knew that she felt exactly the same way. She turned and placed both her arms around his shoulders and pulled herself in close.

"I love you too, I have tried to tell you but couldn't find the words!"

Sam felt that they had melted together. She had never felt anything so totally right as they found themselves kissing intensely. It was almost like very their souls had melted and fused. The kissing continued and became slowly more torrid, sexual and intimate, when a loud shout shattered the moment.

"Sam, Danny's just arrived!" Scottie shouted from the hallway.

Both were jerked back to reality, they looked quickly at each other smiled and quickly composed themselves.

"Not an ideal time for this, is it Mr Thomas?" Sam said with a smile.

"Unfortunately not," Taff responded.

Sam then fixed Taff's eyes with hers and stroked his bearded chin with the lightest of touches from her right hand. "It's too late to change things, Taff, I feel the same, I wanted to leave you out from the job as well, but I guess I knew what you would say. We will do this thing together like soldiers and then we'll sort out our other relationship afterwards."

"Sounds like a plan," said Taff.

Sam then shouted down to Danny. "Hi, Danny, Cinders is just getting ready for the ball and one of the ugly sisters is helping me, we will be down in five."

Taff finished helping her place on her weapons cache containing her lightweight body armour. Sam firstly slipped into her radio harness and made sure that the chest mike was positioned in the right place. The pink coloured wire then travelled inside the right hand arm of her long sleeved t-shirt and down to her wrist, so she could use the button styled prezzle switch to transmit. Taff then helped her hang an MP5K, 9mm machine pistol from a length of bungee cord from her right hand shoulder and then adjusted it. She then tested the length of the doubled-up cord to make sure she would be able to bring it on aim quickly from under her abaya. A silenced 9mm Glock 21 was holstered snugly at her right hip, housed in a leather holster with a front spring break so it could be drawn easily from the same, all-shrouding black abaya. She also wore a SIG 230 9mm short pistol in her favourite ankle holster.

She would also wear a small rucksack to her front under the abaya containing the immediate action 'dems kit', including some of the ECT door charges and some 'crash-flash' grenades strapped by bungee cord to her front. Once Taff had helped her strap this over her weapon cache, all would be covered with the worn-looking black abaya with the obligatory black, full-face niqab completing the effect. At the end of the transformation, Sam would look just like a very poor, and very pregnant girl from Mosul.

Sam and Taff left the bedroom together and met Danny in the main hall of Claymore House.

"Have you seen my baby, Danny?" she said. Parked in the entrance of the hall there was a black, tattered-looking old-fashioned style sprung baby's pram. It contained all the immediate kit they needed for the first actions on the target.

It was a very ordinary-looking pram, carrying an extraordinary payload. Sam's short-barrelled M4, with a Colt manufactured one hundred round drum magazine nestled comfortably next to Taff's Mini-me .556 Light machine gun. Taff had made up the ECT door charges and they were now contained in a small green canvas bag that lay immediately under the weapons. There were also six L60 hand grenades, and a claymore mine vying for space within its confines. All were covered with a brightly-coloured baby blanket with a baby-sized doll snuggled on top to complete the effect. A small digital tape recorder was placed alongside the doll's head to supply the suitable sound effects.

"That's top notch," said Danny. He was genuinely impressed with the solution.

"Yeah," said Sam. "It should let us to get the heavier kit to the doors we need to blow, and Taff had also left behind a little present for anybody who wants to chase us."

Sam lifted the front of the baby blanket and Danny could see the ominous shape of the claymore mine. The mine was mounted towards the front of the pram so its deadly charge would be propelled outwards to its front. Two high-velocity plates welded to the internal metal frame of the ancient old pram held the deadly charge in place and guaranteed direction.

"That looks like it might work Sam, but remember as it says on the tin — front towards enemy, and put the brake on or it will overtake you on the way out," Danny quipped.

"No problems with that, Danny," said Taff, bringing a small car central locking device from his pocket. "It works with this," he held the small device in the palm of his hand, "And it has its own channel, in case of accidents or jammers."

Danny was impressed, the team had thought of just about every possibility. That old saying about 'no plan surviving contact with the enemy' briefly flashed into his mind, but he knew that the better the plan the more chance you had of surviving at all.

Sam looked towards Danny. "See you when we get back," and she held out both arms for a fatherly cuddle.

Danny embraced her. "I will be at the Pershmerga Ops room all the time, and in constant touch with US Air if you need help."

Danny was genuinely finding it difficult to control his emotions, but he held his voice in check. He was old-school, and still liked to lead from the front. He didn't like the idea of his kids not coming back.

"Roger that," said Sam.

Danny shook each guy's hand, finishing with Doc who he walked with to the door.

"Are you sure you are up for this, Doc?" he asked.

"Yeah," Doc replied. "I want to see the look of surprise on the bastards' faces when I give them Taff's present," he said with a laugh. "Plus, there are worse places to be in a firefight than in an armoured vehicle," he said smiling.

Both guys smiled. "I never thought of it like that," said Danny.

"That's what we learn in the Royal Marines, Danny," Doc replied. "The power of positive thinking."

Danny turned and left with the hint of a smile.

"OK," said Sam, turning towards the team, "let's go for a talk-through/walk-through, and then some rehearsals. We have to be at Kalak for 03.30."

Chapter Thirty Three

Kalak

It was a particularly dark and cold Thursday night at the Kalak checkpoint. The air was still and frosty as the team made their final preparations. Sam looked upwards at the inky blackness of the star strewn sky; it had always intrigued her how the most dangerous countries always seemed to have the most beautiful night skies. It seemed that the more dangerous the country was the brighter the stars seemed to shine. She had often gazed in awe at the gorgeous night skies in Helmand. She could not help thinking about what the future held for her and Taff. Was there love written in the night sky, or maybe their imminent demise?

All the disparate parts of the operation were now gathered at the designated form up point near the Kalak checkpoint. This was a large joint operation involving over 300 of Tommy's men and the Brits. The insertion group was paired, Sam with Taff, and Scottie with Pat. The assault group was quietly talking with Tommy Talibani. The Scott brothers, Mac, Eddie and Doc were dressed in ISIS-style Iraqi winter kit: loose black pyjama type smocks and shortened trousers, Iraqi Army boots and loose-fitting desert pattern US Army jackets. The whole effect was enhanced by the beards and the loosely wound black and white tribal shemagh each guy wore.

The Pershmerga guys looked across at them curiously. So these were the Brits they would be working with. The ISIS look did not worry them, it was a tactic that both sides used regularly; the Deash dressing in Iraqi Army or Pershmerga kit and sometimes the reverse was true. Their Commando unit had launched many attacks dressed as the enemy; it only got confusing after the initial contact. Tommy had told them that these guys would wear an orange armband and a British Army hat with the English word 'Army' in orange once the shooting started.

The Pershmerga Commando soldiers were just about everywhere, quietly chatting, joking and constantly checking their equipment. Kurdish music leaked out from some of the vehicles lined up for the assault. Guys who wanted to smoke, smoked. Some of the Kurdish Commandos chatted quietly on their mobile phones to their families. It wasn't like any start-line that any of the Brits had been on before; it was a far more casual affair. This was obviously something that these guys had routinely done in the past. *To them, it is just another start-line,* thought Sam, *just one of many in a very long war.*

Doc, the Scott brothers, Eddie, and Mac then checked the black painted Humvee. Mad Mo poked his head out of the roof cupola and checked the mountings on the GPMG. The machine gun had a heavy canvas bag mounted to its side, containing a belt of 200 rounds of .762 ammunition; every fifth round on the belt was a tracer round. He also opened up another four boxes of the same ammunition, carefully breaking the wire seal that held the cans shut. The belts were all partially removed from the cans; they wouldn't have time to do this during a firefight.

Mo lifted the GPMGs top cover and swept the tray with his right hand, introduced the belt of two hundred .762, until it was pushed against the breach block and then slammed the cover shut. The weapon was now loaded, and all he needed to do was to draw back the cocking handle for it to do its business.

Doc first of all checked the three claymores attached to the front bumper of the armoured Humvee and then checked the firing button in the driver's side; it was a simple firing device, with a U-ring type safety that had to be removed before you could depress it. He also checked the claymore clacker that was on the dashboard on the passenger side. It was the standard clacker that was supplied with the mine; you just pressed two levers together to generate the electrical charge that would explode the detonator.

Eddie and Mac would sit on either side of the gunner.

Eddie was sitting with the bulk of the mighty Barrett 50 Cal upright on its butt in front of him. Mac was cradling his M18 short across his legs. Both operators would drop off before the final checkpoint; they had pre-selected a drop off point, an elevated firing position and their possible targets from the IMINT and the Black Hornet footage. They knew their priority targets would be the engine blocks of the suspected ISIS suicide car bombs before they could concentrate on the checkpoint to support the Pershmerga assault.

Jimmy was dressed in full Pershmerga kit, the same old-style American pattern camouflage and the same body armour and weapons. He would stay with Tommy Talibani to conduct a Black Hornet over-flight before the initial attack. He carried his precious toys with him. It amazed him just how much the little helicopters looked like very cheap toys, such amazing technology in such tiny machines. He checked the battery levels on all the kit; he was good to go. His job would be to check that they were not straying into some elaborate ambush. He would firstly check that the suicide bomb vehicles they had identified were still on the plot. He would then pass that information to Eddie and Mac.

At exactly 0400 hours Taff turned the key that started the Hiace's engine and then drove through the forward chicane of the checkpoint. The extraction group was complete; Sam sat in the back of the van on the extreme left completely shrouded in her UBO (Unidentified Black Object) outfit. The old pram had pride of place in the middle of the van by the side-opening door. Scottie and Pat squeezed in the remaining seats. It was only when you actually tried to squeeze into a fairly confined space that you realised how much space you needed for body armour, weapons, and elaborate disguises.

"Put the air-con on Taff, for fucks sake," said Pat. "Or we'll fucking melt before we get there," he said, laughing.

"It is on," said Taff. "It's just fucked, that's all."

"That's unusual in Iraq," said Pat. "That's the well-known Iraqi factor again."

"A fucking big roger to that," said Taff.

Sam then interjected, "Guys, what do you think the UBO in the back feels like, at least you can see what's the feck's going on,"

"Yeah, sorry boss," said Pat, with a giggle. "But you look beautiful."

"I've got a gun here, Pat," said Sam.

Taff pulled the van up to the right-hand side of the road and waited. There was tenseness in the air, they were rolling on timings, and everything depended on this one 'Sunni sheik' scouting them through the checkpoints. Everybody in the vehicle realised that Iraqi men did not do precise timings too well, that's why every time an Iraqi talked about being somewhere at an allotted time, they used the phrase 'Inshallah' afterwards. If all went to plan, Doc and the assault team in the Humvee would follow about a click behind. Another two clicks behind them would be a mobile attack force of 300, quite angry, and highly armed Pershmerga Commando types, who had a collective axe to grind with the Daesh.

They needn't have worried; this guy had worked with the US Special Forces and obviously had an accurate watch. His Toyota Corolla saloon car flashed its lights three times in their direction one long, two short, and the ICOM that Tommy had given Taff transmitted the agreed brevity code that Tommy had arranged, again three bursts of static from the transmit button, one long and two short. The job was on and the small Hiace van rolled towards Mosul.

Taff spoke to Tommy on the Pershmerga net.

Sam spoke to the Hedges and Fisher guys on their own covert net.

"That's us towards Red Three," she simply said.

"Roger that," said Doc "Towards Red Three."

"Roger that," said Danny over the net "Best of luck guys, and try not to get tagged, it's not good for the company's no claims bonus."

Sam then tested the team's encrypted net.

"Hello all stations, this is Sam, comms check."

Doc answered as he gunned the Humvee's engine slightly and took up his position behind the Hiace van.

"Yeah, it's Doc, Lima Charlie (Loud and Clear)."

"Yeah, it's Pat and Mac, Lima Charlie."

"Yeah, it's Taff, Lima Charlie."

"It's Scottie, Lima Charlie."

"Hello all stations, this is Sam, good luck guys, rolling now."

The small Hiace van pulled forward and rolled towards Mosul.

Hassan the security officer was smiling as he left his house near to the interrogation centre. Mosul was still in darkness as he wrapped his shemagh around his face to combat the icy cold. He was smiling to himself, he felt a lightness in his chest, and he was taking long controlled deep breaths, savouring his memories of the Yazidi girl while they were fresh in his mind; she had been a gift for his excellent work in exposing the British spy. He had enjoyed his evening with her. She was very young and she had been scared. *That somehow made it better*, he thought. He had started by binding her hands and gagging her. He then had knelt beside the bed and prostrated himself in prayer before getting on top of her. When it was over, and he had enjoyed her body and her fear, he knelt to pray again. He had explained to her that it was allowed and halal, and the Holy Book gave him the right to rape her. Sacred texts actually condoned the act because she practiced a religion other than Islam and he was allowed to rape an unbeliever. She had screamed through the gag, she was just an ignorant slave and did not realise that the act was actually drawing him closer to God; it was, after all, a form of 'ibadah' (worship).

The smile faded from his lips as he thought of the important task he had been given. He had been personally selected by Mullah Mohammad to organise and film the execution of the American hostage. Arab social media had been abuzz with the rumours that he was a CIA spy and not the journalist he pretended to be. He would meet his security guys and the video cameraman at the Chechen checkpoint.

He would make sure that he used big Ivan and the German to control him. He would need to control the American so a dose of scopolamine, the so-called truth drug, would be placed in his food before the judgement. It would be enough to make the task easier, he must try to get the American to admit to his sins and the drug would make him more cooperative. The video was important, it must be done well, and he had already sort of composed the scene in his mind.

The Mullah would describe the American's sins, who would be tied and kneeling with the black garbed and masked ISIS man standing behind him. The camera lights would clearly display the black flag of the caliphate on the wall behind them. Everything had to be perfect as he had his reputation riding on this production. He would meet and brief the Mullah and the British executioner who had done such a good job with the spy Sayeed, It would be all over the social media as soon as the event had been filmed, it was an excellent recruitment tool for the Caliphate; if it was done right that is. It should all be complete before the call to prayer and on the websites after breakfast.

Chapter Thirty Four

Covert Approach

Less than five clicks away from where Hassan planned the execution, the Iraqi tribal Sheik had done an excellent job. The small van in which the hostage rescue team travelled had only had to go off-road to wait for a while as he reported on an ISIS patrol that had halted to mount a checkpoint. There was an expectant hush as the whole convoy had stopped, completely silent in the darkness with engines and lights off. Doc had pulled the Humvee over to the side of the road and the lads had dismounted to supply security for the lead vehicle. The Pershmerga column waited, weapons at the ready.

Tommy Talibani shivered slightly in the cold wind as he nervously looked at his watch, his mouth was dry and he had that peculiar empty feeling in the pit of his stomach, it was the familiar pre-combat feeling he had long got used to in the past ten years. The whole plan only had about fifteen minutes of flexibility built into it. If Sam and the Brit teams could not roll on timings, then his task would have to take priority and it would become a conventional Commando attack. The attack on the Raqqa Syrian front could not be delayed and his guys had to keep the Daesh busy for at least an hour.

The ICOM with Sam broke the silence with three burst of static produced by the scout depressing the send button. One long-two short meant 'all clear' and the lead vehicle once again led the way.

Taff looked towards Sam.

"We have about 5 clicks to drop off," he said, consulting his GPS. "That will give us a walk in of about a click."

"Roger that," said Sam. "I'm looking forward to taking my baby for a walk, Taff."

"Yeah, anything to get out of this piece of shit," said Taff, who looked strangely oversized within the confines of the small Japanese side-opening van. Taff subconsciously checked his weapons as if for reassurance. He felt under his jacket and touched the pistol grip of his MP5K, and thumbed the selector lever to check it was on safe. They all knew that chances of discovery become more acute the closer you got to a drop off; everything must look totally normal. It had been planned and rehearsed meticulously; they would exit the vehicle naturally, looking like a normal family group. They only had thirty minutes to make their way across the square to set up for the hostage extraction; they could not afford another delay. He checked the silenced Glock 21 in its specially adapted holster; it nestled comfortably on his hip. He tapped it thoughtfully, *they might need it.*

As the Toyota Hiace neared the outskirts of Mosul, it blended perfectly with the other early morning traffic. The majority of the town was still sleeping, but there were still several families on the move. He remembered that Friday was a special day in the Islamic world. It was the Sabbath and families often came together to pray, and Iraqi families were large. The increased traffic correspondingly increased the risk, there were no safety checks, driving tests or insurance on Iraqi roads, and a minor shunt could derail the whole operation.

Every car seemed to be crammed full as the traffic became busier. The women and children usually occupied the rear of the vehicles with the men in front. Taff looked at the numerous children's faces pressed up against the car windows, illuminated by the Toyota's headlights, pictures of innocence in a world gone mad. He hoped that none would get mixed up in the controlled carnage to come. He knew from bitter experience though that sometimes they did. He had seen graphic evidence of that in both Iraq and Afghanistan.

Taff checked the GPS; it was two clicks to the drop off point they had selected. Doc would soon be approaching his holding point; it was in the area of the LUP (Lay-up Position) they had used for the CTR (Close Target Recce) Sam would call the assault team forward when the hostage rescue team were nearly 'good to go' on the target. A final radio check would establish whether they had enough range for the small Motorola radios. In handheld mode they probably had a range of about two clicks, but that depended entirely on the buildings in between.

Sam pressed the prezzle switch on her covert fit radio.

"Hello Doc, this is Sam."

"Lima Charlie," Doc replied.

"We are going firm now."

Doc looked down the nearly deserted street, with the dipped headlights from the Humvee picking up the shapes of the abandoned Christian houses. It was still pitch black, with just a hint of the ghostly sheen of the lightening sky beginning to make progress against the blackness. Doc peered through the gloom and detected a brief flurry of movement. He quickly switched off the Humvee's lights, picked up the weapon's night scope off the dash and explored the darkness. Two wolf-like semi-spectral figures were clearly visible; their eyes seemed to light up as they looked towards the Humvee. They were two local dogs of unknown breed, whose slat-like ribs gave an impression of their condition as they scoured the empty streets for food. The scope reflected a green image of hopelessness as they stumbled amongst the filth. *A fitting image for what this place had become,* thought Doc.

Talal broke the silence. "Anywhere here will do," he said. "Dad's bike shop was in the next street. We are within a kilometre of the Daesh checkpoint, let's set up."

The team, as per orders, would set up an ISIS checkpoint.

Talal and Mo calmly left the Humvee to check the immediate area.

They moved stealthily, AK47s in the ready position with their distinctive drum magazines clearly visible. Each went to a different side of the road, sometimes kneeling and pausing to listen, sometimes relaying hand signals to each other.

Somebody trained these guys well, thought Doc. They cleared for fifty metres up and down the location before they returned to the vehicle.

"It looks good," said Talal. "We should be about 300 metres from your position, guys."

Eddie checked his watch and GPS, Talal was right; they were only two hundred and fifty metres from their OP (Observation Post). It was a large, three-storey family house with an exterior concrete-stepped outside stairwell that led directly to the roof. The building was deserted and had been at the centre of a firefight before. A low four-foot crenulated, almost turreted, wall enclosed the flat roof, giving the sniper team cover from view and a modicum of protection against incoming fire.

Both the sniper teams removed their kit and equipment from the rear of the Humvee. Eddie slung the Barrett from its sling over his shoulder and then covered it with a dark brown light winter blanket. Mac's M18 was also swiftly slung across his shoulder and covered the same way. He also carried a green canvas bag containing the spare claymore, the Barrett ammunition and all the team's L60 grenades. The claymore would provide rear protection for the OP and the grenades could be rolled down the stairs or thrown into the street in case of a building assault.

"Hi Sam and all stations, that's us foxtrot to golf," whispered Eddie into his comms.

"Roger that," said Sam.

Both guys then casually walked down towards their sniping position.

Sam transmitted the message as she struggled from the

cramped confines of the van. Enshrouded in black, the abaya seemed to catch on just about everything, and with the added burden of the body armour, weapons cache and her weapons with a small back pack of explosives lashed with bungee cord to her front, it suddenly occurred to her that this is what many pregnant women had to put up with. *Not for a while*, she thought.

Taff and Scottie had moved the pram from its position by the door and placed it on what passed for a pavement in Mosul. Pat reached inside to help Sam out of the vehicle.

"Thank you, kind sir," she whispered.

Taff looked towards Sam, she looked quite convincingly like a pregnant poor girl from Mosul. Sam leaned back while pressing her right hand into her back.

"This feckin' front back-pack is killing me," she said quietly.

Taff smiled. "It was your idea boss," he teased.

"Yeah, fair one," she replied, almost inaudibly. Sam walked behind the pram and pulled the blanket back to act out the checking the baby sketch. She moved back the blanket, looked inside and checked the immediate equipment she would need. She then removed the silenced pistol from the holster under her abaya, and with her back to the road and shielded by Taff at the other side, she placed the Glock 23 with the Osprey silencer immediately under the blanket. Within a minute the team were walking towards their target.

Sam then transmitted with the firm's comms. "Hi Danny, that's us at Red Two and dropped off."

Danny was sitting in the Pershmerga Ops room alongside an RAF liaison officer who was held spellbound by the unfolding drama.

"Roger that, Sam, good luck," he replied. "Hello all stations, this is Danny, Sam is dropped off and moving."

All the stations then responded.

"Roger that," said Doc. *Now this is where it gets interesting*, he thought.

"Roger that," said Eddie. They had climbed the exterior steps of the house and had set up the OP. Mac had placed the claymore to their rear, angled down at the steps supported by bricks, the wired up clacker lay in front of them both. The Barrett was loaded and trained towards the Chechen checkpoint. The M18 was mounted on biped legs and lay in the other direction covering the stairs; both operators had removed their MP5K machine pistols and placed them to their fronts with the ejection opening covers upwards, so when they picked them up quickly the pistols' grips were the right way up.

Eddie looked through the handheld night-scope he had removed from his chest webbing. The ghostly green light clearly showed some ISIS fighters were awake and moving around. The ZPU-4 anti-aircraft guns were partially manned and occasionally rotated to the left and right as the gunners adjusted the four-barrel heavy machine guns aimlessly, *probably to keep awake*, thought Eddie. He couldn't detect any extra security. He whispered to Mac, "What does it look like through those, mate?" he said.

Mac was doing the same thing with a more powerful scope. "Looks OK, I have counted six, plus the guys on the ZPU4-s, the ZPU-4 on the roof of the hostage house is also manned. I have seen various people leave that house for the checkpoint."

At the checkpoint Hassan was holding court, he was inside the small building that Ivan, the big Chechen commander, used for his office. It was a small room, cluttered with a desk and a bed and several white plastic chairs. He quietly explained to Ivan and his German second-in-command his plans for the American. Hassan explained the guards would drug the American's rice or water this morning to relax him and make him more compliant.

"Ivan," said Hassan in English; he knew that the Chechen's English was far better than his Arabic. "This guy could be dangerous, he is an ex-American Commando"

Big Ivan laughed along with the German. "No American is dangerous to me," he replied. "I look forward to seeing him die," he said tersely. "I would love to cut his stinking kuffar head off myself."

Hassan felt a shiver down his spine. *Chechens were scary bastards,* he thought.

Taff walked in front, every inch the imperious Iraqi husband, and then came Sam shuffling along; head lowered as per her orders, pushing the ancient pram, with the two other male family members Pat and Scottie, quietly walking separately about twenty metres behind. It became immediately apparent that the progress to the target might be more difficult than they had planned. Iraqi roads and pavements are not repaired at all and a combination of the poor light and the numerous large potholes slowed progress considerably. Sam broke the silence. "Check the GPS, Taff."

"Yeah, we need to hurry, Sam," said Taff. Taff looked at the GPS, they still had at least one click to the main square, and it appeared that they had dropped off to soon. Taff studied the GPS, and tried to work out a shortened route, a small orange dot clearly indicated their current position of the mapping; another orange dot indicated the lock-on left by the source, marking where the hostage was being held. They were close, but they needed to speed up. The group began to walk more swiftly while it was dark and there were few people about.

Sam seemed to step up the pace with the pram and despite the odd pieces of broken ground and the inevitable potholes, they started to make good progress. It was at a price though, you very seldom see people hurry in the Arabic world. The team all knew that a slow approach was more likely to be covert in that environment, so quick was inherently unnatural. They started to look like what they were, people in a hurry, and that was itself a problem.

Taff whispered to Sam. "It's getting light, we need to slow down."

"Yeah, you're right, but we are still behind time, let's just crack on until we reach the square," replied Sam.

"Roger that," said Taff.

The speed picked up considerably as Taff and Sam pushed the pace. They had to make the most of the darkness, as soon as they were in plain sight of the locals they would have to slow considerably. Sam was concerned, the whole operation was designed to run on timings and she had wrongly calculated how quickly they could move across open ground.

The pram was making heavy work of the journey, the wheels squeaked annoyingly and the right rear wheel had developed a visible wobble. Sam was extremely fit, but the constant pull of the backpack to her front was causing extreme discomfort.

Chapter Thirty Five

The Khansa Patrol

They continued to move along the street until they came under the first solar-powered street lamp since they had entered the outskirts of Mosul. The aging lamp, supplied with such largesse by the USA in 'Hearts and Minds' mode some years before, could only now muster a slight glow, but as the team passed under it, not far away, another early morning riser was watching. She saw something that just seemed odd. A lone female was frantically pushing a pram with a man and she seemed in a hurry. She moved away from her male colleagues and carefully lifted her outer veil and niqab to confirm what she had seen. She returned and talked quietly to them from the safe darkness of her black abaya and niqab.

"Brothers, I have seen something quite strange," she said. She was still unsure of herself; Fatima was a twenty-six-year-old British girl by birth, whose parents had fled Iraq when Saddam Hussein had clamped down on the Muslim Brotherhood and her parents had obtained asylum in Britain. She had lived in Birmingham until six months ago. She had hated living with the kuffars and all their immorality.

Her life had changed when she had watched the ISIS movie *Saleel al-Sawarim* (The Clanging of the Swords) on YouTube. She had memorised its tracts, it proclaimed that 'the end of time was coming' when the Muslim Army would be victorious as Mohammad had predicted: 'The spark had been lit here in Iraq and its heat will continue to intensify until it burns the Crusader Army in Dabiq'.

Her family, still in Birmingham, was proud that she would be part of it; they had always encouraged her towards the true path of Allah. It was the perfect, almost poetic simplicity of the violence contained in *The Clanging of the Swords* that had impressed her to her very core, it excited her, it enthralled her, and when the time came, she was glad to leave the moral decay and kuffar Jewish filth of England behind, she rejoiced in her rebirth. When she had watched that film, she had in that instant, totally committed herself to the Caliphate, Dural-Islam, and the blessed 'Islamic State'.

She had therefore been proud to be selected to serve in the Islamic State's Al Khansa Women's Brigade, or religious police. Fatima was happy to be part of Al Khansa, blessed with the duty of upholding the tenets of Sharia in Mosul. She also had the immense honour of carrying the weapons of Al Khansa; an aging AK47 across her shoulder and a length of heavy rubber hose to beat suspected apostates and backsliders. Fatima thought this might be the chance to impress her new colleagues. Some Iraqi families had been trying to smuggle their daughters out of Mosul to avoid marriage to the brothers of ISIS, this in Fatima's mind was a sin against God. *Maybe this is why they are hurrying*, she thought.

She approached the senior ISIS fighter who led their group; Fatima spoke Arabic with a heavy British accent. "Brother, I have seen something strange, a woman with a pram and a man hurrying on the road into the square."

"You are blessed with the eyesight of an eagle," the fighter replied.

He liked Fatima and hoped that one day he could afford the dowry to marry a girl like her, *although Fatima herself is a bit too old now*, it quickly occurred to him. "Let's get to the vehicle and see why they are hurrying."

The two ISIS fighters and Fatima quickly returned to their Ford Ranger pick-up truck. The two males climbed into the front of the cab and Fatima of course had to climb into the back. It would be too immoral to share a close space with men. The patrol then raced off in search of their prey.

Sam whispered into her covert comms, "OK guys, we can slow down."

Taff quickly checked his GPS. "We have about twenty minutes to the call to prayer, we have ten minutes to set up," he whispered.

Sam quickly checked her watch. "Yeah, we are on time," she said, as they adopted a more relaxed pace.

Scottie and Pat had pulled back from Sam and Taff and had separated slightly. It made the scene more believable as the sky lightened a little bit. The front pair looked more natural now, just a husband and a heavily pregnant girl pushing a pram. In another one hundred metres they would be by the Grand Mosque on the main square of Mosul and just five minutes from the target.

Sam was relieved; once they reached the main square they could make better progress. She started to mentally run through her actions on the target, when Taff suddenly muttered into her ear. "Stand by."

Taff had spotted a set of headlights approaching fast; they pierced the darkness and illuminated the front pair accompanied with the sound of a revving engine. Taff whispered into his comms. "Pat, Scottie, ISIS patrol?" he queried.

Scottie replied, "Roger that, it's a Ford Ranger, three up with a woman in the back, looks like an Al Khansa patrol."

"Roger that," Taff replied, feeling for the silenced pistol under his utility jacket. He turned to Sam. "Looks like the shit has hit the fan kid, let me talk to them first."

"Roger that," Sam replied. "But we can't afford to hang about."

Within a heartbeat the Ranger had screeched to a stop just in front of Sam and Taff, as Pat and Scottie looked on from their respective positions behind them on the square. Both guys were well away from the reflected lights from the Ranger's headlights. They observed the passenger door lights go on as the first ISIS fighter dismounted from the vehicle and closed the door. The Khansa in the back dropped the tailgate of the Ranger with a resounding clang and climbed down.

Scottie observed her calmly adjusting her abaya and niqab. She then reached into the back of the vehicle to retrieve her AK47. It was an old model with a shiny wooden butt that seemed to reflect the rear taillights. She slung the AK over her left shoulder and then reached back into the rear of the Ranger again and picked up what appeared to be a length of black rubber covered electrical flex with her right hand.

"All stations, yeah, it's a Khansa patrol," said Scotty.

"Roger that." Sam pressed her prezzle switch twice to confirm the message. Taff did the same.

Scottie continued to watch, he checked the selector lever on his MP5K with his right hand and un-holstered his silenced Glock. He was not close enough for a silenced pistol shot. He waited, Taff was fluent in Arabic and even sounded like an Iraqi, maybe he could talk his way out.

The driver of the vehicle dismounted and slammed the driver's door as he walked around the front of the vehicle. He was short in stature, squat but powerfully built. Taff saw that he was armed with an old American M16 assault rifle, the sort issued to the Iraqi Army. Taff looked as the fighter checked the selector lever. *This guy has done this before*, he thought. Both fighters and the girl walked over to him and Sam.

The fighter from the passenger side, a tall skinny guy with a sneering expression, addressed Taff with a barrage of questions in Arabic.

"What are you doing at this time in the morning?"

"Why are you running, are you trying to run away from the Caliphate?"

The final question was: "Where are your papers?"

Taff knew these were not local guys, they spoke an almost classical form of Arabic, he knew straight away that these two had arrived from Saudi Arabia and had come from rich families. The preferred staff for the religious police was usually Gulf Arabs, possibly because the actual fighters in ISIS generally found them highly-strung and therefore unreliable in combat, although they were extensively used as suicide bombers, such was their rush to get to 'Jannah', or Paradise. Europeans and especially converts were also used a lot to discipline the local population. They were usually trying to prove themselves and were generally more fanatical than the locals.

Taff looked downwards, casting his eyes low so as not to offend. Dressing like the locals was not just about fancy dress he had learnt, the correct body language was also needed. He handed over his ID, his Iraqi nationality document known as a 'tashkira' and his permission papers from the Caliphate. Both men scrutinised the documents in turn, using a small penlight torch to combat the gloom.

"Why were you running?" they said finally.

Sam had reached below the blanket in the pram and turned on the recording of a baby crying before the patrol arrived.

"We are rushing because our baby is ill," Taff replied, with a hint of sadness in his voice. "He is our only son." Taff looked towards the pram. "We'd hoped to see a doctor in town, we are poor people and we've had to walk."

The two fighters seemed happy with the answer. "OK, we hope you can find help Mohammad," one of them said using the name on the ISIS documents.

The Khansa listened intently; she had hoped that she could impress her brothers on one of her first missions. She had her suspicions about the baby and the pram, she came from a large family and the wailing coming from the pram did not seem right, it was too tinny and not loud enough for a baby in pain.

"Wait, brothers," she said in Arabic, with the heavy burr of a Birmingham accent. "Let me check."

She approached Sam and placed herself right in front of her. She placed her left hand on Sam's shoulder as if to control her; in her right hand she held the improvised whip. "Let me look at the baby. I think you are both lying, you are trying to flee the city."

Taff shouted across to Sam in Arabic, "Show her our baby!" and then pressed his prezzle switch three times rapidly.

Sam heard the bursts of static in her earpiece and understood the signal; she leaned over the pram and found the pistol grip of the Glock 23 with the Osprey silencer underneath the baby blanket.

She had turned now, had her back to the Khansa and was leaning over the pram. As soon as she had grasped the Glock with her right hand, the baby stopped crying suddenly; the digital recorder had failed. The Khansa's eyes widened behind her niqab as she suddenly realised that she had been right all along, and she rushed to unsling the AK47 from her left shoulder, dropping the rubber whip to the floor.

Sam sensed the danger behind her and instantaneously straightened and turned quickly to her left, rotating from her hips as she lifted her left elbow to strike the Khansa on the left side of her face. Sam realised immediately that she failed to connect properly, and so almost simultaneously she rotated her whole body, pivoting on the ball of her left foot, brought the silenced Glock up instinctively to her hip and double tapped the Khansa twice in the chest.

PHUT-PHUT!

The silenced rounds impacted almost at the same time throwing the Khansa forcefully back and down. At the same time Taff engaged the two fighters who were standing next to each other facing him. He pulled his pistol quickly from under his long utility vest and engaged both, while they were still slightly stunned by what had happened by the pram.

PHUT-PHUT!

PHUT-PHUT!

He aimed for a double tap to the chest of both fighters; they did not even have time to shout out as they were visibly thrown back by the impact of the 9mm rounds. Taff then calmly stepped over each body and placed another round in each head.

PHUT!

A one second wait and PHUT!

Lightweight body armour and suicide vests had ensured that such a seemingly callous act was necessary.

Scottie and Pat hurried to the scene.

"Let's get this cleared up," said Taff. The three guys swiftly and unceremoniously placed the dead Khansa and her colleagues into the back of the Ford Ranger.

"Did anyone else see that?" Taff asked Pat and Scottie.

"No, mate, I think we're good."

"There was no one else about from what I could see."

Chapter Thirty Six

Final Approach

Sam quickly made an assessment; they were running out of time. "We are behind time guys, are the keys in the ignition?"

Taff checked. "Roger that."

"OK, guys let's use it," said Sam.

Pat and Scottie carefully lifted the old pram into the back of the Ranger and climbed into the back after it. The deck at the back of the Ranger was quickly becoming slippery with blood and Pat slipped slightly as he climbed in. The SAS had required him attend a Health and Safety course when he was briefly a TQ (Technical Quarter Master) in B Squadron. "Not impressed, not very hygienic and quite dangerous," he quipped.

Sam climbed into the passenger seat, struggling with the backpack to her front that had become slightly undone when she had dealt with the Khansa. Taff forced himself behind the driver's side of the cab, barely able to squeeze his bulk behind the wheel, and adjusted the seat.

"That Saudi was a real short-arse," he said.

"Yeah, well he's an ex short-arse now," said Sam.

"Roger that," Taff replied. "Hey, kid," he continued in his broad Welsh accent. "You looked proper pregnant getting into the car just now, you OK?"

"I'm OK, but the bungees have loosened and I am just about to give birth to this Ops kit, so best get us near the target and somewhere quiet so we can get this done."

"They will find the guys in the back as soon as it gets light and they will be quite annoyed."

"Yeah, but it had to be done."

"Yeah," Sam said with a hint of sadness in her voice. "It had to be done."

It was the first time that Sam had killed a woman, she had hoped that the elbow strike would knock her out, but knew straight away that it had not. The double tap was almost instinctive; it was more like muscle memory from all those hours on the range at Hereford and Chicksands. *It was her or me*, she thought, *or more importantly, it was her or my team*, she concluded, and refocused on the job.

Taff neared the objective and was now looking for somewhere to dump the Ranger and its macabre cargo.

Within 200 metres of the operators' final drop-off, the security officer Hassan was briefing the prison staff and the cameraman. Big Ivan's hulking form was propped against the far wall of the office, he sat on the heavily decorated Arabic cushions that the guards used when they took tea. He listened intently as he tried to pick out the Arabic words he knew. They talked quietly in Arabic, with Hassan occasionally struggling over some word or other that was instantly translated by the German, much to Hassan's annoyance. The cameraman had arrived and sat nervously in the corner; he was Tunisian and had performed this honour many times in the past. He was listening to the instructions but also thinking about camera angles and lighting.

He would mount up the tripod and lights quickly outside the room and adjust them quickly as they restrained the kuffar. A large black flag was neatly folded on the desk; this would be placed behind the hostage. It looked impressive on camera, just solid black, that would outline the beheading, with only the Shahada 'There is no God but God', emblazoned across it in stark, unadorned, white Arabic script.

All in the room stood as Mullah Mohammad Al Salah glided

fluidly into the room. He entered with a tall, gaunt-looking black-garbed figure behind him; *he was the Brit executioner that had done such a good job on Sayeed,* thought Hassan. The Mullah was smiling and obviously elated, this was the first time that he had been offered the chance to give a videoed sermon at such an important event. *My words would be broadcast all over the world,* he thought proudly. The Mullah's face was upturned and smiling broadly. He beckoned the guys to sit down and they complied, all apart from the big Chechen in the corner who had not stood up. This annoyed the Mullah and he wondered whether he should reprimand him.

He glanced at Ivan sternly; he was quietly cleaning his nails with a large combat knife. Ivan looked up nonchalantly and smiled, showing a mixture of gold and brown rotting teeth, and raised his hand and waved. The Mullah felt a chill along his spine and decided to let it go.

Less than thirty feet away, leaning against another interior wall, Connor was listening intently. He had known something was being planned through brief snatches of conversation he had heard in English, but mainly Arabic. His Arabic had improved over his period of captivity, fuelled by his desire for survival. Each snippet had been like fitting another piece of a jigsaw puzzle, he thought he had worked out that he would soon be moved and had already decided to resist. He now knew that this was the end game.

The final giveaway had been the break in the usual routine; they always tried to disorientate him by bringing his food at strange times and always before the call to prayer in the morning. His treatment had got a lot worse since the other hostages had been released. It was at about 0400 when the skinny little Brit fuck had brought him his rice, but this time had not said anything, no comments about kuffars or Americans, no sneering, no spitting or pissing in his food. Connor immediately knew that his food or water might have been interfered with in another way.

He had therefore waited until he left, and immediately buried the food under the heaps of squalor that surrounded him; he poured the water into the plastic bucket that served as a chamber pot, although he was choking with thirst. He then checked that the thick steel chain that connected the heavy iron manacle that attached his left wrist to the wall was still loose. It would be his best weapon in a very one-sided fight, but he knew that one of those fuckers was going to die in that room before he did.

When they come for him he would be ready. He would pretend to be compliant and drugged, and then would take his opportunity when it occurred. He then heard the skinny Brit's footfall outside the door. He had long since learned how to recognise their footsteps, the big fat Brit slammed his feet into the ground and shuffled, the skinny Brit walked quickly and was light on his feet. He then heard the viewing hatch on the heavy wooden door bang open on its chains. Connor slumped against the wall and pretended to be asleep as he continued to listen to the fuckers next door planning to cut off his head.

Chapter Thirty Seven

Jimmy's Toy

Tommy Talibani and Jimmy were about two kilometres from where Connor made his plans. They were seated in another black painted Humvee with the black Shahada fluttering slightly from its right rear in the light breeze. The top gunner in the cupola on the roof of the Humvee scanned the direction of Mosul over the sights of his Browning 50 CAL machine gun; they had pulled over on the road that led to the square to enable the Black Hornet over-flight.

Although they were within two clicks of the target, things were not going well. The first Black Hornet had disappeared of the screen soon after flight. Jimmy thought it could have hit a power line but wasn't sure. He opened the Humvee's heavily armoured door, stepped out and prepared to launch the second drone.

Tommy checked his watch, ten minutes to the call to prayer, although that was never exact. *We still have time*, he thought.

Jimmy held the drone as it powered up and then released it upwards this time. The Black Hornet stabilised itself at 300 feet and then started to make its way to the target.

Jimmy stood by the opened door and started to give Tommy a running commentary. "OK, I'm keeping it at height now, that's the quickest way to get it on target in this light wind. At least the wind is in our favour."

Tommy moved into the passenger seat so he could observe

the small tablet monitor with Jimmy. He watched, fascinated, as the drone flew across the still dark but rapidly lightening sky. He could clearly see the shape of the large dome of the Grand Mosque as the drone began to close on its coordinates.

"We need to check those suicide vehicles first," said Tommy.

"Roger that," said Jimmy.

The Black Hornet descended and hovered, Jimmy angled the main night camera downwards from about two hundred feet and both men could clearly see a bird's eye view of the layout of the Chechen checkpoint.

"All looks quiet, looks like there may be ten guys up. The truck bomb is in the same position and the two smaller four-by-fours are unchanged."

Tommy leaned across. "Can you get the precise GPS fixes for those?"

"Yeah, I have done that," Jimmy replied. "The ZPU positions are manned, looks like only the gunners at the moment though."

Tommy knew that was a very encouraging sign, if the Daesh were expecting or trying to mount an attack everybody would be up and getting organised, especially the Chechens who were more efficient than most.

Jimmy moved the control slightly and turned the drone towards the house. Extraordinarily, just at that moment it managed to pick up what looked like a heavily pregnant girl pushing a pram. Sam was on target. Jimmy clearly recognised Taff as he walked beside her confirmed by his relative size compared to hers.

"That's the guys on target," said Jimmy.

"Right, let's roll the guys up mate, let's go to war," he said in his broad cockney accent, he then rapidly spoke into his ICOM in Kurdish.

Two clicks behind the attack force in armoured Humvees and armed Toyota gun trucks started their engines and started to slowly pull onto the main road into Mosul.

Doc and the Scott brothers had heard Tommy's order to move and were standing beside their vehicle ready for the signal from Sam. The wait had not been incident free; a three-vehicle convoy of ISIS fighters had driven past their position ten minutes before. Doc who was behind the wheel at the time rechecking the firing mechanism had just heard Talal say urgently, "Flash your lights three times," which he had done. As the ISIS patrol had passed, it had responded with three flashes, and Talal had given them the unofficial ISIS salute, a smile and a right forefinger extended towards paradise as they drove past. Several fighters responded with similar gestures; their disguise had held out. *But will it work at the checkpoint?* Doc wondered, as he heard the call he was waiting for in his earpiece.

"Hello all stations, this is Sam, five minutes."

"This is Doc, roger that."

"This is Pat, roger that."

"This is Jimmy, roger that."

And finally, "Hello all stations, this is Danny, roger that."

Doc immediately gunned the Humvee into life and started towards the Chechen checkpoint.

At their sniping position Eddie observed the checkpoint through the bors sight of the Barrett. As dawn approached, the sensitive optics enabled the dark shapes and shadows to gain substance. He could clearly see the outline of one of the ZPU-4s that was beginning to be silhouetted against the lightening sky. *That will have to go before it causes mayhem*, he thought. He had received the coordinates of the primary targets from Jimmy and had calculated the precise range and adjusted the bors' sight accordingly. He had loaded five armour-piercing rounds in the top of his lead magazine, although a normal Barrett round could usually cripple an engine block.

Eddie considered their chances; the only downside of the Barrett was its very loud and distinctive 'bang with a very fucking big B' when it fired, always accompanied by a flash from the barrel that was always clearly visible to the enemy. The discharge of gases from the large, double muzzle break at the front of the barrel, designed to eliminate some of the recoil, could also throw up dust that could also give away your position. In other words it was an easy weapon for the enemy to find in a firefight.

Eddie and Mac had improved their survivability considerably by selecting three different sniping positions on their rooftop overlooking the checkpoint. The flat rooftop with its low turreted wall had been in a serious firefight before, and had gaping holes in many places that overlooked the checkpoint. Eddie and Mac would move every time they thought their sniper position had been compromised.

CHAPTER THIRTY EIGHT

EXECUTION PARTY

As Eddie made the final adjustments to the Barrett's scope, Imran was walking across the square towards the death house where ISIS had parked the Save the Children's VW transporter. He was carrying his prayer mat and was deep in thought, and in a quandary. He had gained the permission and the means to leave Mosul the day before. In fact he was disobeying the orders from both the organisations he worked for. Ahmad and MI6 had expected him to have 'got out of Dodge' by now, and the previous day the Caliphate had loaded certain supplies and money that they needed smuggled back to England. One of the ISIS technicians had placed the gear into the covert containers that were built into the vehicle; they wanted him gone then as well.

He had managed to contact Ahmad with some information that he had picked up from the Brit Jihadists he had chatted to. It seems ISIS had found out that the Yank hostage was connected to the CIA in some way. He had told Ahmad that they would probably kill the American after a short Sharia court.

Ahmad had thanked him profusely, but Imran sort of thought that the news did not exactly shock him. He thought that was odd. Imran's main worry was his iPhone, the one he had left outside the hostage house to confirm where the poor bastard had been banged up. It was hidden amongst the rubble strewn around the waste ground outside the house. It was just propped up between a brick and a piece of building tile. It was fairly well camouflaged amongst the other shit, and the odd stray bush, but Imran was sure it would be found.

Ahmad had assured him that he would take care of the destruction of the phone, but Imran could not see how he possibly could. Even Hassan, the brainless fucker, would be able to work out that he had left it deliberately. He would be OK, Ahmad his handler had promised he would be resettled and he believed him, but what of his family? His old Mum and Dad never volunteered to be involved in all this stupid shit. He had broken his Dad's heart when he had gone Jihad. Imran knew what he would do: he would recover his phone before he fucked off back to London. Job done.

Imran looked across the square towards the Chechen checkpoint, it would be the call to prayer soon and that's when he would take his opportunity to find the phone. He would say that he had stayed to say prayers just one more time with 'true believers'. He hurried slightly; the sky was lightening, now every Muezzin in Mosul would be making their way towards their loudspeakers for the call to prayer.

Connor feigned surprise as the cell door opened swiftly and clanged into the wall and the execution party rushed into the room.

The big Chechen was first, his vast bulk filled the doorway and he almost brushed his shoulders on either side of the door as he sprung though it. He immediately stood to Connor's right about five feet away, growling and muttering Chechen like a giant bear focusing on his prey. The well-built German quickly came next and stood to his left, his hate-filled blue eyes and long blonde beard gave him the look of a deranged Viking. Connor made a quick assessment; he was maybe six-two and 200 pounds, he would be a handful. The rest of the execution party filed in the room after them, first Hassan the security officer smiling broadly, then a slightly built little fuck who struggled in with a video camera on a tripod in one hand and a fully mounted camera light in the other. Behind him came the two Brit guards, the one that pissed in Connor's food and the skinny one who had a folded black flag in his hand. Mullah Mohammed Al-Rafdan was the last to enter the room, dressed immaculately in a white Arab robe and smelling of aftershave.

Connor was unceremoniously grabbed by both Ivan and the German and hoisted to his feet. He made himself almost a dead weight, as if he was heavily sedated. The two guards quickly moved behind him and draped the black Shahada flag of ISIS along the wall and secured the ends with heavy gaffer tape. It was all over very quickly and the scene was set.

Ivan and the German held him in the kneeling position while the cameraman checked his angles and lighting. *This will be perfect*, he thought, *better than the last one I filmed, the lighting was sub-standard.*

Connor felt the pressure of Ivan and the Germans bulk both pressing down on him and holding him up at the same time, a firm heavy hand held each of his shoulders. He again pretended to relax his posture as if drugged.

Inside of him, at his very core, he felt the adrenaline start to course through his body. He would take the first opportunity that he could; he remembered the hand-to hand instructor's advice from his time with Delta, 'Strike from ambush if you can, summon up every ounce of violence from within yourself and harness its power and then commit totally, they will not be expecting it, you have the advantage.'

The black-garbed guy with the Mullah took a smallish black combat knife with a serrated edge from under his clothing and balanced it in his hand; he always enjoyed it more when the kuffar could see the knife. *I am going to enjoy this*, he thought. He showed the knife to Connor and quietly whispered into his right ear, "Yank fucker, I am going to butcher you like a sheep and I'm going to enjoy it," he said in a London accent.

Connor again slumped heavily between Ivan and the German. *And if I get a chance I'll fucking kill you as well*, he mentally answered.

Connor again thought of the hand-to-hand guy's advice, 'G-L-F, go like fuck, use everything you have for at least a mad minute — just sixty seconds of sustained violence can help you escape.'

At that very same time, and less than thirty feet away, the team had adopted their entry positions by the doors. Sam and Taff had arrived at the side door to the hostage room and immediately dropped the black rucksack that Sam had endured on the walk in; the Ops kit baby had been born. Taff removed the ECT door charges quickly from the pack and inserted the detonators and ran the lines out. He had to move quickly to wire up four different bangs and passed two to Scottie and Pat. He knew that that both teams would need at least two charges for the heavy wooden doors. Sam had ditched the abaya and now stood with her back to the security office's dirty brown wall. She was holding her MP5K tight into her body in the ready position. Sam looked towards the Chechen checkpoint; she could now clearly see its outline as the sky began to lighten. *We're running out of time*, she thought.

Pat and Scottie had collected their door charges and 'flash-crash' grenades from the 'Ops baby' and had casually walked around to the front of the office and quickly placed the door charges. The sticky side of the ECT was now stuck fast on the outside, and in the middle of the thick double doors. Scottie leaned with his left shoulder against the wall with his MP5K held firmly in the ready position in both hands. Pat held the M57 firing device or clacker for the door charge in his right hand and stood behind Scottie. It was the same device that operated the claymore mine and never failed.

Pat's MP5K was hanging by his side on its bungee cord; in his left hand he held a flash-crash. He had loosened the pin, it was on a one-second fuse, and the grenade would be lobbed into the room as soon as the door was breached. The grenade was non-lethal and designed as a distraction device. The mixture of magnesium and mercury supplied an ear numbing 160 decibels of sound and hundreds of loud explosions and bright flashes that was designed to disorient the rooms occupants

Scottie would go in fast, to the left and low, Pat would go right and high, and then they would double-tap everybody in that room. The team all listened to their earpieces intently, this was the most dangerous time, and this was where they were most exposed. Three rapid bursts of static from Sam's prezzle switch would be the signal when she was ready to breach, and then Doc would take out the checkpoint. The room entry team would then all go simultaneously, it seemed to be the longest wait in their lives.

Doc listened as he, Talal and Mad Mo started to approach within 200 metres of the checkpoint.

Just at that moment, loudspeakers from a hundred different Mosul mosques provided background accompaniment for the chant of the Muezzin from the minaret of the Grand Mosque. The singsong voice of a recorded call to prayer echoed around the square. *ALLLLah Akbarrrr, Allahhhhh Akbarrrrr.*

Tommy Talibani listened; his guys were now running in. *Come on, Sam*, he thought as he willed her to start the attack.

The Ops room was tense as Danny listened into the Hedges and Fisher net. There was an intense silence as if everybody, Brit, American and Pershmerga alike almost held their breath. *What had gone wrong?* he thought.

Inside the death house the scene had been set for butchery. The lights were on and the cameraman had started filming. The Mullah had launched into his denunciation of America and the CIA. *He loves the sound of his own voice,* thought Hassan. The black-robed executioner was now standing behind Connor and holding the black combat knife up for the camera. Connor felt his presence and knew it had to be now, he gave himself a mental countdown. The grip of both the Chechen and the German had lessened, and they were now just more or less holding him up.

He had three separate threats to engage. The primary threat was the guy with the knife behind him. He then had the nasty big Chechen and the German to deal with. There were no firearms within reach, the two jailers had AKs slung over their shoulders but they were out of range. He had thought he had seen where the big Chechen had put his combat knife and it was directly beside his left ear on Big Ivan's right hip. The Mullah was becoming louder. Connor opened his eyes slightly and focused on what he was going to do, the bright video lights hurt his eyes slightly. *Let's roll*, he thought.

Chapter Thirty Nine

Room Entry

Outside the door Sam was ready, the charges were set against the heavy iron hinges because it looked like the door was sealed on the inside. It had taken them extra time to change these around. There was activity in the room; a loud voice seemed to be delivering a sermon. Was it too late? Sam pressed the prezzle switch three times and waited for Doc to take out the checkpoint.

Connor flexed the muscles in his left arm, summoned up all his strength and snatched at the heavy chain to which he was manacled, he punched his arm forward and felt it release. There was a stunned silence in the room as he simultaneously reached for the Chechens knife, grasped it from his waistband and stabbed it hard into his leg: Connor felt the razor sharp knife bite deep and hard. The Chechen grunted more than screamed and Connor's 'Mad Minute' was on.

He slashed with the knife and stabbed the German upwards into his the groin almost immediately. The German screamed as a long stream of blood sprayed from his testicles. The executioner now tried to react, he was scared, he had killed many by slicing through their throats but he had never been in combat. He lifted his knife and prepared to plunge it into Connor's vulnerable back but hesitated.

At the same time, Doc heard the call to prayer as he aimed the Humvee at the Chechen checkpoint.

It was 100 metres away now. Doc held his breath.

It was fifty now.

It was twenty-five.

The black-flagged armoured Humvee came to a stop as a single Chechen who had been half sleeping on a white plastic chair brought his M16 up to challenge them. He then heard shouting in Arabic from the door of the armoured vehicle that had been partially opened.

It was Talal. "Help, brothers, we have casualties," he shouted.

The Chechen stood and barked orders to two of his comrades to go with him.

Doc came up in clear on comms. "STANDBY, STANDBY, STANDBY," and pressed the button.

A huge BANG! and 2100 fearsome ball bearings were explosively launched forward in a deadly arch all around the checkpoint. Mad Mo poked his head from the cupola of the vehicle and pressed the trigger of the cocked and loaded GMPG, and sprayed the ensuing chaos with a long burst of 7.62 Nato standard bullets that ripped through any target he could see.

Taff and Sam heard the ear-splitting explosion. Taff immediately squeezed the two handles of the clacker together within his large right hand and BANG!

The door flew from its hinges as Sam hurled a flash-crash into the room that exploded with a frightening mixture of sounds and lightning. Taff went right and Sam went left — they were in the room.

At exactly the same time Scottie and Pat were breaching the office. Scottie used the clacker.

BANG!

As the double doors smashed inwards, Pat lobbed a flash-crash and they went in. Both teams were in, fast, both high and low and up on aim, just in time.

Both teams were in the two separate rooms simultaneously. Pat was in the security office, and taking right of arc, the flash-crash was still exploding in a thousand little flashes. As Pat quickly scanned the room he saw two prison guards over the sight of his MP5K, they remained shocked and still seated at a cheap white plastic desk. Their faces were ashen, transfixed and bolt upright in fear. They had two short-barrelled M4's on the desk in front of them.

"DON'T SHOOT, I'M BRITISH!" screamed the one on the extreme left.

BANG-BANG! Pat double-tapped him directly between the eyes and he flew back in his chair with the impact of the rounds.

BANG-BANG! Another double tap caught the side of the other security man's head and bowled him over sideways, blood and brains spattering the white coloured wall.

Scottie had gone left. His X-ray had an M16 slung across his shoulder and he was frantically trying to bring it on aim.

BANG-BANG! Scottie double tapped and caught him in the area of his nose and he was thrown back violently by the force of the rounds as if he had been poleaxed.

Sam had gone left, Taff went right and directly onto the right-hand wall. The video lights and camera were still running but this was not what they were expecting to film. The cameraman, wide eyed and trembling, shouted a long, impassioned, "Please, no!" in English as the first two rounds impacted his chest and threw him backwards.

BANG-BANG!

A fattish guy appeared from behind the opened cell door. He then moved his weapon upwards towards Sam.

BANG-BANG!

He caught Taff's double tap in his temple and it cartwheeled him sideways against the ball.

At the same time Sam had brought her MP5K on aim at the black-garbed, masked figure who was just had recovered himself after the flash-crash and was just about to plunge a black combat knife into the dirtied GITMO orange of Connor's back.

She engaged him.

BANG-BANG! The tall ninja figure was thrown back as two closely spaced 9mm rounds in his chest threw him against the green-wallpapered wall.

Sam aimed again at the front of his head when he finally stopped sliding down the wall.

BANG!

Then BANG-BANG! Sam switched target, she then placed a double tap through the head of the big German who was rolling around in agony, holding his groin.

Connor was still held in a bear hug by Ivan on the floor and was repeatedly smashing his forehead into the big Chechen's face, he could feel the Chechen weakening, and he had won. He knew a rescue was on as soon as the door flew across the room and the stun grenades came in. He knew how Brit SF operated; he had trained with them during his time with Delta. One of the Brit prison guards, the little skinny shit, had been leaning nonchalantly against the door, enjoying the show, as the heavy wooden door came explosively in, powered by twenty-seven grains of super powerful plastic explosive. He was now lying under it on the other side of the room.

Sam came on aim as she stood in the ready position behind Connor. "BRITISH ARMY!" she shouted. "MOVE, CONNOR!"

The shout penetrated the mad mixture of hate, self-preservation and blood lust, which still coursed through his body, and he stopped head butting the Chechen and rolled his head to the side.

BANG-BANG!

Sam's double-tap impacted Ivan's already bloodied forehead, the big Chechen's luck had just run out.

Across the square with the sound of the first explosion still sounding in his ears. Eddie engaged the first target with the Barrett.

"Shot," he said to Mac. Mac observed.

BANG!

Mac said, "You're on." Observing through his high-powered binoculars, he clearly saw the impact of the armour-piercing round as it hit the front cab of the truck bomb and penetrated the engine block, and then another in swift succession.

BANG!

Then the black four-by-four.

BANG!

Then the white four-by-four.

"Both on," said Mac.

The ZPU units were next.

Hassan had been playing dead. He had been lying behind the opened cell door; if it were the British Army he could surrender to them. The rapid double-taps had convinced him otherwise and now he was terrified. He quickly leapt up and propelled himself towards the now open space where the outer door had been, in a bid for freedom. He knew they wouldn't shoot him in the back.

"Don't shoot, I'm British!" he screamed.

Taff turned quickly and placed the double-tap.

BANG-BANG! Hassan's body was thrown forward and thumped as it hit the floor; Taff stood over him and put one in his head.

BANG!

"It's big boys' rules here, mate," he said quietly.

Hassan's intelligence career was over.

Sam surveyed the carnage as the guys arrived from the other room.

"Coming in," shouted Pat as he and Scottie arrived at the now opened cell door.

"RIGHT CLEAR!" shouted Taff.

"LEFT CLEAR!" shouted Sam.

"IT'S ALL CLEAR!" he shouted for a final time.

Pat and Scottie entered the room. "Sam, that's three X-rays all dead, no Yankees."

"Roger that," she said.

"We have five X-rays, all dead, Yankee is recovered, and he's OK. Let's check for info before we get him out of here."

The team quickly searched the bodies looking for any intelligence they could glean; they picked up a couple of bloodstained British passports. They took a thumb-drive from Hassan's pocket and they took the film from the camera, but they did not have time for much else.

Taff was attending to some superficial wounds that Connor had sustained; the Chechen had left a large bite mark on his cheek and it seemed that his right knee ligament had been torn in the struggle. He tried to support himself on it but could not sustain his own weight. Connor really didn't know what to say. He looked at Taff, looked at the first friendly eyes that he seen in an eternity and said, "Thanks guys, but I think I'm going to hold you up."

"You are what we have come for, buddy, and we're not leaving without you," Taff replied, extending his hand towards the American.

Sam moved across the executioner she had topped. She had slung her weapon and took out her iPhone; she would now photograph all the faces very quickly. She pulled up his mask.

She recognised him from press pictures at home and grimaced, there was a single large hole in the middle of his forehead where both bullets had impacted so close together that they had pushed his brain out and splattered it on the wall. She took the photo. "Listen to your Auntie Sam, you never take a knife to a gunfight, kid," she muttered quietly.

It was quiet in the room now, outside the room the rest of Mosul was in chaos as explosions and gunfire was heard from just about everywhere. That's when the team heard the whimpering coming from under the door. It sounded like a child quietly crying. Pat came up on aim and went over to investigate. He moved the door with his foot and there was the Mullah, his immaculate robes scorched and blackened with soot from the flash-bangs, crying quietly to himself. He had lost all control of his emotions and prostate by the look of it, and he was gibbering in fear.

"PLEASE, PLEASE!" he shouted in English. "I AM A MAN OF GOD!"

Pat looked at him and immediately came on aim. He sighted his weapon and then found that he just could not shoot such a pathetic fucker. He took the MP5K off aim and let it hang on its bungee cord.

No, there's been enough killing today, he thought. He stepped across to the Mullah and hit him with his signature right cross, developed when he was a middleweight boxing champion in 3 Para, and knocked him out.

Taff turned towards Sam, Pat and Scottie and said, "Right, guys, let's get the fuck out of Dodge," in the exaggerated Welsh accent that he reserved for such occasions. "It's more dangerous than my village on a Saturday night, and that's fucking dangerous."

The Pershmerga had arrived in Mosul, they had spread out throughout the town and the lightning raid had now become a thousand little firefights as the Daesh tried to rally. Tommy Talibani's vehicle had arrived at what remained of the Chechen checkpoint. His cupola gunner hammered away with a Browning 50 Cal to keep the remaining Chechens heads down, accompanying the GPMG of Mad Mo, who continued to fire short, accurate bursts at every opportunity target.

A Chechen climbed into the seat behind the ZPU-4 anti-aircraft gun mounted on top of the office building. The previous gunner lay dead with the biggest chest wound he had ever seen inflicted in his twenty years of warfare from Chechnya to here. He checked the feed tray, re-cocked the weapon and peered over its vast bulk as he directed it at three Kurdish gun-trucks that were engaged in a firefight with ISIS on the square.

"The ZPU at Black-two is getting manned again," said Mac, observing through the binoculars draped around his neck.

"Roger that," said Eddie as he adjusted the Barrett's position.

The new gunner was instantly framed in the crosshairs of the sighting system.

"Shot," he said.

BANG! Mac clearly saw the Chechen gunner ejected backwards from his seat as if swatted by some giant hand.

"You're on," said Mac. That was all the ZPUs accounted for.

"Let's move," said Eddie, and both men made their way to the next firing position, carefully talking the clacker for the claymore with them. They would have to leave soon, their position was compromised and they had seen ISIS fighters trying to outflank them from the rooftops on their right.

Come on, guys, Eddie thought, willing Sam and the room entry team to extract soon, as the first of the rounds from the ISIS fighters ricocheted of the concrete of the roof behind them.

They knew they had to try to stay longer until the team had completely extracted the hostage. The ISIS fighters were slowly making their way behind them, once they had pinned them down, they would attack. Mac was still observing the checkpoint.

"TARGET!" Mac shouted. "An RPG (Rocket Propelled Grenade launcher) man near Black Three."

"Roger," said Eddie. The bors' optic quickly picked out the Chechen by one of the destroyed ZPUs. He was a large man; the RPG seemed small against his bulk. He was aiming the RPG from about thirty metres way from the open ground by the hostage house. He knelt and calmly placed the RPG on his shoulder, its warhead clearly visible and was pointing towards Doc's Humvee. Eddie lined up the crosshairs on the bors sight.

"SHOT!"

BANG!

The Chechen disappeared from the sight picture as by magic,

the round hit him below the left shoulder blade and cartwheeled him sideways.

"You're on," said Mac.

Imran had been lying on the ground outside the hostage house, in a state of semi-shock. As he had approached to reclaim his iPhone, the whole world had exploded around him. The blast from the claymore had thrown him to the ground and he had stayed there. He had tried to move his body lower as rounds had started to impact right across the waste ground; bullets were ricocheting off the ground and pinging into the sky.

He had seen the big Chechen RPG guy get hit with something big. It had catapulted him across the waste ground in front of Imran until his stone dead body came to rest in front of him. The Chechen's very confused looking dead face was now right next to Imran's. He had ended up in the fetal position and was staring with his very dead eyes into his. The Chechen's long red beard was nearly brushing Imran's face. Imran waited and then pulled the Chechen backwards a bit more to provide him with a bit more cover.

He noticed the Chechen had a Czech Scorpion 7.65 machine pistol slung from the dead fighters shoulder. Imran took it, lay on his back under the cover of the Chechen's bulk and checked it had ammo in the long thin magazine. He then cocked the weapon.

I may have to kill someone to get out of this, he thought. *Right, I need to get some cover.* He looked over his shoulder to the extreme left of the hostage house. *At least there I will be in dead ground to all the gunfire on the square*, Imran confirmed in his own mind. He kept really low, his stomach hugging the ground as he belly crawled initially and then ran at a crouch towards the relative safety of the corner of the building.

The firing from the Chechen checkpoint had ceased; from the protection of the corner of where they had held the hostage, Imran crouched low with the Scorpion VZ61 as his only protection as he saw the flames lick higher consuming what was once the checkpoint. The flames were sometimes disrupted by a large explosion of some type, ammunition cooking off, or maybe an RPG round or grenade on a fighter's belt. There was no life, it had been extinguished, and it suddenly occurred to Imran, *every Chechen is now dead.*

Chapter Forty

Imran Decides

The room entry team had gathered themselves; they had conducted an ammunition and casualty report and had let Danny know the current state of play. Danny was elated but now knew that the most important and dangerous part of the mission was to come. The pram had been stripped of its arms. They had swapped their primary weapons. Sam's MP5K was now slung over her shoulder on its bungee cord with a fresh mag attached, its job done for now, and she had picked up and prepped the Colt M18 assault rifle with its drum mag.

Taff had done the same and now had his favourite weapon, the Minimi Para .556 light machine gun. He had checked the 200 round box mag was firmly attached and cocked it. Pat and Scottie had prepped their M4s. All the team had put on their hats emblazed with ARMY in orange and day-glow armbands to identify them as good guys. Connor waited with them and got ready for one more last effort for freedom.

Sam came up on the Hedges and Fisher net. "Hello all stations, check."

"Yeah, that's Doc, roger," gasped Doc, in between firing his M4; he and the Scott brothers were still in a desperate firefight with ISIS reinforcements.

"Yeah, that's Eddie," Eddie and Mac were coming under increasingly accurate fire from an ISIS position on a roof further down the street. Eddie looked through the bors' sight on the entrance to the security office. The final job would be to cover the team's withdrawal and then they could get the fuck out. *Come on, Sam*, he thought as he willed her to move.

Doc tested the drivability of the Humvee as Mo continued to rattle away with his GPMG from the cupola. "I'M ON MY LAST BOX OF AMMO!" he shouted down. The GPMG's barrel was now glowing with heat and getting dangerous to use without a barrel change.

Mo dropped his rate of fire and only chose definite targets. He would need the remaining ammo for the extraction.

Doc willed the Humvee to still drive, it had been hit with numerous rounds of various calibers, including the odd armour piercing round that had gone through the armour of the Humvee like butter and exited the other side without injury to the occupants. He knew they had been lucky, but how lucky. Would the Humvee drive? He placed the automatic gearshift into reverse and the big diesel and quickly responded and moved backwards.

Talal screamed into the Pershmerga ICOM in Kurdish to Tommy in the other Humvee and both reversed at speed. Doc's Humvee bumped furiously over the rubble of battle as they disengaged from the fight at the checkpoint. There was very little fire coming from the checkpoint now, the Chechens were mostly dead but the whole square had become a hornet's nest of buzzing, angry bullets as the Kurds prepared to withdraw.

Doc could only just about see through the armoured screen of the Humvee; although the thick armoured glass had stopped the rounds it had also nearly completely crazed the glass. Doc concentrated on a small area of the screen that had not been damaged and tried to find the security office.

Mad Mo lived up to his name and braved the angry buzz of bullets with his head outside the cupola to try and direct him. "GO LEFT! ANOTHER 100!" he shouted above the din of battle.

Tommy's gunner had been killed and lay in the back, his driver was wounded and he now drove the second black Humvee. The shape of Doc's vehicle was clearly visible through the crazed windscreen, the vehicle bumped after Doc's.

Eddie and Mac witnessed the extraction from the roof of the sniping house. Eddie had managed to take out three of the remaining Chechens as they had fired on the Humvees. He now refocused the scope on the double doors of the hostage house and waited, the bors sight searching the rooftop of the Madrassa and the security office for the enemy. Mac meantime was engaged in his own firefight with the ISIS fighters on the roof of a building 300 metres away. He fired at the flashes of their weapons which seemed to be predominately AK47s and the odd RPD Russian machine gun that seemed to be suffering from a lot of stoppages, which was a big advantage to Mac.

Sam came up on coms in clear, "Change of plans, we are going out the side door." Sam had gauged the amount of rounds being exchanged across the square and thought that an extraction from the front of the building would be too dangerous.

"Roger that," said Doc calmly as he pulled the Humvee up on the waste ground outside the hostage house.

Tommy Talibani pulled his Humvee around to face in the other direction.

Two more of Tommy's vehicles joined them, another Humvee and a brown coloured Toyota gun-truck mounted with a Dhushka. The Kurd on the back of the Toyota was standing totally calmly and firing the Dushka with short bursts, or with single shots, towards a group of ISIS fighters who were trying to regroup at the other end of the square.

Doc came up on the Hedges and Fisher net. "We are good to go, guys."

Taff moved through the opening that had once been the door that they came in. He glanced outside quickly; the Humvees were a fifty-metre dash away at the side of the house. They were positioned to protect them from occasional round coming from the square.

Sam pressed her prezzle switch and transmitted, "We are moving now," as she left the relative safety of what had once been Connor's prison. Scottie and Sam went first and broke right to provide security to the rear and towards the Chechen checkpoint. Taff and Pat, the two taller guys, left the doorway with Connor draped between them, he was conscious but in some pain. The long chain that had once tethered him hung from the heavy manacle that was still on his wrist. Taff picked up the chain and passed it around his own shoulders. Sam was on their extreme right now looking back at the 'Death House' and covering their movement to the rear. *It looked good,* she thought, and she turned to look towards where Doc had parked the Humvees.

The skinny Brit, the worst of Connor's jailers, was conscious. He knew what he had to do, just stay put. He had heard the Mullah's pleading and he had heard what he had assumed was British Special Forces searching some of the bodies. He had rehearsed what to say, he would put his hands up and threaten them with war crimes if they killed an unarmed prisoner. He was hurt, but he was alive, his luck held, they did not check under the door. As his fear subsided he had slowly put a plan together as the SF were preparing to leave. He would be a hero 'Mujahid' after all.

The British SF had left, he slowly and gingerly tested that he could stand up; the only sound in the room was the heavy breathing of the Mullah. Nobody else was breathing. He was angry, he had never fought in a battle, and now was his chance, he thought. He had to act quickly. He picked up one of the guards AK47s, took off the magazine and checked it was loaded. The mag felt heavy in his hands. *It's full*, he thought. He pulled back the cocking handle and slowly and silently fed a round into the breach. He then slowly clicked the select lever down to its bottom position, for automatic fire.

Taff and Pat were struggling slightly with Connor's weight, he had blacked out and the extra encumbrance of their weapons made things difficult. Sam hurried towards them to help; only Scottie remained in the kneeling position with his M18 in his shoulder covering them towards the Chechen checkpoint. Connor collapsed completely, both Taff and Pat now just lifted him bodily between them. The Humvees were only ten metres away now. The doors of Doc's, and two of Tommy's, were open ready for them, and Talal and a Kurd from Tommy's vehicle prepared to help them over the last five yards of broken ground. A fierce firefight was still heard from the Christian quarter, where the occasional boom of Pat's Barrett was also heard.

Imam peeked around the corner of the building; he saw that they were ready to leave. The American was being supported and almost lifted towards the opened doors of the Humvees. He would now wait, and when they went, he would try to find that fucking phone and then 'imshee' (walk).

Imran suddenly spotted movement in front of him at the opening that the rescue team had left after their explosives had imploded the door. He saw a dusty figure stagger through what had once been the doorway with an AK47 held downwards by its pistol grip in his right hand. Imran recognised him as one of the security staff, the skinny British one. He was moving with difficulty and was half staggering out the door. The rescue team had not seen him. He turned towards where the team and the Kurds were trying to lay the American hostage in the Black Humvee, and he brought the AK47 shakily up on aim at their unguarded backs.

"There are moments in life where you have to decide between good and evil." Imran instantly thought of what his father had once said to him, without hesitation he quickly brought the Scorpion up on aim and placed a long burst into the security man's back. He pitched forward dead, the AK47 falling from his hands. Imran then ducked behind the wall as the first return fire from the Brits he had just saved impacted within one foot of him. Imran made a quick new plan: *forget the phone and just get the fuck home to Luton.*

Sam shouted, "CEASE FIRE!" She knew instinctively that someone had just saved her and her team's lives. She saw the dead security man, someone had killed him, and she just did not know whom.

Taff reached into his right hand pocket and pulled out the car key fob to activate the claymore in the pram. It was now outside, parked by the wall of Connor's cell with the nasty end pointing towards the Chechen check point. They knew that civilians would soon be in the area of the square again, so the claymore had to go. He depressed the button.

BANG! The claymore secreted in the pram exploded its deadly cargo outwards harmlessly in the general direction of the checkpoint and the wheeled carriage smashed itself against the building, sending the doll inside spiralling into the air. *That worked well,* he thought, as the team quickly clambered into the vehicles.

Sam ended up face first and draped over Taff's leg in the back of Doc's Humvee with her backside staring into his face as the vehicle accelerated across the square with Mad Mo still hammering away with short accurate bursts at the Daesh.

Taff was quiet for a second. "You OK, Sam?" he said.

"Never better," said Sam sarcastically from her position with her face by Mo's feet, who fired the GPMG, sending a succession of empty .762 cylinders raining down on her head. "You OK?" she enquired in turn.

Taff took a moment and glanced down the length of Sam's body. "Fucking excellent," he said in his broadest Welsh accent. She could feel him smiling.

"I have still got a feckin' gun, you fucking eejit," Sam said.

All the team got the next transmission through their earpieces.

"Hello all stations. This is Eddie, in heavy contact, extracting in five, confirm you have our fix on GPS."

"Roger that," said Taff as he helped Sam correct her position. *This is not over yet*, he thought, as he checked his GPS and located the sniper team ready for extraction.

Chapter Forty One

Withdrawal

The sniper team was quickly running out of luck, they were under a heavy fire now and pinned down. Eddie and Mac were lying on their fronts with their weapons close into their sides. Small pieces of concrete were being splattered from the low wall they sheltered under. They heard the voices of the Daesh below them, loud shouted discussions in Arabic. Both guys now only had their MP5K's as Mac's M18 and the Barrett were out of ammo. Eddie thought about removing the breach block and ditching it, but he knew that a decent engineer could manufacture that quite easily; he would take it with him. Both guys had donned their recognition hats and armbands. They then crawled slowly and carefully towards the rear stairs of the roof and waited. They heard different voices and shouting from the street leading up to the stairs. They were obviously trying to organise an assault. There was a loud BANG! WHOOSH! as an RPG round flew over their heads and upwards, narrowly missing the wall near where they sheltered. Mac peered over the steps. About ten ISIS fighters prepared to come up them. Mac picked up the claymore's clacker. "All right, mate, this is shit or bust," he said.

"Roger that, mate," Eddie replied, "count it down." Eddie had a primed high explosive L60 grenade in his right hand. Five other grenades had been prepped ready for action.

Mac picked up the clacker. "TEN, NINE, EIGHT, SEVEN," he mouthed silently.

The first ISIS fighters were now creeping stealthily up the stairs their weapons held in the ready position.

"SIX, FIVE, FOUR, THREE," mouthed Mac.

They heard Sam in their earpieces but could not reply. "Your location with five gun trucks in two minutes," she said precisely.

The front ISIS fighter was slowly creeping up the steps, the butt of his weapon in his shoulder, looking over the sights of his M4. He sighted his weapon forward, scanning for movement, and then he saw it. It was a dark green, oblong box. He only spoke Arabic and could not write it; he knew very little about England, Europe or America, he only knew they were kuffar and damned. If he could have read English, he could have read the words on the green box, which simply said, 'FRONT TOWARDS ENEMY'.

"TWO, ONE."

BANG!

There was a collective scream as 700 ball bearings splintered downwards, rattling off the hard concrete of the steps and into human flesh. Mac eased the pin from an L60 grenade and pulled it, the lever clunked against the detonator and he then held the grenade and mentally counted down two of the seconds on its four-second fuse. *One thousand and one. One thousand and two*, and dropped it over the wall, Eddie's followed straight afterwards.

Two seconds and:

BANG!

Two seconds after.

BANG!

There was a whimpering sound from below them as the two operators made a break for it. They rushed down the stairs that had become slippery with blood.

"Fuck me," said Mac. "That's fucking carnage." Ten to twelve ISIS fighters were down, some obviously dead, some badly wounded. He looked to his left quickly, there was movement;

a wounded fighter had stood up groggily and had come on aim with his M16.

BANG-BANG! Mac double-tapped him and he went down.

The two operators then ran along the inner side of the buildings towards the junction. The ISIS fighters had recovered themselves and the odd bullet started to rattle off the wall beside which they were running, sending pieces of masonry flying into the street.

The next sound though was reassuring; it was a long ripping burst of a medium machine gun, the unmistakable sound of an FN GPMG that had come from the top gunner on a Kurd gun truck. Both guys saw the dipped headlights of a Kurdish Humvee driving towards them, with the flashes of tracer from the GPMG fire passing over them to the left and high and impacting the ISIS positions on the rooftops.

"That's us, Sam," Mac said into his comms.

"Roger that," Sam replied as the first Humvee stopped and opened its thick armoured rear doors.

Sam and Taff appeared from the other Humvee. Sam engaged the area of some enemy weapon flashes with a long burst from her M18. Taff leaned into his Minimi and supported her from the other side of the street with long sustained bursts to cover the sniper team's extraction. Eddie firstly threw the dead weight of the Barrett into the open door of the armoured Humvee and quickly followed it. Mac let loose a long burst from his MP5K and piled in afterwards his empty M18 across his shoulder.

Sam and Taff worked together. Taff came on aim and delivered a long burst towards the muzzle flashes of the Daesh.

"MOVE NOW!" he shouted. Sam moved quickly back to the safety of the armoured Humvee and covered Taff.

"MOVE!" she shouted, after a long burst of automatic fire.

Taff turned and looked over his right shoulder and dashed, zigzagging while he was running to make his back a hard target. He ran to the door of the Humvee where Sam stood with the butt of her weapon firmly in her shoulder and was leaning forward with deadly intent, firing short bursts to cover his movement, as Taff made his way towards the shelter of the open Humvee door.

Once both operators were in and safe within the vehicle, both Humvees then started to reverse at speed with the top gunners still engaging the weapon flashes of the enemy. The firing was still intense, with rounds skipping up from the concrete road surface and the odd round rattling against the Humvees armour plating. The sound, frequency and accuracy on the incoming fire slackened as the Humvees extracted at speed.

The Kurds were withdrawing now, with individual gun trucks trying to disengage with the enemy from a hundred different individual firefights. Tommy Talibani was listening intently to the Kurdish ICOM net; his face sometimes grimaced as some element of bad news filtered through. The Kurdish casualty rate could only be fully assessed once the Commando Unit had been reassembled back at the Kalak checkpoint, but he was determined not to leave anybody behind.

Tommy's Humvee showed that it had been in the thick of the fight; being hit with a hundred different enemy rounds had visibly battered the armour. The scar from a RPG warhead ran along the whole driver's side. There was a deep gouge where an ISIS fighter had must have forgotten to remove the nose pin before he loaded it into his launcher. The inside of the Humvee smelt of sweat, blood and death. Talal's young cousin, Tommy's gunner, had turned from being a valiant combatant into a respected piece of cargo, and was now lying dead across the back seat. Two ISIS bullets had impacted the front of his forehead and taken parts of his brain through the exit wound; Talal's bloodied shemagh now covered the damage. *He had been eighteen,* thought Tommy, and he had been Pershmerga since he was sixteen. Pershmerga in Kurdish means 'one who confronts death', and Tommy knew that the young Kurd had faced death bravely on hundreds of occasions.

The Kurdish Commandos rolled back in an organised manner, with one unit that had successfully disengaged supporting the remaining units that had not. Slowly and surely the last units were coming up on Tommy's ICOM and reporting that they had successfully disengaged. Tommy had a simple postcard-size chart that he used to check off the Kurdish call signs with a small marker pen. He would stay on the main highway outside Mosul until he had counted all his guys out. His Humvee would be the last to leave.

Connor had been transferred to safety with the other wounded. Sam and the team had voted to stay with Tommy and his group until all were accounted for. Tommy had initially objected but had been impressed by their solidarity. Sam pointed out the more practical reasons why it might be advantageous. After all, they still had the Black Hornet that could be employed to search for stragglers and assess the ground. Jimmy had recharged the battery and could re-launch his remaining drone at any time.

Finally Tommy crossed off the final Kurdish sub-unit and they started their engines and made for home. When they finally rolled through the Kalak checkpoint. Sam gathered her thoughts; they had done it, it was over.

Sam came up on the Hedges and Fisher net; she knew that Danny would have been getting a running commentary from the battleground on the Kurdish radio net. She calmed and composed herself, you never wanted to sound high pitched and panicky on the net, and it was unprofessional, even if you were terrified, as she had been on many occasions that day.

"Hello Danny, this is Sam, SITREP (situation report) over."

A joyful-sounding Danny replied. "Roger that Sam, send."

"Hi Danny this is Sam, we are at the Kalak checkpoint and RTB, (Returning to Base)" She then continued to give a full SITREP in the correct sequence. "We have no casualties, ammo at twenty-five percent for M4, nil for Barrett, 9mm good. Ten

X-rays dead on target, Yankee is recovered and well. We have items of Intel importance, our intention is to RTB and assess, over."

There was a slight pause as Danny recovered his composure, and there was a loud cheer and round of applause from the Kurdish Ops room. It had been the most worrying couple of hours of his life so far.

"Hi Sam, this is Danny. Good job." That was just about all he could think of to say.

Tim and Ahmad had arrived in the Ops room as the Kurdish forces had started to withdraw and now stood behind the seated Danny.

Danny stood and turned and faced the new arrivals. "They've done it," he said quietly.

"We know," whispered Tim conspiratorially in Danny's ear, gently implying that their source had been on the ground when it was happening. "Great job, Danny," said Tim.

"Really great job," Ahmad added. "There is only one thing now to tie up, we have a little bit of source protection to take care of. If you can excuse us Danny, we need advice from the Wing Commander here."

Danny understood immediately. In a world that revolves around the circle of knowledge and the 'need to know', he actually and quite happily, 'did not need to know.'

Danny opened the door of the Ops room and felt the warmth of the winter sun on his face. He sat on a low blast wall outside the Ops room that served as a smoking area. He took a deep breath of the crisp Kurdish morning air, closed his eyes and slowly exhaled. He had a jumble of thoughts quickly flash into his mind, he thought about Northern Ireland, Bosnia, Afghanistan and Iraq and all the shit and suffering he had seen that sometimes he could do nothing to change. This time, unencumbered by government, his team, had made a difference, and he had snatched one back from the darkness. With that final thought he allowed his normally impassive expression reflect into a broad smile.

Danny thoughtfully unwrapped one of his finest cigars that he had removed from his humidor earlier for this very purpose. He snipped the end with a cigar cutter, lit it and slowly felt the gentle warmth of the Cuban tobacco trickle into his lungs. *Well done guys, fucking well done*, he thought.

Ahmad and Tim quietly talked to the Wing Commander, who had been sitting next to Danny in the Ops room. He had been frustrated that his assets had not been needed but pleased that all had gone well. Now these Security Service people had asked some advice and he had responded, but it would need political clearance at the highest level.

Ahmad had promised his agent that he would take care of the phone and now that is what the RAF would do. It was more important than even Source 2030 thought it was. The phone reflected the same technology in its rather tattered body that had also been employed by Jimmy in the bugged laptops. If ISIS techs recovered the phone, it was just slightly possible that the technology could be discovered or even replicated. The phone had to be destroyed in-place.

Chapter Forty Two

RAF AKROTIRI

The RAF Typhoon's two Rolls Royce MK 103 turbofan engines burst into life as Pilot Flight Lieutenant Rebecca Garland rolled the GR4A onto the runway at RAF Akrotiri in Cyprus. Her navigator, Squadron Leader Joanne Erwin, quickly checked the instruments for the flight path into Iraq. Under the Typhoon's sweptback wings hung two pods of three Mark 2 Brimstone missiles. The Brimstone was a very accurate missile made by GEC-Marconi.

It was, as the crew knew, a very special piece of kit and expensive at £108,000 a pop. Weighing only 48 kilos it not only possessed an advanced guidance system for pinpoint accuracy but on impact also produced a low blast area to prevent collateral damage. It was ideal for this job; they had been tasked to destroy a piece of kit that was omitting a homing signal. They didn't ask what it was, the SF had probably left it behind, and they just knew from the briefing that British lives were at risk if they couldn't pull it off.

Mosul was calm and quiet by the next day and Mullah Mohammad Al-Rafdan had fully recovered his composure and was once again immaculately clothed and smelling of expensive French aftershave. The accursed British and Kurds had gone, but luckily they had killed everybody who might have witnessed his cowardice. He had cut a heroic figure with his bloodied and swollen jaw and his explosive stained and bloody clothing. He had shouted, despite the discomfort, and had successfully rallied the ISIS Forces in Mosul after the attack. He made a great show of his fearlessness once the battle was over, he felt no shame, after all, *'it doesn't really matter what they think, it's what you make the idiots "think" that counts'.*

He had ordered a search of the hostage room for bugs and his security guys had found a battered iPhone hidden near the security building. As soon as the tech guys arrived he would uncover its secrets and pursue the investigation, someone would pay. He looked around his office; it was full of expensive furniture and high-tech equipment. He really didn't like the fact that the walls were bare but that's the price you paid to be part of an Islamist organisation. Not for long though, his accumulated funds now topped five million US dollars and were safely secreted in his bank in Dubai. He smiled as he daydreamed of how he would spend it. A knock on the door disturbed his musings; the two tech guys were here.

Rebecca identified the signal from the target, the cross hairs of the aiming system automatically locked onto the signal. She carefully checked the area for any civilians. She observed an armoured Humvee outside the office, just on the outside of the cross-sights of the Typhoon's aiming system, but that looked ISIS military. She had checked again, no civilians, and so she removed the safety and pressed firing the button. She watched the Brimstone streak towards the target.

He held the phone; it was a standard iPhone 5 covered with a tatty black leather case. He would ask the techs not to damage it too much if they did not need to, he could replace the cover with a more ornate one and maybe use it. There was a sudden roaring sound. He looked up, his eyes widened, a blinding streak of light seemed to be seeking him out, coming straight for him. He screamed, he felt pain, he felt intense heat, and the lights went out.

Rebecca saw the missile impact; it seemed to enter through

a window of the building that the signal had been coming from. There was an explosion; a blinding light, and the mission was a success.

"Right, Jo, job done," she said as she pulled the GR4A into a tight turn and rolled it in a mini victory roll and headed for home. "Back to Cyprus in time for tea and medals," she joked.

Chapter Forty Three

A Wedding

The wedding photo told the whole story. It was a conventional wedding with unconventional guests, between two very unconventional people. Sam looked radiant, her beautiful long hair fell in a bright blonde torrent across her brocaded silk dress that pinched in at her tiny waist and shaped outwards to the ground. Her face glowed in happiness as her bright blue eyes seemed to light up the whole scene. Taff's bulky form looked slimmer as he stood dressed in a light grey top hat and tails, his shoulders somewhat straining against the constraint of the suits, shoulder pads.

Danny stood next to Sam, dressed in a similar manner to Taff, although his suit seemed to fit him better. He had just had the honour of giving Sam away. The slightest trace of a tear of happiness welled up in his eye. Sir Ian Cameron was standing close to his son Connor next to Kenny from the London end. All the other faces were beaming at the camera, Pat, Scottie, Doc and Mac, with Eddie standing on the right of Mac. The sight of the two Scott brothers on the right emphasised the Kurdish link, both resplendent in the Scott family tartan. Tommy Talibani stood on the extreme right; he had managed to get a week away from the war.

Not on camera, Tim and Ahmad looked on; photos were not the Security Services' favourite things. *A happy wedding photo was a good a place as any for a story to finish*, thought Ahmad. He

279

had more work to do now, Imran was in deep and producing excellent results. He was changing the whole dynamics of the London Islamist scene, and he had therefore saved many lives.

Every picture tells a story, thought Tim, *it was like a brief moment in time frozen and recorded forever.* But a simple glance at this one would not reveal the true story, the majority of this story would remain untold. The team's heroics would never be discussed, Imran's act of bravery would never be mentioned, and no medals would be awarded. The only thing that would be considered in the future was that his organisation now knew a trusted agency, Hedges and Fisher, which was ideal for the more unconventional jobs that they might need completed without the complications of Parliamentary oversight.

As the church bells rang in Belgravia, an audible bleep sounded in the ear of the duty tech monitoring the laptops that had been sent to Syria. Nothing had been heard from them for nearly three weeks. The tech immediately reached for the phone to summon the duty officer. The receiving monitors were all suddenly going crazy, a thousand intercepts at the same time.

"What's up?" said the duty MI6 officer entering the office.

"It's happening," said the tech, "the whole network's going mad."

"We need the whole task force in, at least twenty linguist techs."

"There are literally thousands of intercepts, it's hoovering up all the email, all the Yello and Firechat stuff. We have an intelligence goldmine here."

The duty MI6 guy was elated; three weeks of waiting and then just before they closed the thing down, success. He dialled the encrypted emergency number to let Tim know.

GLOSSARY OF TERMS

ANA Afghan Army
BOLO Be On the Look Out for
BMP Russian troop carrier
CTR Close Target Recce
DHU Defence HUMINT Unit
The Green Bean US coffee shop at Camp Bastion
FRU The Force Research Unit
Humvee High Mobility Multi-purpose Wheeled Vehicle
ICOM Radio system used by the Taliban/AQI/ISIS
ISI Inter Service Intelligence
JSG Joint Support Group
OMINPON Morphine Syrette
OOB Out of Bounds Area
ML Royal Marines Mountain Leader
MOE Methods of Entry
NDS Afghan Intelligence Service
QBO's Quick Battle Orders
QRF Quick Reaction Force
RTA Road Traffic Accident
REME Royal Mechanical Engineers
ROE Rules Of Engagement
SAS Special Air Service
SHIN BET Israeli Intelligence Service
SBS Special Boat Service
SRR Special Reconnaissance Regiment

Coming Soon...

A Falling of Angels

W.T.Delaney

CHAPTER ONE

The fat old man parted the dusty, nicotine stained blinds of the small kitchen window. A shaft of light pierced the interior gloom of the council flat to further accentuate its shabbiness. The window was partly open. The old man heard normal life outside, children laughing, neighbors chatting, and the odd laugh and shout from a game of football that drifted in on the still summer air. He frowned and slammed the window shut and closed off the dank, darkened flat from the everyday ordinariness and normal comfort of suburban life. This was the safe house for the brothers that were coming.

He actually felt safe in the safe house, but only once he had shut the kuffar-noise out. He was safe in this place, it was thousands of miles away from his homeland, where chaos reigned and people died by the thousand.

At the moment. He thought. *But that's going to change soon, when the lions of the Caliphate come – these kuffar bastards will know the same pain. Suffer the same agony.*

He smiled. "Inshallah."He muttered silently under his breath.

Once he had checked all the windows and double-checked the reinforced front door, he removed a small laptop from a dusty black leather briefcase. He then fumbled with the connection between the laptop and the power point projector. He then connected the USB thumb drive, squinting through his thick black-framed glasses. A grunt of satisfaction signified his little conquest over technology. The power point projector buzzed into life and projected a picture onto the wall.

They say that every picture tells a story, but sometimes it's where and when you see the picture that conveys the real meaning behind it.

A good wedding photograph is a joyful moment forever frozen in time.

It was Sam and Taff's wedding photograph and it presented a happy image. Any neutral observer's eye would also be immediately drawn to the beauty of the bride and the happiness that seemed to radiate from her face. The couple's joy was recorded forever by the split second it had taken for the cameras shutter to record the image. Sam and Taff's arms are lovingly entwined. They are smiling, looking into each other's eyes, totally connected, in love, and centrally framed amongst the smiling faces of their friends.

The image in this context though, looked strange. The black and white photograph really belonged in a family wedding album. It was now projected over-enlarged and grainy, onto the slightly uneven, plaster filled, and dusty beige wall of a Luton council flat. It shimmered ominously and seemed to flicker, almost like an old silent movie film. It was almost ghostly. It also presented a somewhat different image to the man who observed it.

They also say, beauty is subjective and in 'the eye of the beholder'.

"Kuffar bitch." he muttered venomously under his breath.

Reflected in the dim light emanating from the power point projector, the fat old man's eyes glittered with hate.

He grunted and his long white beard seemingly quivered in disgust, as a delicate looking index finger, with an overgrown fingernail pressed the remote and:

Click

Another picture filled the screen.

This was a close up of the bride, with one strange addition. The low cut bridal gown that had previously emphasized her shapely figure appeared to be crudely obscured by black marker pen.

The old man grunted with distain and:

Click

Another slide appeared, this was a Google map image of a location somewhere in the highlands of Scotland and then:

Click

The spindly elongated finger depressed the button again and:

Click

The picture changed to be replaced by a quaint white walled Scottish croft cottage. Newly painted, and adorned with hanging baskets of flowers to each side of the freshly painted red front door.

This is where the kuffar she-devil lives. He thought.

"Your time is coming." He muttered almost silently.

He then picked up the large black 'Bowie' style combat knife lying alongside the remote control. He lifted it and grasped its hilt gently, as if it was an almost sacred object. He felt the weight of it and assessed its balance. It looked huge and bulky in his podgy hand. It was a foot long and made of black carbon steel. It looked out of place in the old man's hands. The harshness of the black cold steel contrasted with the smooth aged spotted skin. After all, they were hands that had never produced anything or held any other tool, or even planted a seed. These were the hands of a cleric, a Mullah, a thinker, not a doer. He slowly turned the knife almost lovingly in the dim light generated by the projector.

The knife glistened along the blades razor sharp serrated edge. As he slowly turned the knife he felt a thrill in the pit of his stomach as he visualized its final function. He enjoyed the mental image of suffering and his wizened mouth arched slightly under his snow-white beard into a broad smile, contrasting his tea-stained teeth with the silky whiteness of his facial hair.

"The brothers are arriving soon," He said quietly.

The brothers are on their way from Europe to drag you to hell, you kuffar bitch. He thought

And this knife is God's instrument to put you there, the knife of the martyr you killed, Captain Samantha Holloway.